Leaning

a novel

Melissa Dawn

Learn to Curve Publishing, LLC

First edition

ISBN 978-1-7340002-0-7

Printed in the United States of America

Learn to Curve Publishing, LLC
Upper Marlboro, MD 20774
Learn2curve@gmail.com

Also by Melissa Dawn
Goddess of Wisdom and War, a short story

Table of Contents

Part 1
Sunrise

1

As the sun brushed the edges of the sky, Patrice poured a cup of dark roast coffee then sat on her chaise and read a passage from her father's book, both essential to waking up. *Memories eternally live in secular souls awaiting daylight and writhing nightfall. Peaceful habits in life lead into peaceful souls.* The worn black leather book was read every morning and placed gently on her dresser at night. Each morning she fanned through the poetic passages and read from wherever her finger landed. Her way of keeping him present. There were moments when her heart ached knowing that memories of her father continued to fade each year.

Patrice remembered him mostly by the stories told and the preserved images of pictures. Her mother's stories about her father's endless animal analogies, "Don't let that bear of a thought roar in your mind." And his equally distributed frustration with basketball playoffs and partisan politics. Patrice kept the family photo album her mother gave her in the center of her coffee table with a small candle on each side.

Leaning

Flipping through it refreshed her memory of his cropped hair cut, bowed legs, and mahogany skin. Sometimes, she caught a waft of his smell, Irish Spring soap and aftershave. Her last vivid memory of him was from the first day of third grade. That morning, he played an oldies station in the car while driving her to school.

"Dad?! Can we please listen to some real music?"

"Ha! You don't know nuthin' 'bout real music!"

He grinned at her with fake disdain and swayed his head as he drove. He playfully swatted at her hand when she reached for the radio knob to change the station. Within five minutes, they pulled into the parking lot and he waved goodbye singing, "Ain't no mountain high enough!" She giggled, waved back, then mixed in with the shuffle of students walking into school.

It was a week and a half later, on a Thursday afternoon, that Patrice's mother sat on the living room couch with a morbid trance draped on her face. Patrice and her sister Michelle felt the death before they were told. Their mother's shaky words squeezed through her cries. She said something bad had happened to their father. He had been driving home from work when he was side-swiped by a driver having a heart attack, which sent his car spiraling into oncoming traffic. Patrice, her mother, and sister stretched their arms around each other for hours. The guttural groans of pain filled the house for days. They stayed home from work and school for a week, cocooned in the grief that permanently altered them into a family of three.

When Patrice took a shower the morning of the funeral, the water stung her skin, which hadn't been washed in the absence of her mother's reminders to do so. A week later, her body returned to school but left her spirit at home. She didn't raise her hand once in classes or talk unless she had to. Lunchtimes were spent in her favorite teacher Ms. Adams' classroom, away from students who stared or awkwardly asked what happened to her father. Ms. Adams would sit in a seat next to her and eat in silence. By the end of the first week, Ms. Adams gingerly handed her a journal with a pastel yellow cover titled "Speak." Patrice wrote in that journal daily for months, until there were no words left. The overwhelming lesson from losing her father was that pain—aching, hollow, heavy pain—never goes away. But it yields a little after a time and gives way to more memories of good times.

As Patrice finished her coffee, she peeked through the curtains in her bedroom and was happy there wasn't a cloud in sight. After drying off from her shower, she stood in front of the full-length mirror peering at her reflection. Studying the aesthetic summation of three decades, she struggled to focus only on the perks as her eyes gravitated to early signs of sagging. She was grateful, though, that the shadows of aging weren't prominent. She dealt with her recent thirtieth birthday fairly well—a spa day with her girlfriends replete with mimosas and massages—but she couldn't help but fondly remember the buoyancy of her twenties for a brief moment. A day of spa lounging was a far but comfortable cry from wheeling into Miami with a suitcase full of skin-tight dresses, mid-thigh skirts, and five-inch heels for her 21st birthday.

Patrice always liked her caramel brown skin. Her long legs. And her curves. The thing that made a woman a woman. She coined "curvy and swervy" in her teens as her moniker.

She knew that what men loved, contrary to popular belief, were hips. An old boyfriend once took a picture of her laying on her side then later gave it to her as a 16 by 20-inch framed canvas photo. She warmed with embarrassment and pride when she looked at it. But that tribute to her body was now long gone along with all the rest of his things and gifts when that relationship ended.

Patrice sipped her coffee as a flicker of nerves rippled through her stomach. *Time to get dressed,* she thought. She had a couple of hours until her 10:00 a.m. interview, but she had to manage that time wisely. She entered her closet and pulled out suits. Why she believed that picking clothes the day before was a jinx, she didn't know. But she adhered to it without fail. Now she faced the decision head-on. Her gaze bounced from one suit to the next. *What energy do I want to exude?* A suit that hugged her curves too much would give a sense of desperation. A more traditional suit would age her a few years. She needed the right blend of class and sass. After a few minutes of indecisive 'hmm, nah, maybe,' she grabbed a suit and laid it on the bed.

Patrice slipped on a black lace bra and panty set before donning the emerald green three-button skirt suit. She thought it gave a nice contrast to her newly dyed, golden brown shoulder-length mane. She could always get a wash and roller set from the Dominican salon to last a full week, which made it worth the price. But she was lucky to get in to see her hairdresser Tiffany early yesterday morning, so she only had to maintain the style overnight. She gave herself one last glance in the foyer mirror, smiled with confidence that danced in the corners of her lips, then walked out the front door.

After exiting the Dupont Circle Metro Station, Patrice briskly made her way up Connecticut Avenue for two blocks. She had chosen tan three-inch heels that were low enough to hustle in and high enough to give her butt the right amount of bounce when she walked. She crunched through the fall leaves imagining she was walking a runway. Without coffee to help squelch her bouts of nerves, she instead reminded herself that she already had a job lined up no matter how the interview today went. She had interviewed at Prestige Public Relations last week and was unofficially given an offer.

"We would love for you to consider coming on board. Pending a background check, you could start next month!"

The job was hers for the taking if she wanted.

The interview she was headed to was at a firm in the heart of the city. Patrice looked forward to the possibility of working in Washington, D.C. Her current firm was tucked away in the corner of a Maryland suburb. And given that Maryland *was* already considered the suburbs of D.C., working there felt too far removed from city life. Granted the job was near her apartment, but working so far out of the city felt too subdued. She liked the peace of her neighborhood and the sound of crickets at night, but it would also be nice to work around the corner from several bars if she wanted to have a happy hour drink. She enjoyed the taste of city life during college but working there would be different.

Patrice was grateful that the fall weather was tame enough for no jacket to be needed. So, she didn't have to cover up her suit. *And no rain in the forecast! Being soggy at my interview ain't the vibe I'm looking for.* She checked out the buildings as she walked by and noticed several bars and restaurants. She thought about how much fun it would be to work in Dupont Circle. For the most part, D.C. was like any other city. Coffee shops and restaurants, with a scattering of specialty shops and food stands. Clusters of tall buildings, bars every few blocks, traffic-ridden streets, and the smell of exhaust. At any time of day or night, there were shoals of people on the sidewalks and crossing the streets, always hustling like they were late for an appointment. But Patrice loved the pulse of D.C. She described it to her cousin, who visited from New York last fall, as a soulful song that had a semi-southern rhythm with a touch of the north. Like a southern martini with a northern olive.

Patrice entered the twenty-story, glass-front building, and took a deep breath. She savored the smell of dry-cleaned suits and blended flavors of coffee creamers wafting from the cups of people ebbing and flowing in and out of the building. She inspected herself in the mirrored elevator for runs in her pantyhose and breakfast remnants in her teeth. As she stepped off the elevator onto the eighteenth floor and into the foyer of the office suite, she heard the administrative assistant utter a monotone greeting into the phone,

"Good morning, York & Newton Public Relations. This is Monica. How may I direct your call?"

As Patrice walked up to the front desk, Monica dimly smiled then waved her off to sit in the lounge. *Did she just flick her hand at me?* Patrice wondered if she should make herself more of an apparent nuisance by announcing that she was there for an interview, but she decided to wait and see what happened when Monica got off the phone. She took a seat in the lounge area. She had planned for the usual fifteen-minute wait that agencies put interviewees through to make them squirm. She had also preplanned her selection from the expected array of superficial to scholarly magazines that ornamented the coffee table in the lounge. She imagined other interviewees busying themselves by painstakingly deciding between mindlessly flipping through pictures of celebrities versus the pretense of intellectual stimulation by getting engrossed in a research article while waiting. Such a decision about reading materials wouldn't seem so important if they weren't trying to distract themselves from the reality of what job searching meant in this town and this economy. Even the most confident, competent, experienced person was acutely aware that they were just one of the hundreds of job-hunting people walking the same corridors to the same waiting areas and looking at the same coffee table of magazines. Given that context, simple decisions became major ones, and in an odd way, kept the worry of the real major decisions at bay. *Black Enterprise it is!* She picked up the magazine and fanned through the pages. What she hadn't planned for was hearing a familiar voice.

"Good morning Ms. Pearson!"

The voice wafted into the lounge from the doorway. She briefly froze. Her eyes barely focused. She blinked a few times and stood, placing the magazine back on the coffee table. As she rose, their eyes met and she smiled widely.

"Hello, John."

He flashed a shiny smile.

"Patrice! You know, when I saw a resume for Patrice Pearson in our stack of potential interviewees, I thought,

'It couldn't be?'" He paused, peered at her, then continued, "But here you are." He paused again. "Welcome to York & Newton."

Patrice attempted her best nonchalant tone despite the distinct pulsing of her heartbeat and her tightening throat. She cleared her throat, hoping for the best, but her voice caught in her throat like a dry piece of toast.

"Y–, Yes. Well, I'm, I'm excited to be here."

She managed a confident smile and asserted her hand for a firm handshake before they got clammy. She tried again to use her words.

"Well good weather today. I'm glad it wasn't a soggy one like yesterday."

She silently winced. *Geez. Really Patrice? Weather small talk? Come on. Do better.* She politely smiled and listened as John talked about getting caught in the rain yesterday coming back from lunch. Patrice glanced at his tailored suit. She surmised that his tie was one of those attempts a woman made to be a part of her husband's business world. A way of making her presence known. It had a bold gold paisley design with a silky sheen. A tie that a man wouldn't buy for himself but would wear if his woman bought it. Patrice reached for her purse on the coffee table, steadying and steeling herself. *Okay, here we go.* As she turned to face John again, he outstretched his arm in the direction of a long hallway and stepped out of the way.

"Well, let's get started."

Patrice followed his gesture and started the journey to the conference room. She tensed thinking of the rough start she was off to. *Mike Tyson's so right. Everybody has a plan 'til they get punched in the mouth.* She felt his eyes move over her body as she past him and heard his breathing change. She grinned inside, realizing that she reclaimed a little leverage.

"So, your first interview will be with myself and our CEO, Trevor Edwards –."

Patrice tuned out at that point. Her thoughts raced. She calculated how to factor John into how she planned for the interview to go. As they reached the end of the hallway, she tuned back in.

"I'll give you a tour of the agency, then you will have a visit with HR."

They turned a corner and walked up the next hallway. Patrice glanced from the corner of her eye as he ran his hand over his tie. She saw the glimmer from his left ring finger. She picked up her pace as they walked up the hallway, which was laden with abstract paintings, toward the conference room. She kept her pace slightly faster than his. She wanted to keep things professional. *We're not old friends. No casual banter*, she thought. John cleared his throat and sped up. Patrice thought back to her research on York & Newton. *How could I have missed that he worked here, much less that he was a senior executive?* She fought the urge to shake her head at her poorly executed search skills. *And what was he doing in public relations anyway? He was a business major. He could be in a hundred other fields.* She had to make the best of the situation. *Maybe the past is the past.* But this thought quickly disintegrated in the interview. A switch had flipped. The grilling questions lobbed across the conference table from John had her head swimming with insecurities about every one of her responses. She tensed from head to toe with aggravation at John for throwing her off her game.

"Ms. Pearson give us an example of a six-figure campaign that you spearheaded and the resulting profit margins."

Patrice managed to respond to most questions with minor fumbles. But sweat beaded on her back and trickled down her spine. After ten minutes, an image flashed through her mind that helped release some of the stiffness in her body. She reverted to seven-year-old intellect. She imagined hopping on the conference table and mooning John while chanting, "Kiss my asshole, Asshole!" She laughed on the inside. Once her shoulders and back relaxed, rehearsed answers flowed more freely.

"My accounts have resulted in a 22.3 percent increase in M & B's overall revenues in the past year, and 18 percent over my full tenure."

When the half-hour mark approached Mr. Edwards distributed folders to John and Patrice, then reviewed the company's goals and mission. Tension crept back up her spine. *Geez, if this interview was recorded, I'd look like a sweaty, fumbling mess,* she thought and sighed silently. She glanced at John's bald head. *Ha, looks like a chocolate-covered banana!* A flash of biting the banana ran through her mind, and it felt like she was biting his head off. She cleared her throat to keep from chuckling aloud. As the forty five minute mark approached, the interview finally wrapped. She was spent. *Oh God, we still have to do the tour.* She sighed. *Shoot me now.*

The tour wasn't as painful as she anticipated. York & Newton was comprised of twelve offices, a conference room, a kitchen, bathroom, waiting lounge, and more than a fair share of gold-framed abstract paintings. Once they finished the loop through and landed back at the lounge, Patrice masked her surprise at John's next offer.

"Well, it's early for lunch, but how about we grab a coffee and bagels?"

Patrice paused for a beat before responding. *Is this a peace offering?* She felt like a sputtering mess of burnt coffee on the inside from the grueling morning, but turning down an offer from a hiring influencer was not an option. She remembered her lunch plans with her boyfriend Sean, but she'd just send him a text saying that she was running late. Patrice and John took the elevator down to the first floor and walked to a coffee shop. She breathed a sigh of relief as she sipped her dark brew and took a bite of her maple walnut scone. Luckily, the conversation ended up being as generic as corn flakes.

John droned on about, "York & Newton's mission has been—"

Nothing but facts about the firm's productivity and future projections. *Geez, did he look this data up for the interview, or does he actually keep it all memorized?*

They arrived back at the lounge a half-hour later.

"Diane from HR will be in shortly to give you the forms packet for the background check. And, you'll be hearing from us soon. Take care, Patrice."

They shook hands and Patrice managed a wide but weary smile.

"Looking forward to it."

He disappeared down the hall. She was grateful that Diane arrived with the HR packet within a minute. After the brief discussion, Patrice thanked her, grabbed her purse and headed to the exit. She sped passed the front desk to the elevator and gave Monica a hand flick mixed with a wave in place of saying goodbye. *Bye, grouch.* Once in the downstairs lobby, she darted from the building and hustled to the Metro train to meet Sean. She plopped on a seat, and foraged around in her purse for an antacid to settle her swirling stomach. She chewed on two while focused on a boy bopping his Black Panther action figure along the top edge of the seat in front of him, much to the annoyance of the grimacing man in the seat ahead and to the oblivion of the boy's mother who was nodding off beside him. Patrice settled in for the twenty-minute train ride. *This day's been 48 hours long. And it's only 12:15 p.m.*

She replayed the interview in her head and cringed. She thought about John's casual comment about his profit margins, which happened to be triple the value of hers, then popped one more antacid tablet. She thought about what it meant to see John again after all these years. She couldn't quite name the feeling. Familiar yet vague. Relieving yet tense. But mostly unsettling. *Would it be weird to work with him? I don't know. Maybe.* As her metro train stop approached, she stood and waited near the doors to exit. She decided to be done with mulling over the morning once she walked off the train. She straightened her skirt, then hopped off and headed to lunch.

A few days later Sean was spending the night over at Patrice's. They cooked and ate a spaghetti dinner together then, both exhausted from their days, readied for bed just after 10:00 p.m.

"Sweets, I'mma check whether my son called."

Patrice knew Sean used that excuse to satisfy his curiosity about who was calling her. His son Micah never called on her house phone for Sean, though he had the phone number. She wondered why, after three years, he still didn't refer to his son by name around her.

She obliged, "Okay babe."

Sometimes she liked Sean's possessiveness. But mostly because he didn't take it too far. She sat in bed propped up against a pillow with a book in her lap. She peered intently out of her bedroom door into the living room. She enjoyed the contours of his back as he hovered over an end table with the cordless phone. She thought about what was his best physical feature. *Definitely his back. And his chest.* After checking Patrice's voice mail, Sean turned and headed to the bedroom. He stopped short before entering and leaned into the door frame with a curious look.

"Who's John?"

For a brief second, Patrice's breath caught in her throat. She attempted to sound relaxed.

"Who?"

She casually picked up her book and fanned the pages.

Sean clarified, "John Blackman?"

Patrice adjusted her body against the pillow.

"He's the senior executive at York & Newton that interviewed me a couple days ago. Did he offer the job?"

Sean handed her the cordless phone to check the message herself.

Sean and Patrice first met three years ago. At the time, she lived in Hyattsville, one of the more urban neighborhoods in

Maryland. Sean was just past being a rookie having been in the Prince George's County Police Department for two years. Patrice awoke after midnight to a fire alarm screeching in her apartment building. The blaring noise blended into her dreams, until the loudspeaker coaxed all tenants out of the building. She jolted awake, grabbed a coat, her purse, and her pet rabbit before running out of her apartment. Outside the building, the lights from two fire trucks, an ambulance, and a half dozen police cars illuminated the front of her building. The scene was a whirling haze of commotion. Police officers questioned everyone about anything they might have heard or seen that night or in the last few nights. Patrice stood where she could see all that was happening and be in earshot of conversations. She overheard a neighbor mention calling 911 after smelling smoke. Another neighbor had heard a screaming woman.

Sean was the first officer Patrice noticed. She guessed that he was about six feet tall. He sported a low fade with a jaw-lined beard. His milk chocolate skin glowed under the lights of the busy night. *I bet he looks delicious after a game of basketball, glistening and breathing all hard.* She smiled at the thought. She watched him jot down notes and ask tenants' questions. He finished interviewing a woman with two kids, then looked around for the next tenant to talk with. He glanced at Patrice, and a subtle smile lifted the corners of his mouth. Had she not been watching she might have missed locking eyes with him for the brief moment that they did. He approached with a confident yet starchy cop-gait. Once closer, he pointed to the rabbit nestled in the crook of her arm.

"Is he friendly?" He gestured with an open palm for tacit permission to pet her rabbit.

"Yes, Pebbles. She's sweet. Little nervous with all this noise and commotion though."

He rubbed Pebbles between her ears and on her chin, and she nuzzled his hand. Sean gazed at Patrice as he spoke.

"I think she likes me."

Patrice's face warmed. *Say something cute*, she thought.

"Any idea what started the fire?"

She winced. *Is that all you could come up with? Geez.*

Sean noticed Patrice's body shiver from the cold air.

"We're still investigating. But we should be wrapping up shortly. We have hand warmers. Let me grab a pack for you."

When he returned, he opened two air-activated heat packets and gave them to her. His hand brushed hers and she tingled. After almost an hour outside the tenants were allowed to re-enter. Patrice later learned that a woman was found unconscious after being assaulted and robbed in her apartment. Her pots boiled over causing a fire that quickly spread to the apartments next to hers on the fifth floor.

It was two months after the fire and Patrice was coming out of the Safeway supermarket. She fumbled around in her purse one-handed to grab her car keys while holding four bags of groceries in her other hand. She heard someone approach.

"Need some help!"

Sean moved in with his hand outstretched to help carry her bags.

"Oh. Hi! Thank you!"

Her car was a few feet away. She pressed her remote to unlock the doors, and silently cursed for not parking further away so they had more time to chat. He scanned her bags as though itemizing the contents.

"Dinner for one or two?"

Sean flashed a smile and Patrice grinned widely.

"For one. Frozen lasagna, salad, and wine!"

He tilted his head gazing at her.

"Well I have enough pork chops for two. That's if you're interested in trying my cooking." He grinned. "I might even *make* dessert."

She glanced at his arms and her gaze continued to his body. His t-shirt flattered his toned chest.

"Hmm, a man offering to cook dinner *and* dessert? That may be a once in a lifetime opportunity!"

Over dinner at Sean's place they chatted about the night of the fire, how long he'd been an officer, and their versions of life in Maryland. Patrice learned that he had a pet snake and joked about whether a rabbit and snake could co-exist.

"You never know," she joked, "rabbits are agile!"

He grinned, "But snakes are fast!"

Their second date was days later at her place. They cooked together while listening to R&B. Through the years, cooking dinner and enjoying music was a mainstay in their relationship.

Patrice's attention returned to her book and Sean, who was flipping channels mindlessly in her bed.

"He left you a message to call him back at your earliest convenience."

She smiled. "Great. That's a good sign. I'll call in the morning."

Sean wondered aloud, "That was the day you were late meeting me for lunch, right?"

She labored through a swallow. Feeling the dryness of her throat, she reached for the bottled water on the nightstand.

"Yeah. Remember, I got on the train going in the wrong direction. I didn't realize it because I was busy on my phone researching the firm to learn more in case I got called for a second interview."

Patrice wasn't sure why she lied, again. She didn't like lying the first time around. Or why she didn't mention that John was her college boyfriend. Or that they went for coffee after the interview. She wasn't hungry by the time she met up with Sean and faked a sudden craving for the lightest item on the menu. Salad. *To be fair*, she thought, *my nerves were so bad that day I couldn't eat much anyway.* She glanced at Sean, who laid back in bed. She gently rubbed his blanket-covered leg and felt his muscles relax.

Sean squinted playfully.

"Yeah right. You were giving all my goodies away to some no-good bum."

He slid his arm around her waist, pulling her in and softly smacking her butt. She kissed him as she wrapped her arms around him.

"Babes. I got all this at home, and you think I would shack up with a raggedy runner-up? Come on now."

Sean smiled and she grinned. Then they kissed. Soft at first then insistent. The inquiry ended, but not before Sean added a quick comment.

"At home huh. Your home or mine?"

Patrice ignored his comment. *Really? Right now? In this moment?* She peered longingly into his eyes. He kissed her more intensely while sliding sensually over her. The warmth of their skin intensified as they enveloped each other. After lovemaking, Patrice drifted off to sleep snug in his arms.

Hours later, Patrice awoke to the sound of Sean sternly whispering into his cell as he leaned on an elbow toward the edge of the bed.

"What? Why wasn't I immediately informed of this?"

She could barely see through the darkness of the bedroom. She shivered, annoyed at the draft she felt now that he had released her from his arms. He continued into the phone,

"Alright, I'll be there in 20. Wait 'til I get there."

Hearing those words cleared her grogginess like a windshield wiper. She sat up.

"What's going on?"

He leaned over and kissed her cheek then slid out from the covers. As he dressed Patrice sat up straighter in bed, readjusting her camisole to cover her chest.

"Did something happen?"

He seemed deep in thought.

"Sean?"

He answered, "Yeah. Sorry to wake you. I have to head to the precinct. It's okay though. Go back to sleep."

She frowned with irritation. Standing near the bedroom door, he glanced over his shoulder at her. She scowled with frustration at his vagueness.

"An officer's wife is in the hospital in critical condition. I don't know much more than that. Go back to sleep sweets. I'll call you later."

Patrice crossed her arms as she heard the front door close. *Back to sleep? No chance in hell.* Sean leaving in the middle of the night for police work made her a nervous wreck. It didn't happen often, but when it did, she felt the full weight of what it meant for him to be an officer. As a cop, he could be in danger at any time. But the threat felt more ominous at two in the morning. They intentionally never talked about how many times he'd encountered imminent danger or about times when he had to discharge his weapon. But she knew either occurred more often than she could handle knowing. That night, she tossed around in bed for hours before drifting off. When the alarm blared, she swore it was within minutes of falling asleep.

2

"Hey, dad!"

Janelle jaunted into the foyer of the house to greet her father John at the door with a hug. At five feet and seven inches, she was on her way to being on par with him.

"Hey, Sugar." He smiled and squinted at her. "Well, you're happy today! What's up?"

She feigned confusion, "Nothing dad. I can't be happy to see you?"

He smirked, "Uh-huh. Sure."

She trailed him into the kitchen and sat at the counter.

"It's been really cool at school. Everybody's wearing a different color of Vans shoes on each foot. The black and burgundy looks really chill together."

"Oh yeah? Did you buy some when Lily took you shopping last weekend?"

"Well. No, we had to buy clothes. I really, really needed some new jeans and t-shirts and sweaters and stuff."

John sat at the kitchen counter.

"Oh good. So, you got what you needed."

Janelle's smile shifted to a pensive focus.

"Well, yeah. I just –, wish I could get those Vans."

He smiled at her.

She continued, "I have a little money saved. But –, I didn't want to use all of it."

John sat quietly peering at her. Janelle put her hand on her hip and smirked.

"So you're really gonna make your fifteen-year-old daughter spend her itty-bitty savings on some shoes when you make bookoo bucks? Don't you want your daughter to look fly? And not be broke?"

John put his arm around her shoulders.

"You're already fly! Plus, you probably have more money than me. What's in these pockets?"

He playfully shook her as if to get money to fall out of her pockets. They laughed. Then the clatter of toddler footsteps approached as three-year-old twins Jasper and Jasmine scampered out of their bedroom and down the steps bounding into the kitchen.

"Daddy!"

"Hey, Sugar Beads!"

They were both rattling off their request in unison.

"Daddy, I want lit critters. I want gummy."

John scooped them up in his arms.

"What? What's that?"

Moments later, John's wife Lily appeared at the kitchen door.

"They want Little Critters gummy vitamins. They've been talking about it since they saw the commercial this morning."

John glanced up.

"Oh, okay. I got it now. Hey honey! How was your day?"

Lily smiled and said it was fine.

He asked, "Have they had a snack?"

She shook her head then disappeared from the doorway.

Janelle leaned on the kitchen counter as John sat the twins at the kitchen table then grabbed juice boxes and fruit cups from the fridge. He signaled to Janelle to grab bags of chips from the pantry. John bit into an apple and spoke between chews.

"How did your art project go? Did you get the mountains to look realistic?"

She grinned.

"Of course! You won't believe what I used though. I crumbled damp paper towels and brushed them with watercolor to get the gray look I wanted, then I brushed on corn syrup. Then I sprinkled flour on it to look like fresh snow. And voila! Snow-capped mountains!"

She flipped through her phone to show him pictures. He smiled and gave her a fist pound.

"Nice!"

* * *

John was fifteen when his parents split. His father — everyone called him Black — was hardly around after that. Black moved out and left Maryland for New Jersey to do traveling sales work. When he came to visit, he stayed at his sister's house for a week, and arranged for John to come over on the weekend. Those visits often came to mind when he smelled pancakes or rum. One of those summer weekends was when John met Janelle's mother Shellie.

On a Saturday, John sat on a recliner listening as Black slurred and babbled on about the ways of girls and women. That morning his aunt cooked pancakes in the kitchen while Black watched TV in the living room with a fifth of Johnny Walker in one hand and a rum glass with Coke on the end table beside him. He doled out advice during commercial breaks between watching sports.

"You know John, you almost had a white mother. You didn't know that huh?"

John glanced at his father, shook his head, and wondered if Black was about to reveal some secret.

Black slurred on, "I was with Heather for years before I met your mother. She turned on me though."

He took a sip from his glass.

"You know, to a white woman, a black man is always going to be less than her. And a white man is always going to see a black woman as a conquest. That seed grew in their psyche centuries ago. And it never dislodged." Black paused. "But then I met your mother. She's a handful. A whole lot to deal with. Stubborn and thinks she knows it all."

John glared in Black's direction at times when he wasn't looking. He felt an urge to defend his mother but knew it wouldn't make a difference. The next commercial break, Black slurred on about how hard it was for a man to be the leader of his family when he was still just a boy at heart.

"Deep down, we all just want to play marbles and kickball, catch bugs, and kiss a girl when we get the chance."

Black laughed. John gave a stiff appeasing smile.

The next break, Black returned to talking about John's mother.

"You know me and your mother only dated three months before she was pregnant with you?"

John shifted uncomfortably while he listened.

"It only takes one time son. Remember that. Just one. Always make sure you use rubbers."

John nodded, "Yeah, I know."

Black insisted, "You hear me? Every time."

"Yeah."

"Don't get caught up. These cute little girls turn into scheming women."

As soon as Black passed out on the couch, John told his aunt he was going to hang out, then bolted out the door into the fresh air of the spring day. He walked two blocks in the neighborhood to a friend's house. He had met Tony months earlier on one of his visits to his aunt's. Tony was grinning when he opened the door.

"Yo, got some fly girls over!"

They headed down to the basement, and as they rounded the corner at the bottom of the stairs, John saw two girls his age sitting on the couch. Tony whispered that he already picked the one he wanted to talk to. John sat next to the other girl. She smiled and passed him a joint. Everyone called her Shellie. She was staying with her grandmother up the street because her mother had moved to New York. She said she was going to move to New York in the summer when school was out.

After they met that night, John and Shellie hung out every weekend that he visited his aunt and talked on the phone during the week. They only had sex once, at her grandmother's house when she was out on a grocery run. He had used a condom, but he didn't put it on until after they started having sex. When he stayed with his aunt two weeks later, Tony said Shellie had moved.

Shellie popped up at his aunt's house, six weeks later, fumbling through saying she was pregnant. Stunned, John's only words were,

"By who? Me?"

He later said felt bad about that, but it was all he could say. Her words had jolted him like an electric shock. She said there was a chance that the child wasn't his, and that she was willing to take tests to be sure once the baby was born. He took a few days before telling his family, knowing the lectures would come like trains pulling into a station one after the next.

John's father offered nothing more than, "Boy, didn't I tell you don't get caught up? And what you go and do? Get caught up. Just gotta learn the hard way, huh?"

His mother, aunts, uncles, and grandparents all gave him some version of a speech about responsibility. His mother's words stuck with him most. She told him that if there was any chance that it was his child, he needed to be there and help as much as he could. Because that was the Godly thing to do.

"When you become a man, you give up your childish ways," she said. Sometimes she would give him her own euphemisms in place of the religious advice.

"Be a father right from the start. You were grown enough to lay down. Then be grown enough to stand up."

Days later, John went by Shellie's grandmother's house and told her he was going to be there all the way through. Every weekend he visited Shellie, whether his father was in town or not. He went to every prenatal appointment that he could and bumbled through asking the doctor questions about the baby's development.

Any doubt that Janelle was John's child was absolved when she was born. She was 6 pounds 11 ounces — the exact weight John's mother said he was at birth. She had a widow's peak and a birthmark on the top of her right ear, just like John. He wasn't in the hospital room when she was born, but he sat in the waiting room with his mother for hours. When they were allowed to go into the room, he cupped Janelle's head in the crook of his arm, the way his mother taught him and hummed, "I'm here baby girl. Daddy's here."

Janelle was one year old before John fully realized Shellie had problems. He came out of the bathroom one day and saw her put a pill bottle back in her grandmother's purse and shove her hand in her pocket. He also found out that she had isolated herself from everyone in her family except her grand-mother, who was actually her step-grandmother.

John questioned her, "Why doesn't your mother come around? Doesn't she wanna meet Janelle?"

"My mother's too busy living her life in Jersey."

"I thought she was in New York."

"Right. Exactly. She's always moving around. She don't have time for me and Janelle."

When John turned eighteen, he talked to his mother about having Janelle live with them. When he brought it up to Shellie, she didn't put up much of a fight. She packed up a few of Janelle's clothes, bottles, and the Pack n' Play set. And with a kiss on Janelle's forehead, Shellie waved and wiped tears away as John carried her to her new home. He bought Janelle clothes, bottles, blankets, and a convertible crib in the next few weeks with every penny he earned from his job at Target. Shellie would come by once or twice a week, then disappear for weeks at a time. As John finished his senior year of high school, he attended school half a day, then worked at Target four hours a day before picking Janelle up from daycare. He worked at Checkers on the weekends too. He earned enough money to cover daycare costs and clothes, while his mother covered food and diapers.

When John got the acceptance letter from Howard University — the only college he ever talked about attend-ing — he deferred admission and instead went to community college. This allowed him to have only a ten-minute commute home from the campus and made it easy to pick up Janelle from daycare. His mother took over caring for Janelle many evenings, while John attended college classes, studied for tests, typed research papers, and worked at a local gym on Fridays and weekends. When it came to Janelle, he tried his best to be what he thought a father was supposed to be. When Janelle grew older and asked about her mother, he told her some version of, "Your mom had a lot of problems that got really bad. She stopped coming around. I wish I knew why. But I'll always be here. And grandma too. We'll always be here."

***

Now at fifteen, Janelle was a tenth grader, diligent about her school work and skillful on the soccer field. John faithfully attended her soccer games, and always watched from the same place in the middle row of the metal bleachers. When they caught sight of each other, each lifted an eyebrow. Their quiet greeting. Janelle had practice after school three days a week and matches two Saturdays a month through soccer season. On the few days when John was late for Janelle's game and had to sit in a different seat, she glanced furtively at the bleachers every couple of minutes until she saw his wave.

"Go Pele!" he would shout.

She would roll her eyes and shush him with her finger.

3

Sean pulled into the parking lot behind the precinct at 7:30 a.m., his mind churning with thoughts about how the day would unfold. His precinct was located midway down a bustling block of Pennsylvania Avenue in Southeast D.C. He darted his eyes around as he entered the building, glancing at every passerby. Having a precinct on the block didn't stop crime from happening there, though it slowed it down.

When Sean got the call in the middle of the night that his old partner's wife had been attacked in her home and was unconscious in the hospital, he couldn't bring himself to tell Patrice. It would have guaranteed her no sleep for the rest of that night. Plus, he figured it was better to have more info on what happened before saying anything. It had been a couple of years since Sean and Patrice hung out with Mitch and Annabelle, but she and Annabelle were close enough to call each other on their birthdays and holidays, and text funny memes. Patrice even watched their two kids when an impromptu business meeting ran over for Annabelle while

Leaning

Mitch was out of town. When he did tell Patrice the next day, she was upset about Annabelle and sad for the kids. Her first question surprised Sean.

"Did Mitch seem broken up about it?"

"Don't know. I haven't spoken to him yet."

She paused pensively.

"There's something about him I never trusted."

Sean walked into the precinct and made his way past a sea of desks and officers to his office. He motioned for two of the officers to follow. They glanced at each other, then fell in tow. Once seated, Sean shuffled through the folders on his desk.

"So what do we know at this point?"

Greg Wilson and Jeff Dannon were Sean's go-to guys on his squad. They both had been on the police force for at least five years, kept their noses clean, and understood when it was necessary to grind down to get the job done. Wilson flipped open a notepad.

"So far, everything checks out Sarg."

He updated Sean about the details of Annabelle Gibson's case. Sean asked rapid-fire questions about evidence found at Mitch and Annabelle's home, the whereabouts of every family member, and what Mitch had to say when questioned. Wilson and Dannon answered what they could. Sean stood and paced behind his desk, his hands shoved into his pockets.

"Alright. So, what have we got here? No forced entry to the home. No proof of anyone else being in the home besides the residents. Mitch was out at a bar. So, he potentially has a verifiable alibi for his whereabouts. Annabelle and the two kids were in bed. He believes someone came in and assaulted her. Someone she knew. The kids didn't hear anything, but his daughter woke up and found Annabelle in the kitchen unconscious."

Sean paused. *Did Annabelle have someone over that night? Was she seeing someone behind Mitch's back?* He tried to remember if Mitch ever said that she had messed around. He thought about how sweet and endearing she was and couldn't picture her having an affair. *Unlikely, but possible,* he thought. He stopped pacing and faced Dannon and Wilson.

"One of you go over to the hospital. Stay for as long as you can because if Annabelle pulls out of her coma, I want her questioned. If you have to leave, get another officer down there on post. Do we know where Mitch is? Is he at home with the kids or at the hospital?"

"Hospital," Wilson said.

Sean considered how much latitude he should allow for the emotional difficulty of the circumstances. *Is it heartless to question him now?* Sean decided he would be doing Mitch a favor by questioning him now if the case turned out to be a murder investigation. He doled out more directives.

"We need more info from the neighbors. Somebody saw something." Sean paused. "As soon as those reports are done on the interviews with the neighbors, I want them on my desk. And I need all of Mitch's case files."

Wilson and Dannon filed out of the office, got Sean the files he asked for, and made a few calls from their desks. Then they both headed out of the precinct. Sean read through the files while taking notes. Then he leaned back in his seat and exhaled loudly. He hit number five on his speed dial,

"Mitch, man. I'm sorry."

"Dude, this shit is crazy."

"I know man."

Sean paused, brimming with discomfort.

"I know it's a rough time. But, you know what I'm about to say."

"I know."

Sean continued, "We need to get this on record as quick as possible."

Mitch was silent for a few seconds. "Yeah, I know. I'm leaving here now. I'll, err, be there in twenty."

Sean looked through case notes. He re-read certain lines. About Annabelle having old and new bruises on her torso and thigh. A gash and bruising near her left temple. That there were signs of a struggle. And that she appeared three months pregnant.

Sean looked up as Dannon came to the office door and stood.

"Sarg, Wilson is at the hospital and he—."

Sean motioned for Dannon to enter the office and close the door.

Dannon sat down.

"Wilson saw Mitch sitting in his car. He was making a bunch of calls and it looked like he was sending a lot of texts before pulling off."

Sean's brows furrowed.

"Alright. Thanks for the update."

When Dannon stood, Sean motioned for him to sit again. He looked at his watch realizing twenty-five minutes had passed since he talked to Mitch. He hit the redial button. This time, he was less concerned about showing sympathy.

"Listen, Gibson, this can't be sloppy. We need this to be by the books. From top to bottom. You need to be here. Now."

Sean hung up without waiting for a response. He glanced at Dannon.

"Alright. Talk to everyone you can at the bars around Gibson's house. If he was there, we need a time line for when he came and went. And anything else anyone saw."

He leaned back in his seat as Dannon left. *What the hell am I going to tell Hodges? Maybe I can delay giving him an update until the morning.* An officer knocked on Sean's open door within seconds.

"Sarg. Lieutenant Hodges is here."

Sean's jaw tightened. *Shit.*

Hodges stood through the brief meeting in Sean's office. He reminded Sean that any cases involving police officers had the immediate potential of being a scandal. He asked about the key info in the case and wondered what the risk of death was for Annabelle. He asked Sean if he could be objective enough on the case if it became a homicide. Sean confidently assured Hodges that he could handle it while also having a plan in case he couldn't.

"I'm prepared to turn the case over if I believe my judgment becomes compromised at any point."

He threw out some names of other sergeants that could take over. That seemed enough to calm Hodges down.

4

Patrice sat in her office planted at her desk typing documents, putting together PowerPoint slides, and sending emails all morning. She plowed through paperwork with a new zeal. She wanted as many loose ends tied up in anticipation of soon starting a new job. But by 11:30 a.m. her light was dimming. She sipped the last of her second cup of coffee and took the empty mug as a signal that it was time for lunch.

Lunchtime was when she decided she would call York & Newton. She had another firm's offer in her pocket, but she really wanted to be where there was the most growth potential. York & Newton was progressive enough to provide just that. She pulled up to a Deli shop at 11:50 a.m. She grabbed a soup, salad, and sandwich—her hunger growling for all three. Then made the call in her car before heading back to work. She wanted to be tired from a long morning when she called John. She needed the weighted blanket of weariness to keep her from sounding too eager. *Eager beavers don't give off confidence. Or negotiate well.*

"York & Newton Public Relations. How may I direct your call?"

Monica's monotone voice sparked Patrice's annoyance, which she quickly squelched to sound polite.

"Good morning! This is Patrice Pearson calling. May I speak with Mr. Blackman please."

Monica transferred Patrice to John without delay.

"Patrice, Good morning! We were hoping to hear from you."

He paused. "Listen, we were quite impressed with you, and we're prepared to offer you the position. Are you still interested? Or has another firm snapped you up?"

Patrice smiled, enjoying her leverage.

"Yes, I certainly am interested! Thank you for the offer."

John transferred Patrice to Trevor Edwards to discuss pay and compensation. A discussion moved from salary, benefits, and vacation, to office space. Patrice learned years before that she needed to negotiate like a man if she wanted a man's salary. Another lesson from a book in her father's collection. By the end, she secured more than she had anticipated. Her chest thumped with exhilaration. But she still held out on accepting the offer, and Mr. Edwards transferred Patrice back to John.

"So, sounds like you will be coming on board," he exclaimed.

"Well. I am quite appreciative of this opportunity. I'd like to have a day or two to consider."

She heard him pull in a breath.

"Absolutely. So, we'll talk shortly then. Looking forward to having you on board. That is, of course, *if* you decide to take our offer."

Patrice talked with Sean over dinner that night. He told her to consider if there was anything else she wanted before accepting the offer, because now would be the time to ask for it. She brimmed with pride over negotiating all that she wanted. She only held out on accepting the offer for appearances. The other firm wasn't offering anywhere near the benefits package and salary that York & Newton was. She called John the next day right at 9:00 a.m. She smiled into the phone.

"I am officially accepting your offer of employment, and I'm excited to come on board."

After hanging up, she could hardly focus on work. She was anxious to start in three weeks, and wished it was tomorrow instead. Public relations was a field that could look quite different depending on the firm one was with. York and Newton had a reputation of giving associates more creative autonomy than most companies, which she would gladly welcome. She didn't hesitate before she started planning her new office color palette.

That night, she thought through the reality of her and John now being coworkers. She considered how to bring it up to Sean and when. She already missed the organic opportunity to say it when he asked about the voice message. But she knew he wouldn't be keen on her working with her ex. *He would have an attitude whether I told him or not. I need to focus on what's best for me.* She fell asleep trying to sort it out in her mind.

The next morning, before work, Patrice stopped by Morning Roast, a local deli and coffee shop. They were pricier than the average coffee shop, but she limited herself to going there no more than a couple times a month to justify the cost.

She ordered a hibiscus mint latte and an egg with pesto croissant. As she got back into her car and took the first sip of coffee, her breathing shallowed. She felt the pressing down of an elephant's hoof on her chest. Her vision blurred as her breaths shortened. She closed her eyes, which felt much more disorienting. So she popped open her eyes again and stared out of her windshield with nothing particular in focus. She fumbled for the window button and had trouble coordinating how to press it to open the window. When it finally worked, she inhaled as deeply as she could but still couldn't get enough air in her lungs. She thought, *Oh my God, is this an asthma attack?* She grabbed at her chest, the hoof still compressing it. *Oh my God, it's a heart attack.* Her eyes darted to her phone leaning in the middle console. She couldn't coordinate her movements enough to pick it up and call for help. *Oh my God, am I going to die?* She stared outside. She fumbled for the door handle, and tried to wrap her fingers around it for what felt like an eternity. Finally, the door opened with a few inches of space. She looked at her feet, willing them to lift into the door space. But they wouldn't move. *Oh my God, I'm gonna die. Right here, right now. Oh my God.*

Her chest felt tighter and tighter, only sips of air squeezing into her lungs. Her heartbeat echoed all around her like surround sound. She leaned herself to the left. Her left shoulder slowly pressed on the door. Then her body weight propelled her to the left, and pushed the door further open. She plopped onto the ground, landing with a successive thump, bump, and thud. She laid on the ground, not yet feeling the pain of her head slamming against the car door as she fell to the ground. Her heartbeat reverberated through her whole body. She sprawled her body on the ground and used her feet to push herself back so that she had enough room to spread her feet under the car. With full extension of all her limbs, she laid flat on the asphalt of the parking lot. She couldn't tell if it felt hot or cold. *Oh God, I gotta do something.* Her eyes darted all around her.

Patrice saw the shadow of a bird land in a nearby tree. Then she remembered something. She repeated words in a barely audible whisper, "Bird. Breathe. By. Blue. Booze. Butt."

Her vision was now blurry. She blinked, her eyes finally releasing the building tears that now rolled down her face. She blinked and blinked and blinked. Finally, she could see the blue of the sky. When a cloud came into focus, she traced the edges with her eyes, all the way around.

She whispered, "Cloud. Coo. Cut. Crud. Cab. Cloud."

As she rounded back to "cloud," she finally felt the hoof lift an inch. She sucked at the air. Oxygen seeped in. She shut her eyes for a few seconds. She blinked and focused on another cloud and traced the edge with her eyes again.

She whispered, "Dew. Deer. Door. Die. Do."

After a few minutes, the hoof had lifted. *Thank God.*

She sighed, thankful to have enough air in her lungs to do so. She pressed her palms on the ground and slowly sat up. Pieces of gravel embedded in her skin. A breeze blew, and the wetness of her sweat-soaked blouse gave her goosebumps. She glanced down at her wet clothes. She finally rose to her feet and dusted the dirt and dried leaves off the back of her clothes. It was only then that she scanned the area for anyone who might have seen the events of the past few minutes. She was relieved that she had chosen a far corner parking spot, located near a dumpster and a curb. Her private cove for an unexpected meltdown. She took a deep breath, glanced once more at the sky, then got back in her car. She was grateful that she remembered that word trick. She had heard it on a morning talk show episode about how to deal with a panic attack by focusing on the present.

"Try saying as many words as you can think of that start with a letter. It will help to focus your mind."

As Patrice turned the ignition, she ignored the wetness of her clothes that stuck to the leather of the car seat. She called out of work and headed home. When she got home, she immediately ran water for a bath. Soaking in the tub she thought about her parking lot incident — as she later came to think of it — and wondered, *What the hell was that?* She had never experienced anything like that before. She thought back to that morning show episode and remembered that one of the triggers to having more panic attacks was worrying about having one. That was when she decided to put it out of her mind. After all, one raindrop is no storm. She shifted her thoughts to her new office space. She imagined the way the sunlight entered from the window and the direction the desk was facing. *Gotta move it across the room to get as much light as possible.* She decided that after her bath, she'd order the wall art and desk items she'd saved online for the office.

At some point soon, she would have to tell Sean about her history with John. But for now, she couldn't deal with it. She laid soaking for over an hour, turning on the hot water faucet every few minutes to keep the water temperature comfy. Nearing the end of her bath, she slowly ran her hands over her hair. She felt the roughness of leaves stuck in the crown of her hair from the parking lot.

5

Janelle emerged from a side entrance of her high school with her friends, a hand mirror in one hand and a make-up remover wipe in the other. School was out and she was going straight home since soccer practice was canceled. She knew her stepmother Lily was off from work and at home with the twins who had colds. Janelle swiped repeatedly at her lips with the wipe until all that remained of her bright red lipstick was a slight tinge of pink. The first time she forgot to remove her preferred makeup, Lily caught one glimpse at her walking in the door at home and banned her from using even lip gloss for a week. When they had a conversation about it, Janelle didn't fully understand why Lily had such an issue with bright makeup.

"Ma, nobody cares about this stuff but you."

Lily shook her head, "It matters. Everything we do sends a message about us. Fifteen-year-old girls don't need to be wearing makeup that attracts men. Don't rush to be grown, sweetheart."

Even if Janelle didn't feel decades behind her friends' makeup skills—they were now all perfecting eyeshadow shading while she still struggled with getting the cat-eye look down pat—she still didn't see why makeup had age specifications in Lily's eyes. *It's not like dating. I'm not going to get pregnant from lipstick,* she thought. But Lily had lightened up over time, so Janelle never complained too loudly. Lily was now okay with some bolder lipstick and eyeshadow colors, but certainly not the bright red Janelle preferred.

Janelle and her friends walked past clusters of students standing on the sidewalk outside of the school. Her friends giggled, and one poked her chin out.

"There goes Trey!"

One of her friends tugged lightly on the bottom of Janelle's t-shirt and teased her as they walked past the boy.

"There goes your boyfriend!"

"What? Girl no." Janelle averted her eyes until it would have been awkward not to look. Then she glanced at him and waved. He smiled and gave her a nod. She thought Trey was cute from the first time she saw him. He came to watch a soccer game once because his sister was on the team until she broke her leg and was out for the rest of the season. After that, he smiled whenever he and Janelle passed each other in the school hallways and complimented her when she was in earshot.

"I see you girl. Them soccer legs are everything!"

Janelle would blush every time.

Trey waved Janelle and her friends over. Everyone stood filling the air with continuous chatter and cracking jokes.

The conversation ended with Trey keying Janelle's number into his phone. She walked away with an extra swing in her hips, knowing he was watching. She and her friends walked toward the neighborhood across the street from the school where they all lived.

One of her friends teased, "Look girl, Eminem's staring at you again!"

"No, he's not."

Her friends whispered in unison, "Yes he is!"

Mason leaned against a fence with a friend. His lanky yet strong frame was balanced by his calm manner. As Janelle and her friends passed, she glanced at him, and they low-key smiled at each other. Once out of earshot, one of her friends nudged her.

"Um, Apple, you better let him know you're taken. Trey might get jealous."

Apple was the nickname Janelle earned after loudly answering "Apple" to a teacher's question to which she hadn't been paying attention. Instead, she was staring out of the window watching the first day of football practice. The boys in tights were way more engrossing than the class discussion about the symbolism in the book Brave New World.

Janelle teased back, "Um, Trey's not my man."

She took a peek behind her while adjusting her backpack strap. Mason gazed in her direction.

Another friend chided, "Looks like Eminem's trying to get the boyfriend title!"

Janelle smirked, "His name's Mason."

Her words were more emphatic than she intended.

"Oh, is it? I see!"

Janelle smiled, "Plus, how do you know he wasn't looking at your Beyoncé bootie?"

Janelle laughed while her friend did a quick wind of her waist and bounced her butt around. They erupted in laughter.

Janelle's friends didn't know that she and Mason knew each other. They met two months ago when he walked up an empty school hallway as she exited the gym. They both were leaving school late for different reasons. Mason was talking with the football coach about if he could have a chance to play this school year since he was signing up so late. Janelle had just left a school pep committee meeting and decided to take a look at the gym to get some decoration ideas for the upcoming pep rally. She stepped out and immediately fell in step with Mason as he walked by.

"What's your name?"

"Mason. And you're Janelle right?"

She nodded, surprised that he knew her name.

"Why are you always looking at me?"

He shrugged, "Cause you're *fine*."

She beamed and he smirked.

"You must be looking at me to know that I'm looking at you."

She grinned, "Maybe I am."

They reached the side doors of the school and walked outside.

She inquired, "Where are you headed?"

"Why? You coming?" He glanced out of the corner of his eye. She continued alongside him. They walked two blocks to the neighborhood elementary school. As they headed up the walkway, she saw a boy's head turn toward them. He smiled and walked in their direction. He was a shorter, skinnier version of Mason, with a higher-pitched voice and fearless face. He and Mason did a handshake that included three taps and a hand dip. The boy shook Janelle's hand while giving her the once over.

"Dang! Now that's a fine dime!"

Mason rustled his brother's hair.

"Boy, watch your mouth. Sorry about that, he thinks he's cool. This is my little brother Lawrence. He's eight."

Lawrence immediately whispered, "No, I'm Los, remember."

Mason teased, "Sure Lawrence."

"Nooo, it's Los. Dang."

Janelle was amused. She smiled at how bashful Los looked when he realized he hadn't released her hand from their handshake. She liked the kid already.

6

Patrice and Sean were playing spades at her friend Jen's house on a Saturday night. She and Sean had inexplicably won two rounds in a row. She was usually the weak link, but somehow was making all the right plays that night. After the games, the group separated by gender. Men gathered in the basement, and the ladies lounged in the living room. Patrice and Jen laughed about a mutual friend's oversharing on social media. The friend posted a picture in a yellow bikini with the caption, "My husband is refusing me in this. WTF?"

Jen complained, "Um, why do I need to know when anybody but me is having sex? Keep that to yourself honey."

Patrice chimed in, "Exactly. And while we're at it, I don't need to hear about anybody's ingrown toenail, favorite holey sweatpants, or bloated belly. Geez."

Jen's seven-year-old son trotted downstairs from his bedroom saying he was hungry. She grabbed him some chips, a Jell-O cup, and a juice box, then disappeared up the stairs with him for a few moments. Patrice had ignored her phone

Leaning

buzzing the first time she felt it, but when it buzzed again she checked. It was her mother calling, and there were two missed calls from her too.

Sean searchingly looked around for Patrice and thought she was in the bathroom. When someone else came out of the bathroom, he glanced around again for her. He eventually spotted her on the back porch on her cell phone. He walked over and waited at the sliding door for a few seconds before knocking on the glass. She turned to him, motioning for him to come out.

"Mom. I can't make her do what she doesn't want to. I've tried. You've tried. So many times."

He sat and listened to her end of the conversation about her sister Michelle. Patrice rarely brought her up. Her mother had a lot to say about it though. He stood behind her and wrapped his arms around her waist. She wrapped her free arm around his arms.

He whispered, "Tell her I said 'Hi.'"

"Mom, Sean said –." Patrice smiled and handed him the phone.

"Hey, Ms. Barbara. Haven't seen you in a while. How's everything? You still racking up at the pool halls?"

Patrice's mother's laughter could be heard echoing through the phone. Sean had a knack for bringing out the playful side of her. After a minute, he handed the phone back to Patrice who was shifting her weight from one leg to the next. The straps of her sandals were denting the top of her feet. He slowly backed her up to the bench in the corner of the porch. He sat down and nestled her on his lap.

"We're at a friend's house having dinner Ma. I don't want to keep being rude. I'll call you tomorrow, okay?"

After hanging up, Patrice sighed and plopped her phone back into her purse. She leaned into Sean's chest and brushed his leg with her hand. After a few moments of silence, she turned to put her arm around his neck.

He queried, "What's going on?"

She tilted her head sideways.

"Mom loaned her $200 last week, and now she's afraid Michelle's on a binge."

Sean listened silently.

"I don't get why she still thinks we're going to find some way to save my sister. We've tried. We've put her in so many programs. Spent so much money. I finally get it. You can't save an addict. Not one that doesn't want to be saved."

He nodded. Then she changed the subject.

"Anyway. So, what's happening with Annabelle?"

She had noticed Sean responding to texts while they were playing cards earlier and figured something was happening with the case.

"She's still in a coma."

Sean tensed up. Patrice asked, "Do you think she'll pull through? I wonder if she'll have brain damage."

Sean said, "She could. There's no way to know for sure."

"I should call the kids at their grandmother's. Couldn't hurt to hear a familiar voice."

"Yeah, that would be good."

"And Mitch, what's he doing?"

"He's looking for leads."

Patrice knew Sean couldn't give her all the details of the case, and what she knew was already more than she should. She usually didn't press for info, even when he was involved in a case that was in the media, but this was different. She knew Annabelle. She'd been in her home, and played with her kids.

"You know babes, maybe the department saw something about Mitch that you didn't. Something off. Maybe that's why you got promoted and he didn't."

Sean gave a slight nod.

"The thing is, all we have is circumstantial evidence, nothing solid. I'm hoping something surfaces."

He looked at the sky.

"Anyway, let's not cloak the night with this talk."

Patrice stood.

"Enough said."

She slid her hand in his, and they headed back inside. After another hour, game night wrapped up and they headed out the door.

Usually, Sean would seem annoyed at how a full stomach immobilized Patrice. But to her surprise, after they said their goodbyes to everyone, Sean gave her a piggyback ride to the car while she carried her sandals in her hand. She looked up and saw the sky was clear, with the exception of two stars.

She pointed.

"See those over there? That's us, babes. Two stars in a world of endless possibilities."

After a pause, Sean said,

"Yeah. That's us alright. See how far apart they are? That one's living over in Greenbelt and the other in Silver Spring."

Sean turned his head towards her so she could get a side view of his smirk. She sighed loudly. He let her down from his back and opened her car door. She felt uncomfortably full.

She lamented, "Do we have to end the night on a bad note? We just had fun."

His brows furrowed as he drove off.

"How does talking about living together make it a bad night?" She poked lightly at his rib.

"See what I mean? See how you're acting? I didn't mean it that way. I'm just saying I want to chill and enjoy the night. Why start fussing?"

She rested her hand on his leg as he drove. She reclined the passenger seat to get comfortable for the ride to her place. Sean kept his midnight blue BMW X4 in clean and pristine condition. She'd never even seen him eat in the car and she certainly never asked to eat in there herself.

Patrice had been thinking about the two of them taking a trip. They hadn't gone on one since they took a short cruise to Nova Scotia last fall.

"Hey babes, how about Atlantic City for a weekend getaway? Do you have any weekends off soon?"

"A lot will depend on the posture of Annabelle's case. I'm supposed to be off the last weekend of this month. But, I'll have to see how things go."

"Okay. Well, how about we plan for it? I'll get a refundable hotel room just in case. But I'm sure your squad can handle the case for a couple days without you. And hopefully by then maybe Annabelle will be out of the coma."

Sean nodded. Minutes later he glanced over and Patrice had drifted off. She woke up when they went over bumpy road. Glancing at him, she asked, "You okay?"

She leaned towards him and slid her hand between his headrest and the back of his head to rub his neck. He peered at her for a few seconds before nodding.

7

"When are you going to take my advice and practice that weak shot of yours?"

Sean teased his brother Ron. They had just finished a game of pickup basketball and were heading to Ron's new condo.

"Yeah, yeah, yeah. I told you, I live a busy life. Basketball comes in tenth after divorce proceedings, my kids, my dental practice, unpacking –."

Sean chimed in, "And all these random chicks you've been hooking up with?"

"With what I'm going through, I'll take any enjoyment I can get. And you act like there's been a dozen women. We're talking three dates."

Sean gave a conceding nod as Ron continued,

"It's crazy. I thought nobody would go for a divorcing dentist with four kids and a gut. I'm an old man."

Sean protested, "Hey, who you calling old? I ain't but a couple years behind you, remember? And I ain't old." He

58   Leaning

added, "Plus, pockets matter more than pouches. They're not worried about your gut if your pockets bulge too."

"Tell me about it. Man, dating is expensive."

They sat in Ron's living room drinking beers.

"Anyway. What's happening with you? How's Patrice?"

"She's good. Getting adjusted at the new job."

"I thought you two were moving in together. Weren't y'all looking at places?"

"Yeah, sort of." Sean paused. "I don't know. Every time I bring it up, she has an excuse not to talk about it."

"What? A female with commitment issues? Now that's rare."

"No, not commitment issues." Sean defended her. "I don't think that's it."

Sean wasn't quite sure where Patrice's head was about moving in together. It was weird. Most women he knew would be pressing to move in after a year together. Because the quicker the move in, the quicker the marriage proposal. Before Patrice, he never gave it serious consideration. But with her most things felt natural. Flowing without effort. They were together most nights. She was good with his son. She accepted him being a cop. Well, to the extent that she could. Him having a job that could result in death at any point wasn't a thing to accept so much as it was something to learn to live with.

Living together first came up as a joke. Sean teased her about the two stuffed dresser drawers she used at his place for her clothes.

"Dang, you sure you don't need part of my closet for your stuff? Those drawers can't hold anything else without the bottoms falling out."

She poked lightly at his rib.

"Yup, let's switch. Let me have the closet, and you can have these drawers back."

He laughed.

"Wait, I was talking about just a part of the closet. You talking about the whole thing. Now how is that fair?"

She shrugged her shoulders.

When they quieted, he said, "Maybe we should split the closet. That's what would happen if we were living together."

When they first talked about it, Patrice seemed on board. He had the bigger place, a third story condo and a balcony with enough room to have a few people over for outdoor entertaining. They had talked about how they would mix their stuff. That he had the better dining table, but her living room set was newer. And she had all the kitchenware so his handful of dinged pots and scratched pans could go. He had a king-sized bed, so her bed could replace the futon in his second bedroom. It all just made sense.

Marriage floated through Sean's mind at times. Last year while shopping for Christmas gifts, he walked into White Premiere jewelry store to take a look at rings. The ample, shapely clerk quickly approached and knowingly led him over to engagement rings. She explained the four C's to him—cut, clarity, carat, and color. Living together, though, was a necessary step in his eyes before a larger commitment. *How can you really know if you get along without seeing every-thing. Tripping over shoes, dealing with toilet seat issues. What about bill paying? And lost keys? You can tell a lot about a person based on how they handle losing keys.* But what started off as mutual interest shifted to Patrice being skeptical and then to her avoiding the topic altogether.

"Babes, seems like there's so much to sort out still. I don't know if it all makes sense yet. Are we getting rid of our stuff that doesn't fit or getting a storage space? Who's going to pay for it? Are we keeping separate bank accounts? What long-term parking options does your condo have for my car? Let's figure things out first."

But those figure-things-out conversations never happened.

Sean was irritated whenever he thought about it. Knowing in your bones that someone loves you doesn't mean every-thing works out. He wasn't much for "I love you," but he knew she felt loved. That wasn't their issue. He wasn't sure what was holding her back. He vacillated between flat out asking her, "What's the deal?" and deciding that if it was meant to be it would happen naturally.

Sean's thoughts returned to Ron, who was checking his voice mail messages. He could hear the voice of Ron's soon-to-be ex-wife, loudly screeching through the phone.

"Look, I'd appreciate it if you would come tomorrow to get the last of your boxes so that I can change the locks. And you need to have your mail redirected to your place. Also, Nina was playing in the closet and got crayon on one of your white shirts. So, you'll need to get it cleaned before wearing it. I'll expect you tomorrow at 5."

Ron lamented, "She is *not* making this easy. Not by a long shot."

Sean offered, "Yeah. Give it time. It's hard to go from mar-ried to single mother."

Ron shook his head.

"The thing is she's not a single mother. Single woman maybe, but not a single mother. I have the kids Friday through Sunday. I pick them up from some of their after-school practices, feed them, and get them home. I've cut back my hours at the practice. Sometimes I'm the one to get them from school if they're sick. It's not like she's on her own figuring this all out while I have them every other weekend." He paused. "I didn't stop being a father because we're not together. I'm there."

Sean conceded.

"You're right. I wasn't saying you weren't a good father."

Ron gave a knowing nod as Sean continued.

"Just saying that she's being nasty right now because it's rough adjusting to everything plus you not being in the house daily and available all the time." Sean paused. "Plus, it's not like you skipped a beat with starting to date again. I'm sure she knows that." Sean smirked at him. "Who are you seeing tonight?"

Ron smiled. "Ty! She's sweet. Good job, no kids, own place, own car."

Sean feigned shock.

"Wow! You want a woman with no kids? Wow!"

Ron retorted with a grin, "Hey, my four kids is exactly why I don't need someone with kids. I can't do the Brady Bunch thing." They laughed.

The next day at the precinct, Sean rubbed his temples and leaned back in his office chair, listening to Mitch give an update on Annabelle, who was still in a coma but showing signs of responsiveness.

"One of the nurses said Anna opened her eyes this morning for five seconds. That's the longest time so far. I think she's trying to make it back. It's just a matter of time."

Sean had visited Annabelle once since she'd been in the hospital. He and Patrice went after work one night. They talked with her as though she was awake, updating her about celebrity news and their upcoming Atlantic City trip. Patrice went back one other time to take her a Peace Lily plant. Sean thought about visiting again, but Lieutenant Hodges had already questioned his objectivity at the start of the investigation. He had to keep his focus on solving the case. Sean didn't have the sense that there was foul play on Mitch's behalf. But something was off. *Someone had been in their house. But no one seems to know anything about who it could be? A stranger? Someone she knew? Someone Mitch Knew?*

Sean thought back to when he and Mitch first met in high school. Back then, attention naturally fell in Mitch's direction. They had three classes together during their senior year and Mitch usually walked into classes grinning like he was remembering an inside joke. Light skinned, long and lean, he was a natural at whatever sport he tried and a decent enough student. Sean didn't gravitate to the light the way Mitch did. They lived in the same neighborhood and would hang out after school a few times a month, smoking, playing video games, and talking about girls. Mitch kept a steady girlfriend and usually a helping of other girls on the side. Sean had the same girlfriend through most of high school. Mitch walked into situations confidently and expected positive outcomes. He had planned to start in the junior management program at his father's car dealership once he graduated. Sean, on the other hand, spent senior year dealing with a pregnant girlfriend who was due a month after graduation. He had to figure out how to support a family. His job as a busser at TGIFridays wasn't going to cut it. They seemed to be on different life paths.

When they both joined the police department around the same time, their lives had come full circle. For Sean, being a cop meant a large enough paycheck to have his own place, pay for childcare, and fly out to see his son several times a year—his girlfriend and infant son had moved to Illinois for her to go to college. Mitch petered out quickly on the management track at his father's dealership and came to the police department ready for a new start. He had married Annabelle, and they had their daughter within a year of the wedding. Sean and Mitch seemed to find a rhythm as partners. Same as they did in high school. Sean had Mitch's back on several occasions, and Mitch returned the favor. Within a year, it seemed like Mitch was going to move up the ranks quicker than Sean.

But the tides turned. Sean's focused, careful approach was now giving him a leg up. He made some high-profile arrests that were by the book. Internal investigations took notice of his airtight paperwork, and top police brass were more than happy about the police department faring well under public scrutiny. Within a year of joining the force, he was assigned to special cases and didn't think twice about Mitch not being assigned with him. Sean enjoyed the attention when higher-ups came to their precinct and knew him by name.

Mitch's resentment about Sean being promoted to Sergeant wasn't obvious at first. It was cloaked in kudos.

"Man, you deserve this. Hard work pays off!"

Eventually, the "Brown nosing the brass" and "Good lackey" comments surfaced, thinly veiled as ribbing. Sean took them in stride. He knew that Mitch's fate was his own to deal with. Sean was measured and careful. Mitch was showy and carefree, an approach that Sean knew had a low ceiling.

Today, in Sean's office, Mitch stood to stretch his legs. They'd been hunkered down for the past hour. Sean questioned Mitch about the night his wife was assaulted and the events leading up to that night. Mitch admitted to hitting his wife in the past during arguments, but swore he hadn't done so in months and definitely not the night in question. He insisted that he didn't know she was pregnant.

"Mitch, this doesn't add up. You say you didn't know she was pregnant, yet she told some of her friends that you were pissed about the pregnancy and wanted her to get an abortion."

Mitch's jaw tensed.

"They don't know what the hell they're talking about. She never said anything to me about being pregnant. We weren't trying to have more kids."

Sean's head tilted, his hands tensed on the armrests of his chair.

"So, you can understand my confusion. We're talking more than one friend giving the same story."

"Exactly. You don't see how off that is? That they have the same story to tell?"

"Fact still remain that there are multiple accounts that you knew about the pregnancy."

"And you think they're more credible than I am? So, now my word isn't enough, Sergeant Robinson? What her friends say counts more than what I do?"

Sean took a deep breath.

"Following up on leads is standard procedure. You know how this works. All possible leads could be something. What's your concern here?"

Sean didn't bother to mention that Annabelle's friends volunteered the information to Wilson while at the hospital. No special efforts were made to find out about the pregnancy. Mitch shoved his hands in his pockets.

"I told you everything there is to know. Don't have shit to hide."

Sean leaned forward in his seat.

"Okay. So what's your problem?"

Mitch turned toward the office window. He took a deep breath and remained quiet.

Sean pushed, "Hey man, if there's something I need to know, better now than later. Later looks like a lie. Or cover-up." Sean paused. "If Annabelle dies, and I hope to God she doesn't, this becomes a murder investigation. At that point you become the prime suspect and the hunt is on for foul play."

Both men stared at each other. Mitch chuckled.

"What? I'm supposed to be shook?"

Sean glared.

"Shook? For what? I thought you had nothing to hide?"

Mitch stiffly smiled.

"We done here, Sarg?"

Sean slowly nodded. Mitch walked out and slammed the door behind him.

8

The Blackmans sat poolside on an unusually warm fall evening. With a clear blue sky and a light breeze, they splashed around and lounged for an hour before night rolled in. Outstretched on a lounge chair in a white bikini, Janelle had ear buds in and silently sang along to her favorite playlist on her phone while texting Mason and two other friends. Her peace was pierced when John's voice permeated through her music.

"Hey, Ms. Missy? How about joining us over here!"

Janelle grew warm with embarrassment as a few people at the pool glanced her way. She popped up and headed over to the kiddie pool to prevent a second call out.

She whispered as she got close, "Really dad? Does everyone have to hear our family business?"

He chuckled.

"What family business? Ain't like I'm telling the story of when you were born or when Lily and I met."

Janelle sighed and rolled her eyes as she planted herself on the edge of the kiddie pool. She splashed water at her brother then her sister, who giggled and clumsily splashed her back. Jasmine bobbed around in the water in a watermelon swimsuit, while John and Jasper had on matching green shorts. Janelle and Lily were both wearing swimsuits they bought a month earlier. Janelle was proud that she picked Lily's out.

When Lily and the kids went to the mall for back to school shopping last month, Janelle sifted through the end-of-summer sale racks for a swimsuit.

"I found some. And look!" She showed Lily a hot pink string bikini. "This would be cute on you!"

Lily grimaced.

"Oh no. Too much flesh on display."

Janelle shook her head.

"Ma, you still have a hot body for having had two kids. Why do you keep bagging it up in tankinis?"

"Because I'm not 18 anymore."

Janelle's eye widened with exasperation. "So? Does that mean you're supposed to swim in garment bags?"

After Janelle showed Lily a couple of choices that she shut down without a second thought, Janelle asked a flurry of questions. She took an inventory on what Lily liked—color, coverage, and design—before she returned to the racks and pulled out more options.

"Okay Ma. I'll pick out five. Then you have to pick at least one out of the five. Deal?"

"Wait a minute," Lily protested, "I might not like any of them."

"You will. Now I know what you like. Let me work my magic!"

Janelle perused all the swimwear racks, and smiled when she found a few good ones. She pulled hangers and hooked them on her hand, building a stockpile of nine options. She knew Lily would balk at the larger-than-five pile when she went to find her in the athletic wear section of the store.

"Okay, before you fuss about how many, let's keep in mind that I'm trying to get a paradigm shift to happen here. So, I need some latitude to make that happen."

Lily laughed.

"What do you know about paradigm shifts?"

Janelle winked then displayed each swimsuit on the ends of the nearby racks. Eventually, Lily picked what she liked and they each walked out with two swimsuits. Janelle patted herself on her back.

At the pool, Lily played with the twins in her peach bikini top and high-waist bottom swimsuit. The sun made the red undertone of her fair skin glimmer. Her short cropped medium brown hair dripped from splashed water. Janelle noticed Lily glance in John's direction a couple times. He obliviously focused on bouncing a beach ball to the twins.

Janelle used to see John and Lily kiss, hug, and whisper to each other and always wondered what they said. Lately, they seemed like ships sailing past each other in the night. She used to be able to ask one parent about getting rides to sports and sleepovers, and that parent knew the other one's schedule well enough to say who would be available to drop her off and pick her up. Now she had to ask both Lily and John separately about availability.

Janelle had heard the story about how John and Lily met several dozen times. She knew the story so well that she could tell it word for word. But what used to be a twenty-minute story had now whittled down to a three-sentence telling that lacked a cute beginning and fairytale ending. Janelle last heard John tell the full story at a cookout they had last summer. He launched into his tale with a beer in one hand and cigar in the other.

"I had bought a townhouse a few months earlier. I was so glad to be done with apartment living."

Janelle sometimes heard him add that he was glad to be done with shady landlords and that the last straw was almost getting into a fight with the last one, who John suspected was going into his apartment when he wasn't home. He didn't add that part at the cookout.

"I had a corner plot in a row of townhouses, which was half a block from a bus stop. Janelle was eight-years-old then. She loved her new, bigger room. Plus, she got to stay at her school since we stayed in the same school zone. When we first moved in, I had to post signs and shout from my window to get neighborhood kids to stop traipsing through my backyard, using it as a shortcut to the public bus stop. It stopped for a couple months."

Janelle remembered him reseeding the dirt path in the yard and the grass growing within weeks. The trail was barely noticeable after a while.

"But then I saw the dirt trail in the yard pop up again. So, I got dressed on mornings in the guest bedroom so I could keep an eye out of the window to see which kid it was. Lo and behold, it was no kid!"

He grinned.

"On the third day posted at the window, I see this woman hustling across the yard. I couldn't see her face too much, but those hips were moving."

He shook his head and grinned like the memory was fresh in his mind.

"I saw her go by everyday for three days. And everyday I tried to figure out a non-creepy way to meet her."

Janelle thought, *Isn't it creepy to sit and think about how not to be creepy?*

"The next morning, I went out on the porch ten minutes before the time I usually saw her and waited. But then I chickened out. I thought, "Go in the house you psycho. She'll run as soon as she sees you sitting here.""

He shook his head with embarrassment.

"So, I retreated."

Janelle grinned at how corny her dad was and couldn't decide if he was cornier when this was all happening, or for how proud he was when retelling the story.

Next, he said he woke up in the middle of the night with a winning idea. The next morning, he prepped to leave home earlier than usual and he went to the bus stop. He was going to take the bus and train to work. He timed out when to get to the bus stop, so there'd be a couple of minutes before the bus arrived. But when he saw the bus coming in the distance and no sign of her coming up the trail, he cursed aloud. When he turned to head home, he finally saw her hustling up the trail. The bus pulled up before she did. So, he asked the driver to wait.

They boarded the bus and he let her pass by to find her seat first, then he sat catercorner from her. She smiled and mouthed, "Thank you."

He held onto everything he wanted to say to get conversation going. Just waited. Lily pulled out her phone. When she smiled at something, he exaggeratedly tilted his head and said, "You're not going to share the joke? I want to laugh too!"

She turned her phone so he could see the screen.

John saw a meme of a bull walking into a shop and breaking dishes as his humongous body swayed. The caption said, "So, I heard there's a china shop around here." They looked at each other and laughed. Three days later, they sat at a Longhorn Steak House chatting over dinner and ended the night with drinks at a nearby lounge. He found out about her car being in the shop for repairs that were taking longer than estimated. He later offered to give her rides to work, which she obliged. They rode together for a week before her car was fixed.

"And that was how we met."

He wrapped up the story by saying that he didn't tell Lily about how he planned their "spontaneous" meeting until they had been dating two months.

Lily's response was, "Look at you. Little schemer! You told me your car was also getting repaired that day and that's why you had to take the bus."

John shook his head, "You know good and well you would've been creeped the hell out if I was sitting in my backyard waiting for you to walk up. Trust me, my way was a much better approach."

Janelle remembered her first-time meeting Lily one day when she came home from school. Lily was in the living room drinking a glass of juice. John introduced them, saying that Lily was his friend.

Janelle asked her, "Do you like the juice? I mixed grape juice, fruit punch, and apple juice together in the jug. It's very berry cheery juice!"

Lily smiled widely.

"It's delicious!"

Janelle took to Lily quickly, and Lily often told John she felt instantly connected to his sweet, funny, doll and action-figure loving daughter. They had arts and craft in common and would go to craft stores together. And Janelle preferred Lily to help her with homework and with friend problems. Seemed that Lily and Janelle's connection was all John needed to be ready for the next step. He asked Lily to marry him after dating for six months. Janelle remembered her grandmother saying to John, "Son, when you find the right one, why waste time!" John and Lily planned a fifty-guest wedding in the space of four months. They married in a private room at Ruth's Chris Steak House, then honeymooned in the Bahamas.

The Blackman family wrapped up at the pool and headed home. Jasper and Jasmine were out like a light within minutes after their baths. The next day, Janelle left school through the side door as soon as the bell rang for dismissal. She had gone to her locker before the last class period to stuff her backpack with the books she was taking for homework. She made it to the spot she and Mason had made a routine of meeting in five minutes. Yet still, he beat her there.

"You must be dipping out of school early. How do you get here this fast?"

Mason donned a cocky smile, "Skills lady. Skills!"

Janelle and Mason would text each other from morning to night. They texted about everything—happenings at school, funny memes on Instagram, family issues, friend situations, and what they had to do after school each day. Janelle had soccer practice or a piano lesson most days, and Mason had to either pick up his brother from school, go to driver's education classes, or hang at a friend's house. Whenever there were a few minutes of time between school and after school activities, they would meet up at the park. Most days Mason was there before Janelle, leaning against a corner streetlight playing a game on his phone. Today, Janelle walked up and snatched his phone. She saw that he was on Instagram. She scrolled through his page. *Let me see what girls are on here commenting about.* He tried to get it back by wrapping her up in his arms. He smiled, and she giggled. They walked in step into the neighborhood. They lived a neighborhood apart, a fifteen-minute walk from one house to the next. It usually worked out that once a week neither of them had after school obligations, and they could walk around together.

They would walk down different streets looking at yards and cars. Or they'd go to the park and sit on top of the monkey bars. Sometimes, Mason would bring Cheetos. Today, he switched it up with a bag of Onion Rings. As they finished the bag, Mason fanned his nose.

"Whew, you need some gum."

Janelle nudged him.

"Speak for yourself dragon breath!"

They laughed. Mason told her about how his driver's ed classes were going. She couldn't wait until she could start in a few months. Just before setting off on their walk home, Mason sidled in closer atop the monkey bars. He brushed a crumb from her lips. Her skin warmed like the sun was beaming just on her. She closed her eyes as he leaned in. She felt the softness of his lips and relaxed into a kiss. Moments later, they sat quietly, until Mason crumpled the Onion Rings bag and tossed it like a basketball into the trash can that was a few feet away.

"Skills!" he said, while grinning with pride. She nodded.

He asked, "What are you thinking about?"

She glanced at his lips.

"I kissed a white boy."

Mason feigned a surprised look.

"Whaaat? Stop the press. This is big news!"

"Be quiet, idiot."

"What? The world needs to know you kissed a white boy."

"Well, I'm just saying."

He glanced at her.

"You upset about it?"

"No." She shook her head reassuringly. "It's not that. It's just, you know. That it happened."

They climbed down from the bars and walked home. She replayed the kiss in her mind. She always wondered what it would feel like to kiss. If she would know what to do, or if it would feel weird. She grinned. *Not weird at all.* She barely paid attention as he talked about his cousins coming to visit next week. When they got to her driveway, they hugged and kissed again before Mason turned to head home.

Janelle tried three times to start her homework that night. Each time she reread the same sentences over and over. By the third try, she decided she would wake up early in the morning to do the work, instead of spinning her wheels all night. She laid across her bed and listened to music while playing Candy Crush on her phone. She thought through talking with her parents about hanging out with Mason. She wanted to spend more time with him, more than a few minutes after school. *Maybe he can come over to the house sometimes.* She played through how the conversation would go with her parents. What her dad would ask and how he would seem about it. Up until now there was only one boy whose house she had been over, but that was a short-lived crush. This was different. Mason was different.

Well before Janelle and Mason knew why, they knew *they* weren't a good idea. Everyone acted like interracial dating was a 21st century norm that no one batted an eye at. Yet, there was usually a tinge of judgment and a slight head lean when it was talked about. Janelle and Mason practiced omission. She talked about all her friends around her parents, except Mason. And he never said her name to his friends or family, only that he liked a girl.

Janelle felt a surge of excitement. She wanted to talk about Mason to everyone now. She even wanted to talk to her birth mother. In rare moments that Janelle didn't talk much about, she wondered about her. She had no real memories of birth mother. And there were no pictures to jog her memory because her father had none. Janelle was three when she last saw her mother at a family member's funeral, or at least that's what she was told. She did have something of an image in mind when she thought of mother though. Janelle pictured a teenager, pregnant yet slim with her hair always in a messy ponytail and with dirty fingernails. She wasn't sure where she conjured the image from. Perhaps from Janelle knowing she was almost the age her mother was when she had her. Or maybe from her father's descriptions, that gave broad strokes of info. Janelle used to ask him questions.

"Do I look like her?"

"Yeah, you do. You're the same complexion. And your eyes, mouth, and hands look a lot like hers."

"How did she smell? Was she funny?"

"I don't know how she smelled. Like soap maybe. And she was fun to be around. She liked to laugh. And sleep a lot. Just like you!"

Janelle didn't ask much now. She saw the uncomfortable look that would wash over her father's face. She didn't want to make life complicated by asking about a ghost. Sometimes she wondered if her mother was dead or alive, or if the wondering was going both ways. When she was twelve, she once saw a woman at a park who waved at her. Janelle thought the woman looked familiar in a strange way. Like she knew the woman somehow, but didn't. She was too far away to see her face clearly, though. *Maybe that was her. She could be anywhere. Or maybe she's gone.*

9

Patrice sat at her desk for the past two hours and pored through data on past and current York & Newton accounts. She was on her third hot beverage. Trying to limit her coffee intake to no more than two cups a day, she sipped on the last of her mug of mint herbal tea. Her first week on the job, she was at the office ten hours daily, more to observe than to work. She arrived early and as she passed by each office, looked to see who else was in. She stayed late and paid attention to who also did. By the second week, she asked questions of every coworker, checking to see who was the go-to person for particular information. Now in her third week, she looked for patterns with who headed up what accounts, and watched how the hierarchy of the office showed itself in meetings. In large part, she'd figured out the rhythm of the office, and now it was time to figure out where she fit.

Going from a small firm to a large one was like going from swimming in a community pool to contending with the ocean. The first order of business was she had to up her suit and shoe game. She previously mostly wore shirts, blouses, skirts, and slacks to work. Now suits were the daily attire. She always loved her shoe collection, but she was well aware that most of them weren't going to cut it for corporate America. She even got a new coffee mug. Her favorite office coffee mug with a bear roaring, "Don't try me. You'll lose," never made it into her new office. She now preferred a mono-grammed black mug with gold trim. It matched the decor she chose for her office. Patrice ordinarily prided herself on not living on credit. If she didn't have the money in her bank account to cover a purchase, then she didn't buy it. Credit cards were only for racking up points for mileage discounts. But she quickly made an exception to upgrade her wardrobe and office decor. None of her old office baubles, vases, and wall pictures made it into her new office. First impressions, contrary to popular belief, were being formed for at least a few weeks, not just the first time meeting someone. She need-ed to establish the look she wanted to be known for, without wasting time buying one suit per paycheck. The 30 percent salary increase she negotiated would cover the spending. She would pay off her credit card within a couple of months.

Patrice was glad that Monica, the testy admin, had re-signed before Patrice was on-boarded. Now there was a new friendly eager-to-please admin at the front desk. Leann had a much more pleasant vibe to walk into on mornings. York & Newton had several projects at various stages. There was adequate work to go around and noticeable, albeit unspoken, competition among associates. Patrice had sized up John's in-fluence and professional persona. He was a conduit to Trevor Edwards. John was respected and confident, always able to back up anything he said. Comfortable with sharing the spotlight, he quickly allowed new associates to start teething. In consultation with Trevor, John gave new associates creative latitude on at least one project within weeks of starting. She noticed that he transitioned from business to casual with ease. He often had lunch with colleagues or Trevor, most days of the week. It seemed to be his way of building good relationships.

During Patrice's first week, she was nervous about whether her past with John would come up. *I don't even know what he thinks about our past at this point.* It didn't take long for her to realize that if it came up, it wouldn't be him initiating it. He never made reference to knowing her before, much less their relationship. At first, she had moments of stirred up anger about their abrupt ending. Then she would think, *Girl please, that was a lifetime ago. You've moved on.* But, those thoughts went nowhere beyond the fleeting moment they existed in. Still, it was hard to see him make familiar facial expressions and not say, "I know what that face means." Hard to erase history, even when unacknowledged.

Patrice could see the John she knew was still in him. In his eyes, his laugh, his humor. But he was as different as he was the same. More centered, with a clear focus and planful approach. He had that air of responsibility that married men with kids invisibly had on their shoulders. Certainly, John having a child when he was still one himself, was a big influence on the man he became. Having a child at a young age also kept the child in him alive. Patrice passed by his office one afternoon and heard him teasing whichever child was on the other end of the phone, using a Scooby-Doo voice to say that he was bringing happy meals home after work. She was certain the child wasn't old enough to know the character, but was probably giggling uncontrollably on the other end.

Occasionally, over the years in quiet moments, Patrice wondered what happened to John after they broke up. It was like he fell off the face of the earth. No friends ever told her, "Hey, you'll never guess who I ran into." She never saw him in the friend lists of her friends on social media. There was no instance where that vaguely familiar-looking guy across the room in the club, or in front of the line in Starbucks, or at the other end of the aisle in the grocery store was actually him.

* * *

Patrice and John met during their first year at Howard University, the D.C. HBCU that was an epicenter for black power, growth, education, and love. Patrice was all set to start college the fall after high school graduation, but an opportunity came up that took her across the pond. Her uncle came over one evening after calling excitedly to say, "I've got an offer you can't refuse!" Her uncle had co-founded Y.E.S., the Young Entrepreneurs Shine entrepreneurial program, years before, with two of his frat brothers. It had grown from 12 to 122 program graduates in four years.

"So, this is going to be our first time expanding to overseas. In addition to having D.C. and New York opportunities for our attendees, London is our newest location!"

Patrice was flabbergasted.

"Are you serious?"

"Of course! Plus, the program is now for three months. So, you'll spend your entire summer before college in the program. But it'll be worth it."

Patrice left the day after graduating high school. She was in London and unpacking her clothes in her room at the host family's house by nine o'clock the next night. The Y.E.S. program included visiting various companies to learn in detail about the business structure, and interviewing for internships in a field of choice every two weeks. Patrice beamed when she called her mother after she landed a six-month internship at a Public Relations firm in London.

"Mom, guess what! I was just offered the internship at Sumpter and Associates!"

Patrice ended up deferring her admission to Howard for a year. By the time she started college, a year after living abroad, she felt worldly and ready to face anything. She had seen the business world up close in London by day and managed to get a tattoo and stupidly drunk more times than she cared to recall by night.

Meanwhile, John had initially planned to go to Howard right after high school. One afternoon a month before high school graduation, his mother sat him down.

"Honey, I have only one question. How are you going to manage Janelle, a full load of classes, and having a life?"

John spent the next few weeks rethinking how to make the puzzle pieces of his life fit. Howard would be a fifty-minute daily commute from home, over an hour and a half each day. Every configuration of a schedule was going to be too disruptive to the flow in Janelle's life. By high school graduation day, his plan was revamped to staying close to home until Janelle was at least in elementary school. He went to community college instead, earning an associate degree in business administration, then eventually transferred to Howard University for a bachelor's degree in business.

While at community college, one of John's professors had set him up with an internship that shaped his vision about being a black man in business. He interned for a large international company with more departments than could be counted on fingers. He spent most of his time bringing coffee and donuts to meetings, making copies, and shadowing employees. But he paid the most attention to Thaddeus, a 26-year-old black, well-liked phenom in the public relations department of the company. Thad had enough business suits to wear no repeats for two weeks, and of course more than one pair of dress shoes. He was easygoing but put in his work daily, researching new projects and keeping his head down until it was his time to shine during meetings and presentations. John observed Thad prepare for presentations and was shocked at the actual amount of time and attention to detail that it took to pull off a sharp presentation. He realized that looking confident, being reliable, and being ready took a lot of behind-the-scenes sweat equity. He discovered his blueprint for success in business.

Patrice loved her first semester at Howard. She and her roommate quickly became close friends, and her classes were fairly easy. Her second semester wasn't as smooth and fun-loving. Her occasional sinus infections were now coming in tow with migraines that had her down for the count a couple days at a time. She was stuck in a windmill of playing catch up on class projects and taking make-up exams while keeping up with current assignments. *Geez, when is this semester gonna end?* A month into second semester, Patrice was sitting at a desk near the middle left of a large lecture room. She was two-thirds of the way through finishing a quiz and feeling like she should have studied more because she had guessed at half the answers. She was congested and tired, the remnants of a sinus infection that had just caused her to miss two days of classes. She glanced up as a classmate ventured up to the front of class to turn in the quiz on the professor's desk. She first saw the back of him as he walked by. *Hmm, who is that?* He had a sexy swagger. She could hear the swish of his jeans with each step he took.

When he turned around to walk back to his seat, she saw his face and smiled to herself. *Hmm, okay!* She watched the sway of his navy blue with white-strips polo sweatshirt, zipped down enough for his white undershirt to show. His brown skin glowed from the sunshine pouring in through classroom windows. His eyes were round and deep-set under full eyebrows. She was relieved that he didn't look in her direction. She wasn't ready. Her ensemble — a ripped sweatshirt being held together with 'I love HU' buttons and stale smelling jeans stained with dried drops of mumbo sauce — was not the first impression she had in mind.

The next class, she came prepared. Patrice's roommate laughed as she dressed and primped before leaving their dorm room.

"Girl, is Obama coming on campus and no one told me? Who are *you* gettin' all nine yards upped for?"

Patrice smirked and kept pushing bobby pins in her hair to keep it in place. She had her braids up in a bun, and her baby hairs tamed with gel. She strutted into class with a fitted sweater, freshly washed jeans, and her newest pair of suede boots. As she walked into class, John and two other guys were standing near the back. She saw him look up as she passed by. She slowed her pace slightly as she scanned the room for a free seat. When she sat down, she noticed a few moments later, John was sitting two seats over in the row behind her. When she turned to reach in her purse, they made eye contact, and smiled.

The next day of class, John caught up with her walking to Blackburn Cafe. After introductions, he launched into asking her thoughts about class.

"What was up with that last quiz? We didn't learn any of that in class. And I was paying attention."

Patrice's mood sank. All he wanted to talk about was class. But she obliged by rambling on about her confusion about the quiz and her congestion. This became his trend. She couldn't figure him out. He talked about stuff—tests and quizzes, upcoming parties, his fraternity—but never made a move. He smiled a lot but never flat out flirted. Never asked her out, but he would show up. He would be in front of whatever building she had class in, and they would walk together for a few minutes before their next class. Or he would text her saying he was on campus, and they would link up on the Yard, the sprawling green, brick paved epicenter of campus. Or at Blackburn or the Library. They met up one day and Patrice stared at his coffee cup when she walked up to him outside of class.

"Man, I never have time to grab coffee before class."

He offered her his cup, of which she gratefully took a sip. She saw it as a sign of connection beyond friends.

After they both failed the midterm exam, they decided to study together for the next quiz and do research for their final class project. They met at Founders library and hunkered down for two hours. Both were exhausted by the time John got up and stretched.

"Alright Mami, I think I'm good. I've got all the research I need for my project. How about you?"

John leaned over Patrice as she sat at a library computer searching for research articles. She seized the opportunity to look into his eyes. *Damn! Gorgeous!* she thought.

She said, "Yeah. I'm good too."

He took a step back to give her room to stand up. He helped her put her binder and books in her bag and put her coat on before gathering his stuff. As they walked out, he put his arm around her shoulder, and she slipped her arm around his waist. When they got to her dorm, he pointed to his cheek. She kissed it. And there it began. John and Patrice. No discussion about being together. No checking if they each were dating anyone else. No deciding on an anniversary date. No fuss, no confusion. Just John and Patrice.

They debuted as a couple at the Howard fashion show at Cramton Auditorium. They low-key color coordinated their outfits, she in a white top with brown and gold jewelry, and him in a brown and white polo shirt and a white hat. They both wore matching wooden rings that they bought at a vendor on campus. Her friends teased her that she looked spoken for. He friends said he was officially off the market.

They fell in step easily without much coordinating. John didn't live on campus but came to campus early each day he had classes. He would go to her dorm, they'd have breakfast, then walk to class. Between classes, they'd grab lunch, or go to the library. Or sometimes back to her dorm to smoke. Patrice secretly loved walking through the Yard with him by her side. To her, it felt like they had a force field around them that only they could see. All that mattered was whatever they were talking about. When they made love for the first time, it felt deep and familiar like they had been intimate all along.

John was the first boyfriend Patrice dated that had a child. It wasn't what she imagined. He was nonchalant about being a father. Maybe because he became one before he fully understood the weight of it. She met his daughter, Janelle, a handful of times. She was a cute, curious and chatty kid who loved her father's attention. John would take Patrice out to his mother's house for dinner on an occasional weekend. He didn't say much about Janelle's mother, other than she had problems and wasn't around. His mother had been helping raise Janelle while he finished college. Patrice never pressed for more information than he would give, knowing that she didn't offer much about her family issues either.

Patrice and John had their good times and fights, but always rebounded together. John was set to graduate a year before Patrice and at the beginning of his senior year, he started job hunting. She was supportive at first. But what was initially, "That's great. I'm excited for you," devolved into, "Well, are you sure you want to work there?" and "I heard they're real trifling there." It wasn't that she didn't want him to be successful. She did. But she felt left out. Dropped to a lower rung on his ladder and less important than his fast-approaching new life. They still spent time together and he was attentive as usual. But now there were other things vying for attention. And it was hard to feel like a special rose with other roses in the bouquet.

They chilled in her dorm room one evening and she turned into a snapping turtle, biting at everything he said. When he got tired of it and left without saying goodbye, she burst into tears and couldn't sleep that night. Instead, she ruminated on the conversations they had in the past months. Not one involved talking about the two of them after graduation. After awhile, John showed up less. When they did hang out, arguments erupted when jokes turned into sarcastic quips about "being petty," and "everything ain't about you," followed by not talking for a day or two. And each time they made up, it wouldn't be long before another argument disrupted their flow again.

Then there was the message. Left on an answering machine with all the warmth of a cold winter night. Full of break-up phrases like "not working out," "still want to be friends" and "need to focus on what I need to do." Everything crumbled suddenly and quickly. Closure wasn't an option. All their years together amounted to dismissive words rattled off in a three-minute message. Seven years later Patrice walked into York & Newton. And just like that, John was back in her life.

10

Sean's alarm beeped from across his bedroom after being snoozed three times. He got up to turn it off and got back in bed. In another twenty minutes he was going to be late for a meeting with Mitch. When he finally got up, he skipped showering and shaving, and got to the precinct at 9:10 a.m. When he walked into his office, Mitch was already sitting in there with an extra coffee.

"Thanks."

Sean scooped the cup up as he walked behind his desk, sat, and took a sip.

"No problem. Rough night?" Mitch's eyes darted to Sean's stubble.

Sean nodded.

"Let's get to it. I want to go over some of these details about your whereabouts the night in question."

He unlocked his drawer and pulled out a file.

"You left your house after an argument with your wife. Then you returned approximately three hours and forty minutes later after your daughter called you. She sounded frantic and said that your wife was unconscious on the floor, and there was blood."

Mitch looked on intently as Sean spoke.

"Yes. Except the fact that you keep saying wife and daughter, like you haven't been to our house and played on the floor with my kids. Everything else is accurate."

Sean continued, "You say you were at Bento bar around the corner from your house and that you spoke to the bartender while you were there."

"Yeah."

"I had an officer question the bartender and some of the patrons that were there that night. People remembered seeing you. But for brief periods. Ten, fifteen minutes at a time."

The times people remembered were inconsistent, but Sean didn't mention that part. Mitch shifted in his seat.

"Well, I was there. I stepped out to smoke a few times. Went to the bathroom."

Sean nodded.

"What time did you say you got to the bar?"

"Like 9:50 p.m."

"And you left when?"

"Approximately 1:00 a.m."

Mitch trained his eyes on Sean.

"Sean. I didn't try to kill her. Or have her killed. And I didn't hit her. Not that night."

That much seemed consistent with the evidence. There were old bruises and new ones—old bruises on her arms and new bruises centered on her torso.

Mitch's voice lowered, "We have problems. But I don't want her dead. I love Anna." He lowered his eyes to the floor.

Sean calmly spoke,

"Do you know if she ever had an affair?"

"She wasn't like that."

Sean squinted at Mitch.

"Why did you lie about not knowing about her pregnancy?"

Mitch's voice raised, "I DIDN'T know she was PREGNANT. She didn't tell me. I didn't know. She wasn't even showing."

Sean continued unphased, "What did you argue about that night?"

"A bunch of bullshit."

Sean waited for him to continue.

"She found some charges on our credit card. She thought I was messin' around."

Mitch's darted his eyes back and forth across the room. Sean leaned in.

"You know Mitch, I'm willing to bet that you weren't at the bar all night. You went, but then you left." Sean stared intently at him. "Where else did you go that night?"

Mitch stared at the floor. Then in a low voice,

"Safina."

Sean squinted at Mitch, slowly leaning in with a raspy whisper through a clenched jaw.

"You're *banging* Hodges' wife? Are you *fucking* crazy?"

Mitch opened his mouth to speak but didn't. Sean stood so fast the desk shook as he pushed the seat back.

"Anything else I need to know?"

Mitch shook his head. Sean grabbed his jacket, the case file, and headed for the door. He left Mitch sitting in his office.

Sean waited until he was in his car and on the road before he called Lieutenant Hodges. He told him that his wife needed to be interviewed in connection to the case and that he would have more details once he spoke with her. Hodges was surprisingly calm. Sean assumed that his wife gave him a heads up. Then he called to set up the interview with Mrs. Safina Hodges. She was agreeable and made herself immediately available. She offered to come down to the precinct first thing in the morning.

At 7:58 a.m., Safina Hodges sauntered into the precinct donning a red suit and six-inch red bottom heels. She strutted through the precinct back to Sean's office with her suit-clad lawyer in tow. Even as officers stood from their desk to ask if she needed help and who she was there to see, her pace never slowed, the click of her heels high-pitched and measured. When they reached Sean's office, they stood at the threshold. Her lawyer stepped forward into the doorway.

"Sergeant Robinson? I'm Gerald Harmon, attorney for Mrs. Safina Hodges. We're here for the interview."

Sean stood and showed them to the seats in front of his desk. After limited pleasantries were exchanged, it was down to business. Sean recorded the interview, making sure to follow procedure. He didn't want bones for Hodges to doggedly latch to. Sean had heard that she had an online business of buying and selling designer clothes worn by celebrities.

"So, how's business?"

"Thriving."

She crossed her legs as though bracing herself. Sean pulled out his notepad.

"Alright, let's begin."

He announced for the recording who was being interviewed and who was present in the room. Then he commenced questioning.

"Mrs. Hodges, when did you first meet Officer Mitchell Gibson?"

"At a Christmas event, two years ago, held by the police department. My husband introduced us."

"Do you know his wife, Annabelle Gibson?"

"No."

"So, you have never met her?"

"No."

"Have you and Officer Gibson had a sexual relationship?"

"Yes."

"For how long?"

"Sixteen months on and off."

"Are you still involved?"

"No."

"When did the affair end?"

"When I found out that his wife was in the hospital."

"Was your husband aware of the affair?"

She paused for the first time before answering.

"He is now."

Her tone was sharp. Sean glanced at her then continued.

"Where were you on the night Mrs. Gibson was assaulted?"

"I was at a fundraiser event in Frederick until 6:35 p.m. I traveled thirty-five minutes home. I cooked dinner then spent time watching a movie with my kids. When they went to bed, I called Mitchell Gibson. He came over an hour after our last text. He probably arrived around 10:35 p.m. He entered my home and did not leave until about 12:30 p.m."

Her eyes never left Sean's. He jotted down notes.

"How did he seem?"

"Fine."

Sean rephrased his question.

"Did anything about his demeanor or action seem out of the ordinary?"

"No."

"Had he been drinking?"

"Yes, I could smell alcohol on his breath."

"Did he mention anything about his wife that night?"

"No."

"To your knowledge, did they have marital problems?"

She smiled patronizingly.

"Yes. Every marriage does."

"What kinds of problems did they have?"

"I don't know."

"How did you know they had problems?"

"He always spoke negatively about her."

"What did he say?"

"That she wasn't as sexy as me, and that she was slipping in bed."

"Did he ever indicate intent to cause her harm?"

"No."

"Or to get divorced?"

"No."

As the questioning continued, Sean tensed and she relaxed. By the end, he wasn't sure what to think about her confident manner, other than knowing she was prepped by her lawyer to answer the questions, saying nothing more and nothing less. *She looks like a good lay. And a piece of work. Definitely not worth the headache.*

Two days later, Sean plopped down on Ron's couch along with two other friends. They were back from a game of pick-up basketball.

"Ron, you slower than molasses with those beers. I'm dying from thirst here."

Ron quipped, "Wow, you real demanding for someone from the losing team."

Everyone laughed. Somewhere in between joking around and drinking beers, Sean's mind drifted to earlier that morning. He could see Hodges raging toward his office from the front of the precinct and slamming Sean's door so hard that the blinds lifted then slammed against the glass windows. Hodges showed up within ten minutes of the Safina interview ending. After what seemed like an hour-long meeting, Sean called Mitch to come back into the precinct, let him know he was suspended and had to turn in his badge and gun. Hodges' words were on repeat in Sean's head.

"Focus on building a case on Mitch. And keeping this out of the press." Just as Sean was about to object, Hodges stood to leave. "If you can't handle it, I'll assign someone else. You decide."

Hodges was ready to proceed as though the Gibson case was already a murder investigation. But the only ground for investigation at this point was assault, possibly with intent to kill. Annabelle had only shown limited signs of coming out of the coma for several weeks now. She had episodes of dangerously low blood pressure then spikes of high blood pressure that took hours to get back to baseline. But she was breathing on her own and had brief moments of physical response when people were in her room, especially her kids. Her eyes would open slightly, or her fingers would pulse a little when touched. Sean thought there was still a chance she'd come out of the coma. So far, there hadn't been much in the news about the case other than one short article in the Washington Post that a police officer's wife had been attacked in her home and was left in a coma. But if this became a murder investigation, it was going to turn into a shit show fast, with Sean first in line to get smeared. He had to make sure there were no holes that could reflect badly on the police department. That is, beyond the possibility that one of their own committed the crime.

Sean shook his head to knock the thoughts loose. He got up to use the bathroom, and before his pee stream ended, he heard his name. It always irked him when anyone called him out of the bathroom when they knew he was peeing. *Nothing is that urgent that it can't wait two minutes.* What irritated him most was that once his stream stopped, he couldn't will it to start again. So, he would have to go again in another half an hour.

When Sean came back out to the living room Ron jutted his chin toward the TV.

"Ain't that where Patrice works?"

Sean heard the channel seven reporter saying,

"Flames engulfed the 1900 block of Connecticut Avenue, in Northwest D.C. at approximately eleven o'clock this morning. Many businesses have been affected by the fire including Starbucks, Smithson Medical Center, and York & Newton Public Relations. Authorities suspect faulty wiring as the cause of the blaze. Thus far, four people have not been accounted for in the three-alarm fire—"

Sean dialed Patrice's cell. Her voice mail answered. He called her office. No answer.

"I'm out."

He grabbed his gym bag and pulled out his car keys.

Hours later Sean was in Patrice's kitchen stiffly pacing. He spent hours that day not knowing if she was safe. When he finally saw her, he felt relief at first. Then anger.

"I still don't get it. It's not computing. How do you *not* think to call me all this time? I'm the last person you think to call? Matter of fact, you still haven't called. *I* had to track *you* down. What the hell? I'm a freaking *nonentity*?"

Patrice pleaded, "Sean, why are you yelling? Is that really necessary right now?"

"Necessary? That's funny." He laughed tensely. "You should've called me. That's what's necessary. When shit like this happens, nothing else is more important. Why do I have to even say that? It *should* be a given. At least, it is on my end."

Patrice sighed.

"Sean, today was crazy. I couldn't believe how unprepared I felt. Everyone was confused, making twists and turns before running out of the building. We thought it was just a drill at first. I just stayed at my desk working. But then I smelled the smoke. And the air looked smoky. Then all hell broke loose. People ran to the elevator, not thinking through that it wasn't going to work in a fire. I ran out of my office, then ran back to get my purse. But I didn't realize that my phone was still on my desk. Every floor of the stairs had more and more people piling out, adding to the jumble in the staircase trying to get down to the first floor. Then Martha started wheezing from the smoke, and I was trying to help her. It was craziness. I didn't realize I didn't have my phone until I was down on the sidewalk. And I was coughing too from all the smoke and running. I was out there with one shoe on too. I had my heels in my hand running down the steps and then dropped one, but I couldn't turn and go back for it. And we were cold because most of us left our coats upstairs."

Sean was stone-faced while Patrice continued pleading her case.

"With everything going on, I just didn't think straight."

His clenched jaw rippled.

"How many times have you called me worried when you heard something in the news? How would you feel if I didn't answer or call back? Would you be fine and calm?"

"No, but I wouldn't yell at you."

He paused his pacing.

"I don't think you understand what I'm saying here. What you do when you're not thinking clearly, when you're caught off guard, says a lot about where your head's at." He stared at her. "You didn't call. You didn't even think to call."

She wrung her hands together.

"Sean, I get why you're upset. But why are you more angry because I didn't call than relieved that I'm safe."

He sucked he teeth, "Come on. Of course I'm glad you're safe."

She protested, "Then why are you still yelling? Do the neighbors *have to* know all our business?"

Sean glared at her.

"So the NEIGHBORS matter more than me too? I don't give TWO SHITS about the neighbors."

She sighed deeply.

"Babes, I don't deal with this every day. I wasn't processing everything. I just wasn't –, thinking straight."

Sean bristled. She continued, "And now I'm just so exhausted. I really need some sleep. I'm really sorry babe, but I just need this day to end. Start fresh tomorrow."

When Sean didn't speak or budge, she turned and walked to her bedroom. Within a minute, he followed then leaned on the door frame staring at the floor. Once Patrice changed into a night shirt and shorts, she walked over to him, putting her hands around his waist and staring at him until he looked at her. Then in a soft apologetic tone,

"Baby I really am sorry. I wasn't trying to make you feel bad. Or make you worry. It was thoughtless of me not to find a way to call you. All I could think about was getting out of there and getting home."

He stared blankly. Then asked, "Who *did* you call today?"

"What? You mean all day?"

"Yeah. Who'd you call when this happened?"

"Nobody. If I didn't think to call you, I sure as hell didn't think to call anyone else."

11

Lily's phone rang as she and the kids headed to the post office on a Saturday morning. She turned down the volume on "*Take me to the king*," which floated through the car from the radio speakers when her mother's call rang.

"Hi, mom."

Janelle chimed in next, "Hi Grandma!"

Then the twins sounded off, "Hi Gwandma!"

Lily's mother, Dr. Mary Redford, cheerily responded, "Hi dears. How is everyone?"

The kids all responded, "Good!"

After a brief conversation with the kids, Lily and her mother chatted.

Lily said, "It's been a busy month at the clinic. We just started accepting another insurance. So, my caseload is growing quicker than I'd like. I picked up four new clients in the past week, and there are more to come."

"Goodness. I remember those days. Hang in there, honey."

"So, what's going on for you, mom?"

"Well, I was talking to Whoopsie to finalize her visit. She's going to come visit early next month."

Janelle, who'd been quietly sitting in the front passenger seat with an ear bud in one ear and listening to the conversation with the other, gave a thumbs-up of approval about her great-grandmother coming for a visit.

Lily questioned, "Oh, she's already able to travel? I talked to her last week, and she still sounded shaky. But she was annoyed with aunt Shirley being there to help her."

Her mother responded, "Well, sounds about right. Needs the help but ornery about getting it. She's been healing well since her surgery. She's loving the weight loss too. I don't think she realized how much the fibroids were a problem. Plus, her doctor didn't restrict her travel."

Janelle wondered what fibroids were.

Lily said, "Okay, good then. Well, the kids are excited!"

"I'm sure!"

"Okay. Well, let's coordinate picking her up from the airport."

Her mother cleared her throat.

"Do you think she can stay with you all? You're closer to the airport and the city. And you have the minivan. It would be so much easier to get around than if she was with us."

Janelle watched as Lily shifted uncomfortably in the driver's seat.

Lily said, "Mom, I know it seems more convenient, but it really doesn't work well to have her stay with us. The twins aren't adjusting well to their new daycare. And potty training has been a struggle. The timing is –"

Janelle had heard Lily fussing before about how her mother loved to impose by putting Lily in the position of being the bad guy and having to say no.

Lily's mother sounded encouraging,

"Honey, Whoopsie would love helping with the twins. You know, she had us potty trained by the time we were two. She can help get that wrapped up."

Lily took a deep breath as her mother continued.

"Plus, John is the best with sightseeing. Remember that year when he took Whoopsie and your aunts to Georgetown when all the holiday lights were up? Whoopsie still talks about that trip."

Lily spoke with a measured tone.

"Right now isn't good timing. John's been focused on dealing with the aftermath of the fire at work. He wouldn't have the time to do much of that right now. They've been working out of a temporary office, feeling displaced and out of sorts."

A dejected voice piped through the car speaker, "Well, okay. If you all can't do it."

Lily kept quiet. Then, her mother continued,

"I will have to figure out my schedule. You know your dad has a golf trip coming up. And I have several important speaking engagements. So, I'll just shift things around. It'll be a bit tricky, but I'll make it work."

Lily exhaled.

"Okay, well I just pulled into the post office with the kids. I'll give you a call back later."

Janelle helped by carrying the return packages while Lily got the twins out of the backseat. As they walked in the post office, Janelle asked, "What are fibroids?"

The next school day, Janelle walked down the hallway to her next class with a friend. She darted her eyes around, barely paying attention to their conversation. She caught sight of Mason up ahead, standing near the doorway of his classroom. As she and her friend walked past, she glanced at him with a fleeting smile then kept walking, nudging her friend to move faster. Janelle wanted to stop and talk to him, so she couldn't understand why she raced away instead. Once they got to class, her friend leaned over and whispered, "What's up with you?"

"Nothing. I just didn't want to be late again for class. Been late all this week."

The next day Janelle took the long way to her classes that were next to Mason's classrooms. For the past two days, she'd taken a different exit out of school. Avoiding Mason was easier outside of school and at the end of the day. In school was harder. As she came up the opposite end of the hall to class, she felt a little relief because she wouldn't have to pass by his class. Later at lunch, she convinced her friend to sit at a different table than their usual. Janelle was cool with everyone at the new table though not close friends with anyone. But having boys at the table meant Mason wasn't going to come over. She sat next to Trey, who smiled broadly when Janelle sat down next to him.

Over the next few days, Janelle sat at the new table at lunch. Trey didn't waste time following her on social media. They started texting a few times a day. A week later, he asked her to come over to his house.

"I've got a bunch of movies that my boy burned. That new Kevin Hart special, and the last Fast and Furious movie. You should come through tomorrow."

"Umm. Let's go to the mall."

"Oh, to the movie theater?"

"No, let's just meet at the mall. To hang out. My folks are weird about me going to friends' houses when they don't know the parents. I'm not really trying to get lectured."

He nodded.

"Alright. Well, my house is a block from the mall. Meet me there and we'll walk over."

Mason's face flashed in her mind and she felt a pinch of guilt. She hesitated, then said,

"Alright cool. I'll be there at like five. Text me the address."

Trey walked her to the next class, and they hugged just before she walked into the classroom. She thought she saw Mason out of the corner of her eye while they hugged, but she didn't dare turn to look.

When Janelle got to Trey's house the next day, she texted him. She stood on the front porch laden with potted plants, wondering how things were going to go. She'd never been to a boys' house without being dropped off by a parent. *This is weird.* He opened the door and waved her in.

"Hey cuteness!"

They hugged and Trey smiled as he took her in from head to toe. Her stomach was caving in on itself. *Just relax, girl. We're just chillin'.* They walked into the kitchen and he grabbed two sodas from the fridge and a bag of chips from the pantry. She stood at the entrance of the kitchen, glancing around.

"I thought we were going to the mall?"

He shook his head.

"Yeah, now I can't. I got caught sneaking out, so I can't go out. But I can have friends over."

He nodded toward the basement stairs. The house was quiet upstairs.

"Where are your folks?"

"They had an after-work thing."

He headed to the basement and motioned for her to follow. She heard zooming cars from the TV. As they rounded the corner, at the bottom of the steps, Vin Diesel was onscreen racing down a highway. Trey launched into proving that Fast and Furious movies were better than any of the superhero movies because of the realness of the action scenes. They sat on the couch and finished watching the movie, which was already halfway over when they sat down. They texted each other memes and videos while watching the movie. They laughed hysterically at a video of different cats swatting at dogs who would turn and run scared.

Trey put his phone down to pull his sweatshirt off over his head. He had on a black fitted t-shirt underneath that lifted when he pulled the sweatshirt up. Janelle briefly saw the side of his abs, and smiled to herself. She wondered if she should finish watching the movie then go. Or say she needed to go now. *Girl, get up. Time to bounce.* She nervously picked at her acrylic nails. Trey laughed and showed her a meme on his phone of a raccoon bathing itself, leisurely lathering up with a soap bar. They laughed and Trey hugged her, pulling her over to his side of the couch. When she didn't pull away, he moved in to kiss her. As their lips met, she tensed. Then she relaxed as she felt him pulling her closer. But when his hand slid from her waist up to her breasts, she pulled away.

He shot her a look of irritation.

"What's wrong?"

Janelle sat up straight. *Why am I here?* She smiled stiffly.

"Let's not, okay."

"Not what?"

She gave him a 'come on, man' look. She asked, "I thought we were just chillin'."

He smiled.

"We are."

She straightened her top and stared at the TV.

"I thought we were going to the mall?"

He leaned back on the couch.

"I just figured it would be chill if we watched a movie instead. Plus, I'm grounded, remember?"

Janelle looked at the time on her phone screen.

"Okay well, I'm about to go."

She got up from the couch, quickly making her way up the basement steps straight for the front door. He trailed behind her.

She wished she was already out of there.

"I'll text you when I get home."

She heard him snicker.

"Girls are so funny. Can't make up their minds what they want."

She spun around and stared at him.

"Seriously, Trey? Don't go there."

He laughed.

"Alright then. See you in school."

As soon as she stepped out of the door, he slammed it behind her. She hustled home. She wondered if Mason would answer if she texted him now. *After you ignored him all week? Doubtful.* As much as she'd been avoiding him, he was the only person she wanted to talk to. She thought about if Mason did text back and asked her what was wrong. She wouldn't know what to say. She just knew she'd feel better as soon as he answered. Even if she couldn't tell him what was wrong.

12

Sean worked late several days in a row. Like clockwork, he could expect a call from Hodges every other day for status updates on the Gibson case, as well as updates on the string of robberies of highfalutin homes in their precinct in the past two weeks. Sean routinely double-checked all the case files of his officers to make sure there were no gaps, loose ends, or questions whose answers weren't being pursued. A couple of reporters had called for comments on the robberies, which he answered handily. But no one asked about the Gibson case, and he was relieved. When the press got a whiff of anything that remotely smelled like a dirty cop, the negative news coverage meant jobs were in danger at the precinct. Usually, somebody had to take the fall when the police department looked bad, to clean up the image as quickly as possible.

After a long night at the precinct, Sean woke up earlier than usual the next day. He looked over at Patrice in bed. The energy had been tense between them for days. He still fumed when he thought about her not calling him the day of the fire. But he knew it was time to move on. *You're gonna have to get over this.* It was only 5:15 a.m., but he couldn't go back to sleep. He slid out of bed and dressed in running clothes. He'd have to be at the precinct for most of the upcoming weekend to prepare for a briefing he had to give to the police brass on Monday about the robberies. So, he figured getting in a run would clear his head and charge him up for the long haul. He stumbled as he tripped on one of Patrice's sandals in front of the bed. She groggily woke.

"Morning."

Sean said, "Sorry I woke you."

She rubbed her eyes.

"No, it was the nightmare that did that."

He sat on the edge of the bed.

"What was it about?"

"I was pregnant with demons that only fed on body parts. Lucky for me, my body could regrow organs. But there was this awful gnawing pain when they were feeding."

"Wow."

"Yeah." She yawned. "I've been trying to step out of my romance novels and memoirs comfort zone to get into fantasy fiction." She shook her head. "I don't think it's agreeing with me."

He reached over and kissed her on her forehead. She watched as he laced up his running shoes.

"You going for a run?"

He grinned.

"Yeah. You coming?"

She squeaked out a laugh, "Um, I just had my liver and kidneys gnawed off. And you're trying to torture me even more?"

He chuckled.

"Not at all. It'll be good for you. Help regenerate your organs."

He tightened the drawstring on his pants.

"Plus, weren't you just complaining the other day about your clothes not fitting anymore?"

Patrice sat up in bed.

"Yeah, and that means I need to eat more salads and less bread. Not blow out a lung on a run."

Sean laughed.

"Wow. Dramatic much?"

Three years ago, Sean joined a running group, Run & Tonic, to prep for a 10K race. He picked them specifically because they met at different parks in D.C. for each training session. He figured it would help keep him motivated to have different scenery to focus on each time. He liked Rock Creek Park the most because it was like being in a countryside park in the middle of the city. And today he figured the 60 degree temperature was just right to get five miles in.

When Sean and Patrice got to the park, it was 6:00 a.m. and there was barely anyone there. He preferred it that way. Less people with dogs to dodge. The sun rays peeked through the trees, and the birds were mostly on the ground picking at the dirt. Patrice took one path to walk and he took another to run. They agreed to meet back at the starting point in forty-five minutes. He got two and a quarter miles into the run and was in the middle of listening to a Jay Z track when his phone rang. When he saw it was Mitch, he answered. Breathing heavy from running he said,

"Hey, Mitch."

After a pause, Mitch spoke in a low stilted tone, "Sean."

The drops of sweat on his skin sent mini jolts of electric pulses. He knew immediately. Annabelle was dead.

Part 2
Noontide

13

Patrice and Michelle were born eleven months apart, both summer babies with sunny smiles like their father's. Although Patrice was older, Michelle grew at a faster rate. By the time Patrice was two-years-old, they wore the same size clothes. While they looked alike, their personalities had no overlap. Growing up, their mother used to say that how they took care of their pet hamsters—and the chosen pet names— showed how different their personalities were. When they brought their hamsters home, Patrice said, "I'm gonna call mine Blossom and Buttercup! Like the Powerpuff Girls!"

Michelle chimed in, "My hamsters are Chewy, because she keeps trying to chew on everything, and Friday."

Their mom asked, "Friday?"

Michelle retorted, "Yeah. I love Fridays!"

Patrice's hamsters were overweight. She fed them often and even gave them table food. Michelle's were underfed. She would forget to put their food out at least a couple of times a week.

Once living on her own, the few times Patrice talked to friends about her sister, she said, "It's complicated with her."

Sometimes she offered nothing more. Even her close friends didn't know much. For years, most of the references she made to her family began with "My mom and I," or "My dad used to." When she told Sean about her sister, she had no choice. One night when they got to Patrice's place after dinner, Michelle was waiting at the front door of the apartment building.

"Hey, Trice!"

Michelle was stooping and leaning against the building. There was a ring of cigarette butts on the ground around her despite the trash can with an ashtray two feet away from her. She looked dingy in a stained white t-shirt and ripped jeans that was more torn than they probably started off. She stood as Patrice and Sean walked up.

"Hey! Is this your boyfriend? Hey, I'm Michelle."

Sean shook her outstretched hand. Patrice's irritation stopped her from saying anything. But she hugged Michelle tightly. They all went upstairs to Patrice's apartment. *Here we go. Again.* Michelle didn't bother waiting to ask for what she wanted.

"So, you'd be so proud of me. I found this really good program in Virginia. It's a 90-day program with three phases. They get you cleaned up in the first ten days. They put you on Suboxone, so you don't have the shakes and sweats while you're detoxing. Then they help you find a job. And then a place to live!"

Michelle asked Patrice for some clothes and $500. The treatment would be paid for through her health insurance, but she needed money to pay someone back she'd borrowed money from, and for snacks and cigarettes in the program.

Patrice agreed to help, but the money had to go to program staff so that Michelle didn't have access to all of it. She took Michelle shopping for clothes the next weekend and drove her out to the program on a Sunday night. By the following Friday, when she called during family hour, the counselor said Michelle had checked herself out.

Most of the time during Patrice's teen years, she felt like an only child. Once their father died, Michelle wasn't the same. They all weren't. By the time Michelle was nine, she routinely refused to do her homework and got into arguments with kids at school. By thirteen, she had run away from home three times. And it wasn't the run-of-the-mill running away to a neighbor's house. She would be gone for a few days and return tight-lipped about where she'd been. No amount of punishment their mom doled out made a difference. By fifteen, Michelle flatly said, "I'm moving out. I can take care of myself."

No discussion, no asking, no childlike deference to a parent. She left with a backpack full of clothes and her art journal.

Their mother, who at the time had been struggling to maintain two jobs, had just been laid off from the higher paying one. So efforts to get Michelle to come back home were disjointed. Shortly after, Patrice and her mother moved from the house to a two-bedroom apartment. Her mother made verbal space for Michelle by saying, "When she comes back you two can share a room."

Patrice nodded and silently knew the room was just hers. The unspoken truth was that dealing with Michelle was easier done from a distance. They received sporadic phone calls from her and a few unexpected visits. She would stay overnight then leave early the next morning. Patrice felt like she'd lost her dad, then her sister too. Somewhere in that time, *their* mother became *her* mother.

Once they were adults, Patrice and Michelle had moments of a real connection. Sometimes when Michelle called, she made some semblance of an effort to connect as humans, not just for immediate needs. After meeting Sean, she'd ask about him when she called.

"So, how's the cop doing?"

Patrice rolled her eyes even though Michelle couldn't see it.

"You know his name. Sean's fine. Thanks for asking."

But those brief moments passed by, easily forgotten, overshadowed by the other moments. The churning wheel of incessant worry about Michelle when she wasn't calling, to her popping up needing help, to Patrice's scrambling efforts to "get her clean for good this time," was tiresome and hopeless. Over time, it became a painfully tedious but customary part of life. Michelle avoided their mother, typically only reaching out after Patrice insisted that she would stop taking Michelle's calls if she didn't make an effort with their mother.

Their mother continued to hold down the worry fort. She went through phases of texting and calling Patrice about whether she'd heard from Michelle and asking details about their last call. She'd devise plans of what they should do to help if Michelle reached out again. At this point, Patrice knew how it would go. Michelle would call. Sound sweet and high, or highly irritated because she needed to get high. Say she'd been working a job with overnight hours and she would be too tired during the day to keep up with life. That would be why she hadn't returned any calls. Then weeks later she would have a story about how she lost the job and that she was short on rent. Then she'd say, "I need a loaner to get on my feet."

Recently, Patrice hadn't heard from Michelle for a few months. Then on an early Saturday morning the phone rang. Michelle was sputtering with rage at being fired for helping a customer to her car and standing out there too long chatting. Patrice listened quietly to the long winding story that had more holes than a golf course. She could hear slurring and the odd tempo of Michelle's words.

"Are you using again?"

Michelle sucked her teeth.

"Are you serious? I'm telling you how they fired me for no reason at all, and you think I'm using? Geez, you're ridiculous."

Patrice shook her head as though Michelle could see her.

"No, I'm not ridiculous. I'm asking for the truth."

"No, I'm not using. I've been clean. I don't have time for that. I'm just trying to stay on track. Save up for a security deposit for my own place."

Patrice softened her tone.

"Michelle, I want the best for you. But I can't keep giving you money. It's not helping."

"That's not true. Of course it helps."

"I don't want to enable you to –"

Michelle interrupted, "There you go with that ridiculous bullshit people tell you. Helping me out is not *enabling*. It's not like you're buying drugs for me."

"I might as well be. What did you do with the last $300 I gave you? How much drugs did you buy with that?"

Patrice could hear Michelle spit on the ground.

"How do you know what I do? So damn high and mighty. I told you I'M NOT FUCKIN' USING. DAMN."

"Hey, hey, hey. Stop yelling."

Michelle took a breath, her voice lowered.

"I'm sorry, Trice. I'm just tired and everything. I've been working overnight shifts for a straight ten days. I'm exhausted. And I have a headache. And now I don't have a job."

Patrice sat quietly listening. Michelle's voice grew emphatic. "Seriously, I'm clean now. I went to that new detox on Georgia Avenue. Been going to meetings too, even though they don't help. But my sponsor crawls up my ass if I don't go. Half of everybody in there's still using. But talking about how their life is so much better now that they're clean. Such bullshit. But I go, drink the stale coffee, eat the dry ass cookies, and listen to the stories of when they all *used* to be high."

A single tear rolled down Patrice's cheek.

"What are you doing with the money from your job? Shouldn't you be getting a last paycheck. And aren't you getting overnight bonus pay?"

Michelle explained with exasperation,

"Yeah. But that's the thing. I'm trying to work my program. Part of the twelve steps is making amends. Paying back what you owe. I owe a lot of people. And every time I pay them back, I come up short on my own bills and rent. But I'm trying to do the right thing. That's the thing, the more I try to do the right thing, the harder life smacks me in the mouth. I can't do this by myself. I'm learning to ask for help. That's what I'm doing now, asking you for help."

Patrice sighed deeply.

"Have you called mom?"

Michelle coughed.

"I was going to call her next. See how she's doing."

Patrice sat silently as Michelle continued.

"Patrice. I just need some money to cover the rent. Dre is being real extra right now. He's still trippin' about some money I took when I was still using."

Patrice cringed whenever she heard the name of Michelle's boyfriend. They had been together on and off for years, and she was none the better for it. Actually, worse off. Seems like he had made some serious attempts to get clean off hard drugs, but would keep drinking and smoking weed and end up relapsing. They each would try to get clean, but unless it coincided with the other doing the same, they would suck each other right back into the vortex.

"Look, the only way I will give you any money is if you come over and take a drug test."

"What?" Michelle's voice screeched. "What are you a drug counselor now? Look, that doesn't tell you anything. First of all, I could beat a drug test if I wanted to. But that's not what

I'm about right now. I don't have time for that." She paused. "I'm telling you that I'm clean and you want me to pee in a cup? Seriously Patrice?"

"That's the only way I'll give you anything."

"I knew it. I knew you didn't care. You love to tell me how much you want to help me. Probably tell the world how much you've tried to save your druggy sister. But when I ask for help, all I get is 'Here, pee in this cup.'" She harrumphed. "I swear, all you really care about is yourself."

Patrice reminded herself that this wasn't who Michelle was. Not when she was clean. She tried a different approach.

"Well, you can come stay here for a while. It'll help you save for a decent apartment instead of having roommates. I could take some days off of work, and we could really hang out, you know."

Patrice truly wondered what could come of them spending real time together. Being sisters again. They hadn't been around each other for more than a few days since Patrice was fourteen.

"I can't. If I leave here, it'll just start a whole bunch of stuff with Dre. He gets his underwear all in a bunch about me leaving him. I'm not trying to deal with that right now. I'm trying to get my life together, not make it worse. I need to clean up my messes. I can't just leave."

"Okay, Dre really should be the least of your concerns. You need to do what's best for you."

Michelle protested, "You don't know anything about Dre. He's been there for me. You wouldn't understand that. Being there for someone when they're down and out. How important that is. Some of us need someone to be there. He saved me. So many times. He brought me back when I OD'd, you know."

Patrice scoffed.

"Please. You're giving him credit for saving you from drowning when he helped push you under in the first place."

Michelle sighed while pleading, "Trice forget about Dre right now. Listen, I can't do this without your help."

The phone fell silent, each of them waiting for the other to bend. Michelle continued,

"You can write the check to my landlord like you did before—"

"Oh no no. I had a talk with your landlord about that. I know you somehow figured out how to cash it the last time and still came up short on the rent."

Michelle cursed under her breath.

"Fine. That's just fine. I'll figure it out. You never really want to help me anyway. You just like to look like you're helping me. Thanks for nothing." She paused. Then laughed. "Life's a bitch when you have a bitch for a sister."

Then she was gone.

***

For as long as Patrice could remember, no one talked about what happened that day when they were kids. The absence of it being discussed became a tacit message to move on. For Patrice, the memory of it was hazy and faded like a centuries old picture. That became another reason to push aside whatever remnants did come to mind from time to time. Patrice was eight when seven-year-old Michelle was gone for that lost hour. An hour that no one, not even Michelle, could account for with accuracy.

It was one of the last days before summer break ended. School was restarting in a week. It turned out to be the last summer their father was alive—he died a couple weeks later. Patrice had a sleepover at her best friend's house, and Michelle was returning home from a four-day gymnastics camp. While their father went to pick up Patrice, their mother had driven four hours, two hours there and two back, to western Maryland to pick up Michelle. Their father was friends with the father of Patrice's best friend. When he got to the friend's house to pick her up, it was over an hour before the adults caught up on life enough for Patrice and her dad to head home. After the drive from western Maryland Michelle wasn't the least bit tired, but their mother sat on the couch and drifted off to sleep. Michelle went in the backyard to practice new moves she had learned on the trampoline.

Their mother wasn't certain how long she had been asleep when she awoke. She later swore it was only a catnap, twenty minutes at the most. Turned out, after information was pieced together, that it was over an hour. After her nap, she fixed snacks for the girls and washed dishes. When she called out to Michelle to come eat there was no answer. She knocked on the girls' bedroom doors. When Michelle wasn't there, the search ensued. Through the house then outside. She could tell Michelle had been on the trampoline because the cover had been unlatched and thrown on the ground. She panned her eyes up and down the street. She called her husband to see if by any chance he came and got her, and maybe took the girls for food. He hadn't, but he and Patrice were ten minutes away in the car and would help look once they were home.

"Start knocking on neighbors' doors," he said.

Their mother hustled down the sidewalk toward a neighbor's house. She looked up the street and finally saw Michelle in the distance, jumping down the street in a light and cheery mood. Their mother stopped in her tracks, infuriated. She wasn't much for yelling—that was their father's disciplinary role. But that day she took over the role like it was an old familiar glove. That was where the strangeness surfaced. Michelle, who used to cry when yelled at, laughed hysterically as their mother shouted at her. She giggled every time she was asked where she had been. She said the candy man took her to a tree house. She said he hugged her a lot and gave her soda. When Patrice and their father got home, he realized right away that Michelle was high. They went to the hospital and a drug test showed she had marijuana and ecstasy in her system. A rape kit was done but there was no evidence of sexual assault. It turned out that the candy man was real.

Bits and pieces of what happened had to be pieced together by retrospective guesswork, mostly based on a similar incident happening to another girl a few weeks later. The girl was given an already opened soda by someone who said he was her brother's friend. She probably didn't drink as much of it as Michelle did, because she had less drugs in her system when later tested. She was taken to a park, touched inappropriately, and told she was dreaming about the candy man. The girl couldn't give a clear description, neither could Michelle, but some teens in the neighborhood had seen a guy walking around during the times the assaults happened. Fliers went up with pictures of a potential suspect, a slim, clean-shaven white male in his late teens to early twenties. Everyone was on high alert after that. He was never found though, at least not to anyone's knowledge.

Even though the details weren't clear about what happened, Michelle was never questioned about it after that day. But things were different. For Patrice her life at that time felt like two sides of a coin. Heads was what happened before that day, and tails was what happened after. When their family got home from the hospital, it was the last time that day was mentioned. A silent agreement to put the day behind them and move on. Michelle continued to be a happy kid who loved gymnastics and wanted to join the circus before going on to the Olympics. But she spent a little more time in her room than she normally did. And she talked about boys a little bit more. And then their father's car accident happened.

None of the changes in Michelle were enough to set off any alarm bells. They could easily and readily be explained by grief from losing her father. Their mother didn't figure out that Michelle was smoking weed and sneaking alcohol until years later when she forgot to put a rum bottle back in the curio cabinet. She insisted that she had never done that before. But it certainly made sense why the rum tasted watered down to their mother when she used some of it to make drinks at a Christmas gathering at their house. Their mother, ill-equipped to handle the unraveling of her child in the wake of grieving the sudden death of her husband, just brushed it off. It wasn't long before Michelle was running away from home.

***

Patrice laid in bed, phone still in her hand from her call with Michelle. She felt like a blast of freezing air had hit her body. She curled up in bed. Her mind flashed to being sick with a cold when she was eight-years-old. Her mother brought her hot chocolate, her dad rubbed her head, and her sister climbed in bed with her and talked about going to the circus.

When Patrice's phone rang again, she spoke as soon as she answered,

"Okay, look, I can give you some—"

Sean spoke with a concerned tone.

"Babe? What happened? You okay?"

She realized it was Sean, not Michelle calling back.

"I just talk to Michelle—" She paused to gather enough breath to get her words out. "She's using again—"

"Okay, I'll be there in a few minutes."

When Sean arrived, he let himself in, stripped down to his boxers, and got in bed with her. Patrice told him about the phone call and about the memories that were coming up. She was exhausted by the end and fell asleep. It was noon the next day before she woke up again. They got dressed and headed to Silver Diner. While Sean ordered a burger, fries and a milkshake, Patrice ordered breakfast foods—bacon, eggs, and pancakes.

Sean quipped, "I still don't get how you can eat pancakes in the middle of the day."

She waved him off.

"And I keep telling you there's no time limit for eating good food."

They ate quietly. Patrice let the food stuff down her worries. When they returned home, Sean convinced her to play a game of Monopoly, the Game of Thrones version that his mother got him for Christmas, that had never been opened. They ended the day watching rom-coms.

14

Janelle waited until near the end of class to beg her fourth-period teacher for a bathroom pass, which he didn't routinely give in the last ten minutes of the class period. She walked to his desk, squirming like she'd held her bladder for so long that she wouldn't make it much longer. Once out of class, she hurried down the hall then slowed when she neared Mason's class. She stood just outside the door. When the bell rang, her heart thumped so loud she thought it would fall right out of her chest. She watched as students poured out. Mason walked out after five students passed by. He glanced her way with an expressionless face and kept walking down the hall. She sped up to keep pace.

"Hey Mase."

He said his words over his shoulder, "Hey Janelle."

Janelle? What happened to Apple?

"How's Los doing?"

"Great."

He bounded down the stairs. She kept on his heels as best she could. Once in the cafeteria he said, "Alright, bye," and walked ahead to catch up with two friends. Janelle gave up and headed over to the table where her friends were. She wasn't going to grab a lunch and even pretend to eat. Her stomach had been folding in on itself all morning. She sat scrolling on her phone, hiding it under the table so none of the school staff on duty in the cafeteria could see her. When one of her friends got to the table with a lunch tray, she looked at Janelle with devilish curiosity.

"Girl, you holding out on me? You didn't tell me you and Trey were a thing?"

Janelle scrunched her face.

"What? No, we're not. Who told you that?"

Her friend pulled out her phone and showed her a picture. It was on Trey's Instagram page. One of the Fast and Furious movie posters. His comment underneath said, "This movie was even better the second time around. Netflix and chill with Bae!" Then he made another comment with kiss emojis that he tagged Janelle on.

She gritted her teeth.

"Oh my God. He is such a liar. We watched a movie, but nothing happened. We didn't have sex. Ooh, he is such a liar."

She glared over at his lunch table. She thought about saying something to him, but stayed put. *Lunchroom drama never worked out well for girls,* she thought. She pulled out her cell phone, this time not caring if staff saw her using it. She texted Trey.

Janelle: *Take that comment off Instagram. You know u lying.*

Trey: *Huh? So we didn't watch a movie? What r u mad about?*

Janelle: *Take it down. NOW.*

Trey: *You trippin'! I got another good one for us to watch next time.*

Janelle's her ears heated up and her breath caught in her throat. She stormed out of the lunchroom and went to the bathroom until the bell rung for lunch dismissal. She barely listened in her afternoon classes. She texted Trey after school, telling him again to take down the comment but gave up after several students had commented on it already. *Damage is done. Shoot. Now what?* She worried that everyone was going to believe Trey. *Nobody questions. They just believe.* The next few days she ignored Trey. She wondered what Mason had heard. After school, she tried several times to text him. She would start typing a text to him, then erase it. *He won't respond.*

Within a week it seemed like Trey had moved on. Janelle saw him walking down the hall with his arm around a girl. A tenth grader with a big butt and an eyebrow piercing. She didn't know the girl well but knew of her. She had a reputation for being sloppy seconds. Janelle couldn't care less. *Maybe now this will blow over.* At lunch that day she walked into the cafeteria with her friends. As she passed by Trey's table, she heard him singing and knew she was wrong about it being over.

"These hoes ain't loyal!"

Trey repeated the song lyric as his friend drummed a light beat on the table. She wanted to scream. Tears welled up. She couldn't think of what to say or do. Her friends shot Trey nasty looks and pushed her along to get to their own lunch table. She fought back tears with all her might, but was losing the battle. They sat at the table, then one of her friends got up and bee-lined over to Trey. She created enough of a diversion—bringing up that Trey was sloppy for getting caught smoking weed in the bathroom last week—to get him focused on something other than Janelle. Soon enough the bell rung, and the torment was over. Janelle and her friends filed out and dispersed to class.

That afternoon Janelle tried her best to be alone at home, staying in her room even for dinner. John and Lily each took a turn checking in on her to see what was going on.

"Hey Sugar. What's up?" John sounded upbeat as he popped his head into her room.

She didn't look up.

"Homework."

"Okay. You okay? You seem—"

She quipped, "I'm fine."

"Hey, what's with the attitude?"

She looked up this time, indignantly.

"What attitude? I'm in my room doing homework. I had dinner. Did the dishes already. You're the one in here asking questions. What attitude?"

John took a step into her room.

"Hey, wait a minute. Obviously, you're having a rough day. And I mean, we all have them. But just remember, I'm not the cause of it. I appreciate that you're keeping your *attitude* under wraps and staying in your room. But I'm checking on you like I always do. Take it in the manner it's meant, with good intention."

Janelle sat up in bed. She kept her eyes trained on the floor and nodded silently.

"We'll be downstairs if you need anything."

He stepped out and closed her door behind him. Within minutes Lily knocked then poked her head in the room.

"Honey? You need anything?"

Janelle stared at her pleadingly. But didn't say a word.

Lily asked, "Do you want to talk about it?"

Janelle shook her head. Lily gave her a sympathetic smile then left.

An hour later, Janelle stepped quietly out of her room and sat at the top of the steps out of sight. She peeked into the living room. Her sister sat in John's lap, and her brother in Lily's. She listened to their conversation.

Lily said, "We haven't been on a date in a while. And I've been wanting a massage. How about we—"

John quickly obliged.

"Sure. Schedule it."

"If you don't want to it's fine. We can do something else."

He shot her a confused look.

"Did you hear me? I said yes, schedule it."

"You said it like I was asking you about getting the furnace cleaned or something."

John chuckled.

"Really? It's not enough for me to agree. I have to say it with zeal?"

He shook his head.

They quieted. Janelle walked downstairs and into the kitchen. She grabbed a bag of Doritos and a Sprite, then plopped down in the recliner. Jasper hopped out of Lily's lap and bounded over to Janelle asking for some chips. As he grabbed chips out of the bag, Janelle looked over at John and mouthed, "I'm sorry," to which he smiled.

15

Patrice hustled around her bedroom getting dressed on a Sunday morning for church. Sean sat waiting in his car outside her apartment. *He's so dramatic. Why does he always refuse to wait up here for me to finish getting ready?* After ten minutes passed, her phone dinged. She checked the text message.

Sean: *Patrice, we're beyond late...*

Patrice: *I'm coming now.*

Five minutes later another ding sounded.

Sean: *Do we have to be those black people? Rolling up to a new church halfway through service?*

Patrice: *I'm coming right now.*

Finally, she hustled out of the elevator. She plopped into the car out of breath.

"Sorry, babes. The heel on my left shoe was a problem. So I had to change outfits to match another pair of shoes."

He rolled his eyes. Glancing at the sweat beading on her forehead he turned on the air conditioner, even though it was

54 degrees outside. She smiled appreciatively. He took the beltway to the new church they were headed to. Their home church, Journey Baptist, had been closed for the past few weeks. A bad rainstorm caused so much roof damage to the already brittle roof, that services couldn't continue while the repairs were being made. Their pastor was a guest preacher today at Mosaic Baptist, where they were now headed. Mosaic was a little farther away, but fortunately traffic was light.

When they walked in the doors of Mosaic, the pews were almost full. There was a hum of chatter and the sounds of patrons settling into seats. Sean and Patrice found seats in a pew near the back of the church. Even though they were twenty minutes late, service was just starting. Patrice was not a fan of sitting near the back of church. Too easy to be distracted. She regretted taking so long to get dressed. She wanted to walk up the aisle to see if there were any closer seats, but she dared not ask Sean given that he hated being disruptive that way and that she was the one that made them late.

They glanced around the church taking in the surroundings. Mosaic was a newer church with shiny flooring and pews. It smelled of pine and rose oil. Different from the hundred-year-old smell of Journey Baptist, which was a musty mix of Frankincense and Myrrh. The congregation looked younger on average than at Journey, with trendier fashion and more youthful energy. Others from their church would be attending services at Mosaic as well until Journey was back up and running.

Patrice whispered, "Look, Anita and Mike came."

Sean nodded. "Yeah. The Nelsons are here too. And Mr. Jimmy. Over on the left."

Sean had been to Mosaic once before, for the christening of a godchild. He gave Patrice some background information about the church before they arrived.

"The pastor's good! And he can *sang*! He was out-singing the choir at the christening!"

Patrice listened, as best she could, to the sermon while periodically scanning the church pews. She struggled to pay attention but heard enough to know the message was about carrying your burdens with grace.

The pastor offered, "Our Savior never gives us more than we each can carry. So carry it well. Amen?"

Patrice tuned in and out. Every now and then she'd hear the organ player hit a bad note and that grabbed her attention. *I wouldn't mind coming back here until Journey opens again.*

Midway through the sermon, Patrice glanced up as a woman walked up the aisle. She was in a flowing burgundy dress and held hands with a little boy and girl. The girl wore a dress the same color as the woman, and the little boy wore a burgundy shirt and gray pants. The woman held both of their hands until they got to the fourth pew in the center row of the church, then released them to slide in and join a man and a teenage girl. Patrice's breath caught in her throat. She squinted, sharpening her view. She saw the man's face when he turned sideways. *John?* He was in a dark gray suit and smiled at the kids. Patrice glanced at the teenager. *Wow, that's Janelle.* She was in a burgundy and gray print dress. The woman switched seats with the teenage girl, and sat next to John.

Patrice's focus pulled even further away from the sermon. She had pictured what John's wife looked like before, but her images were usually frumpier. And shorter. She occasionally panned the church to cleanse her visual palette from staring at the family in the fourth row. She noticed a woman one pew in front of her and a few seats over to the right. The woman leaned forward and seemed to be staring in the same direction that Patrice stared in. Dressed in all black, large dangling earrings, and red bangles, the woman had a Michael Kors handbag that took up a full seat next to her. Patrice watched as the woman darted her eyes, glancing at the pastor then in John's direction.

When the service ended, Patrice and Sean were one of the first out the doors. They stood in front of the church, chatting with church members from Journey. Patrice saw the burgundy and gray clan emerge. She looked at John until their eyes met. He smiled and gave a slight nod. It wasn't long before the woman in black came flitting by with her handbag bumping on her hip. Patrice saw John glance at the woman briefly, just before he and his family packed into the car. The woman didn't once look his way.

Patrice hadn't heard most of the conversation around her, but she laughed when everyone else did.

As the chatter wrapped up, Sean asked, "Let's grab some lunch. What are you in the mood for?"

Everyone dispersed. She and Sean walked to the car. At lunch, Sean talked about funny parts of the sermon, and Patrice nodded along. She'd missed most of what he was talking about. While driving home, she finally spoke up.

"People don't pay attention like they are supposed in church. I saw a woman staring at a married man the whole time she was in there."

Sean observed. "Hmm. Well if you knew she was looking at a guy the whole time, *you* must not have been paying attention to the sermon yourself."

She nudged him.

Later that day, Patrice sat out on the balcony at Sean's place reading. Even with fifty-degree weather, she wanted the fresh air. She was wrapped up in a t-shirt, sweats, and a fleece robe.

Sean poked his head out through the sliding doors.

"You're out here looking crazy. You know you're freezing. Come inside."

"That's precisely why I'm not cold, because I'm out here looking crazy. Layers make all the difference!"

Sean shook his head. His phone rang and when he glanced at who was calling, he retreated inside. Within minutes, he poked his head back out on the balcony.

"Sorry babe, I need to head to the precinct for a couple hours. I'll be back by dinner."

Patrice nodded with disappointment. She wondered if something happened with the Gibson case.

16

Janelle loved all her elderberries. That's what she called her grands—her grandparents and great-grandmother. John's mother was the grandparent she talked to most often. Although John's mother had moved to Florida five years earlier, Janelle taught her how to use WhatsApp, so they messaged each other regularly. Whenever Janelle's report card came out, she would send a picture of it, and her grandmother would send some version of a meme of a gray-haired lady with a cane jumping joyously in the air. It always made Janelle laugh. Sometimes, her grandmother would send her a care package of homemade brownies and a gift card to celebrate her hard work in school.

Janelle saw Lily's parents once or twice a month. She didn't understand what a psychologist and psychiatrist were as a child, though she knew it meant they were "rich" from how nice a house they lived in and the "rich gifts" they would buy. She thought of them as prim and proper. It was at their house that she learned how to keep her elbows off the table, eat using different forks, and take her shoes off when she came in the house.

"But I can eat better this way," was Janelle's usual argument, when she was younger, for why she needed her elbows on the table to eat. Eventually, she learned to appreciate the values they instilled when her friends' parents doted on her for being "such a polite, sweet girl!" She practiced everything her grandparents taught her at friends' houses, albeit to John and Lily's chagrin when she wouldn't do the same at home.

Today, Janelle was excited to see her great-grandmother, Whoopsie. Lily, Janelle, the twins and Lily's mother were on their way to Reagan Washington National airport. Whoopsie was flying in from Georgia to spend the week in D.C. When Janelle got dressed that morning, she could hear John and Lily in the kitchen.

"We're going to stop in D.C. for lunch after picking Whoopsie up. We'll be right near your temporary office. It's up to you to make time to join us."

John dryly responded, "Okay, well. We're still setting up the temporary workspace for adequate functioning." He paused. "I have a presentation at 11:30 so I may run late. But, I'll be there."

Lily harrumphed.

"There's that tone again. Like you're doing me a favor. Come if you want to John. Don't feel obligated."

John sighed.

"Lily. I literally just said I'll be there. Don't make this a thing."

Janelle walked in. She glanced at them both as they quickly averted their eyes. She grabbed an apple juice from the fridge and a bagel from the breadbasket.

"Hey dad, you coming today? Whoopsie said she wanted a picture of the family all together."

John smiled at Janelle and nodded as he headed to the front door.

On the drive to the airport, Janelle felt tension simmer again, this time between Lily and her grandmother.

Lily's mother asked, "So, is John meeting us at the restaurant?"

Lily shifted in the driver's seat.

"He's giving a presentation at work as we speak. He'll come by once he's done."

Lily's mother observed, "He's been such a ghost lately. Always busy."

Lily sucked in a quick breath.

"We've both been busy. There's a lot of running around with the kids. It took some doing to find the right preschool program for them that we were happy with. But they're still fussy at morning drop off. They're slowly getting used to the earlier drop off time. And John's firm is still recovering from the fire. The temporary office space is smaller and harder to function in."

Lily's mother stared at her intently. When Lily noticed her looking, she bristled.

"Dad hasn't been home much either. Are you and dad *okay*? Should *I* be worried?"

Her mother chuckled.

"Don't be silly honey. We're fine." Her mother nodded. "But point taken."

The car fell silent and everyone self-entertained. Janelle had Beyoncé blasting through her ear buds. The twins watched the Craig of the Creek cartoon on the TV mounted in the back seat. Lily and her mother listened to talk radio.

Janelle wondered what book Whoopsie brought for her this time. The last one, *The Curious Incident of the Dog in the Nighttime*, had her crying when she found out what happened to the dog, then loving how the story ended. The books were never ones Janelle would pick herself, but she enjoyed them nonetheless. And they all reminded her of Whoopsie, her smart, fun, young-at-heart ball of energy elderberry.

Before retiring, Whoopsie worked full-time as an office manager and was active in her church, a garden club, a book club, and in the lives of all of her children and grandchildren. She was as dedicated as they come to Lily's grandfather and raised her four children making sure they understood what family meant. Home-cooked meals, family dinners, summer vacations, and the occasional treat of Whoopsie letting them skip school to catch a matinee movie in the theater. Retirement accelerated Grandpa Henry's memory problems and overall decline. He was fifteen years Whoopsie's senior. When his dementia reared its head, Whoopsie took care of him, all the way to his last breath. When he stopped eating, she started preparing the funeral arrangements. She did so with the quiet fortitude of keeping a business running, rather than ready-ing for the death of a life partner. Her only shaken moment was sitting in her car at the end of the funeral. She sat for 20 minutes, tears steadily streaming down her face. Eventually, she allowed her son to drive her to the house for the repass.

Lily pulled the car into an hourly parking lot at National Airport. They all filed out and walked over to baggage claim. Janelle spotted Whoopsie. She had already grabbed her bag off the conveyer belt and had a flower print backpack on while she held someone's baby. When she turned and saw the family approaching, in one fell swoop she passed the baby back to the mother and swung around to greet everyone with open arms. Her lifelong whip skinny frame had given way to a pear shape. But her youthful energy still radiated. She hustled over and bent down to hug the twins first, then her daughter and Lily, then Janelle whom she hugged the longest.

Once they all packed back into the car, Lily drove over to Delilah's Soul Food restaurant in D.C. for lunch and was lucky enough to find street parking on the same block. Inside the restaurant, most seats were filled as the lunch rush was in full swing. The hostess apologetically let them know there would be a twenty-minute wait, so everyone paired off in the waiting area. Whoopsie chatted with Lily's mother, Lily and Janelle looked at a menu and picked what they would have for lunch, and the twins hopped around in a circle on alternating legs saying, "I'm a bunny with one leg!" When the hostess returned to seat them, John came through the restaurant doors.

"Perfect timing! Hey lovely ladies!"

Jasper complained, "I'm not a lady. I'm a boy!"

John rubbed Jasper's head, kissed Lily's cheek, and hugged everyone else.

"Can I join?"

Whoopsie grinned broadly.

"Of course. We need some masculine energy in this hen's nest anyway!"

John and Whoopsie chatted about her senior travel group jaunts and her dating life. She grinned about dating a younger man. At seventy-one, he was twelve years her junior. Lily was mostly quiet, occasionally chiming in to give an update here and there about how work was going and how the kids were doing.

That night after the kids were asleep, John and Lily were in bed — him on his laptop and her flipping TV channels.

She asked, "So, are you planning to spend any time with us while Whoopsie's in town for the week?"

"Of course. It worked out well today didn't it?"

Lily nodded.

"It would be nice if you could take us sightseeing."

John sighed and paused a beat before responding.

"I won't have time. Plus, when did I become the designated sightseeing tour guide? You and your parents all know D.C. just as well as I do. We can have her over for dinner, or go over to your parents for dinner."

Lily crossed her arms tightly on her chest.

"Why is everything all of a sudden an issue?"

"Everything? I just said I can't do sightseeing. How did that become everything?"

"Okay, whatever. Never mind."

Whoopsie's week was filled with family time. Lily took the twins over to her parents' house to play with Whoopsie the first day. Then Lily's mother brought Whoopsie to Lily and John's house two days later. She played on the floor of the kids' bedroom until dinner was ready. Lily insisted that dinner start promptly at five o'clock. So when John got home at 6:15 p.m. dinner was done, and the dishes were being washed. Whoopsie and Janelle went to a movie the following day then had dinner at Cracker Barrel. It was their time to really chat and catch up. Whoopsie gave Janelle the book she chose for her this time, *Don't Judge a Girl by Her Cover*.

"You'll definitely like this one. One of the ladies in my book club said her granddaughter raved about it."

"Cool. Thanks Whoopsie!"

They ordered their meals and waved at an infant in a stroller at a nearby table.

Janelle asked, "So, are you dating?"

"Yeah. It's still strange to me not having Henry around. But I've been a widow for over ten years now. It's time I think."

They talked while eating pork chops for dinner and shared a baked apple dumpling for dessert.

Whoopsie asked, "So, what's going on with school? And boys?"

She winked at Janelle who smiled in return.

"I'm dating a boy. Mason! He's real sweet and cool. He goes to my school. And he has a funny little brother that he walks home from school every day."

Whoopsie nodded as she listened.

"I kinda got nervous and stopped dating him. But I'm going to try to work it out."

"What were you nervous about?"

Janelle shifted in her seat.

"Well, I don't know. Just stuff. But um, everybody hasn't met him yet." She paused. "I want you to meet him. But don't act funny, okay? He's white."

Whoopsie smiled and tilted her head.

"Honey, why are you announcing it like that? You sure you're not *wanting* me to act weird? If you don't want it to be a big deal, don't make it one honey!"

Janelle quietly nodded. Within an hour, Lily came to pick the two of them up from the restaurant. The next day, Whoopsie hugged everyone tightly before her cab arrived to take her to the airport for her flight home. Janelle was happy that she at least told Whoopsie about Mason even if they didn't get to meet.

The next day, Janelle finally felt ready to call Mason. It had been over a week since they really spoke. After school and finishing her homework, she sat on the floor leaning on her bed. It took her half an hour to work up the nerve to call. Her hands were clammy from sweat. She wiped her palms on her jeans then called him on FaceTime.

He popped up on her screen. She could see his bedroom in the background and hear music playing. He was laying on his bed. He said nothing.

She said, "Hey Mase!"

Still nothing.

She asked, "What's been going on with everything? I know it's been a while."

She felt the tension and wanted to melt into the ground leaving just her clothes in a puddle on the floor. He stared at her.

She offered, "I'm just checking on you. Everything good?"

He said dryly, "Yup." Then after a long pause, he added, "Didn't know you cared."

Her heavy chest pressed her into the bed frame. She wiped her palms on her jeans.

"Of course I care. That's why I'm checking on you."

Mason didn't relent,

"But you ghosted though. That makes no sense at all."

"I know. I—"

She hesitated.

"I know I've been acting stupid. I just—"

He interrupted, "And why do I have to walk into school and hear rumors about my girl with another dude?"

His tone was the sternest she'd ever heard him use. Given the circumstances, she didn't have time to pay much attention to the "my girl."

"I'm—, I'm sorry."

"That's it? That's all you're going to say?"

The phone fell silent. Janelle could hear the twins in their bedroom playing loudly. She wished they were in her room to distract her from the sinking feeling in her stomach.

His tone softened as he asked, "Why'd you ghost on me?"

Janelle searched for the words to explain,

"I'm really sorry, Mase. I didn't –, I don't –, I didn't know what to say."

Mason looked confused, "What? I don't get it. One minute we're chillin' every day and everything's good. Next minute you're dodging me and chillin' at some dude's house."

She took a deep breath.

"It got all screwed up. I was just hanging out with him. But we weren't going to hang at his house. It just happened like that, but nothing happened. I left. He just tried to act like something happened. I was there for like ten minutes or something."

"Okay. What about before that? I was texting you. For days. I didn't hear anything from you."

The phone fell silent.

Then she said, "I just want us to chill again."

"Oh okay. Just like that? Is that how it works for you?"

"We were good when we were hanging out. We could talk about anything. We could do nothing and be happy with that. We were great together."

Janelle felt some relief just saying the words. She smiled at him.

Mason stared silently. After a while he sighed.

"If we were so great together, what was the problem?"

She paused for a long time.

"It's like I just thought if we slowed everything down, and stopped talking so much, I wouldn't care as much." She paused. "I didn't want to really like you. Not you as Mason, but you as a white boy. I don't want to have it be a thing that everyone's talking about. I don't want to be out there like that. I know it's supposed to be the 21st century and all, but it's still a thing. You know, nobody in my family dates white people. I would be the only one. It's weird, you know."

Mason listened intently.

"My dad seems all cool about stuff, but then he's weird about some things. When we had the birds and bees talk, he told me that I should always feel strong as a black woman. He said that black boys have to know you're strong so that they can nurture that strength." She paused. "I don't know, it's just I know he's weird about this, even though he's never said it before."

She shifted position, sitting up straighter.

"But, it's so hard not talking to you. I want to tell you the stuff that happens. I really wanted to call you when all that Trey drama happened. But I figured you were pissed. I mean, I would be if I were you."

As the last of her words came out, she felt her chest relax. All the tension she had pent up inside released like a deep long exhale.

They sat silently. He walked over to his desk. Then a song played. She climbed into bed and listened.

"If your love was all I had in this life, that would be enough until the end of time."

She smiled. When Mason finally spoke, his voice was low and raspy, "So, are we together?"

She grinned but didn't answer.

"Come to the park after school tomorrow. I have something for you."

She held up a little drawstring pouch for him to see. It had a gift that she'd made two days before. When they got off the phone Janelle turned off the light and went to bed before her parents came in to say goodnight. She was sleeping within seconds.

17

The York & Newton office was finally inhabitable again and the associates spent the week coming in early to unpack their offices. Patrice and John were perusing the lunch menu at Firefly, a restaurant up the street from their office building. Their table was near the window, and Patrice watched people hustle by. As they waited for their food, they chatted about the most recently acquired client account. There were going to be several new projects to head up, and she was excited that her project palette was expanding. After a while, John changed the subject.

"So, what did you think about Mosaic?"

Neither one of them had acknowledged seeing each other at church a week ago, until now.

"Pretty good. There's a nice energy there. And I like the smell of the place."

He laughed. She looked incredulous.

"What? The smell of a church matters when you have to sit there for an hour, sometimes longer."

He nodded and smiled.

He said, "Your pastor gives a good sermon!"

"Yes! I would like to hear the regular pastor at some point. We only came because our pastor was a guest preacher."

"Good."

She smiled.

"So, how long have you and your family been going there?"

"Four years."

After a beat, she said, "It was real cute that y'all were color coordinated!"

"Yeah. We had a themed event to go to after at one of the church member's houses."

By the time their food came, she dug in quick to ease her hunger pains as she hadn't eaten breakfast. She finished her salmon in minutes then watched as he finished his food.

"Did you notice the woman in the black suit at church?"

He looked at her expressionless as if waiting for her to continue.

"She was several rows behind you. Kept looking your way the whole sermon."

John took a sip from his glass of water.

"She's an old neighbor and family friend. She moved out of the neighborhood but seems to return to the church on occasion."

Patrice leaned back smirking.

"She was looking at you like she was *your* friend."

She paused then continued,

"She even seemed pissed outside of church. Damn near ran past in the parking lot."

He raised his eyebrow.

"Wow, you saw a lot."

"Well, I was taking everything in about the church since it was my first time there."

He didn't say anything. She continued.

"Well, she was pretty."

He glanced at her, "She's taken."

Patrice smirked.

"Whatever. I'm just saying she's pretty, not that *I* want her."

She stared at him curiously. John's voice dropped an octave. "Look. You can assume whatever you want. But, there's nothing there to explain."

Patrice yanked her head backwards and popped her eyes wide open.

"Wow. Okay."

His tone was incredulous, "Well, seems like you're reading a lot into her looking at me." He paused, shook his head, then continued. "We were in the same social circle for a while. Then she and her husband moved. And that's it."

"Okay."

Patrice glanced out of the window.

"Well, you were both sitting in the rows ahead of me. You were just in my line of sight."

John sipped his water.

She continued with a lilt in her tone, "We really did like your church. Sean had been there once before and liked it then too."

John glanced at her and chuckled.

"So this conversation wound you up so much you needed to bring it back to your boyfriend?"

She scoffed.

"Don't flatter yourself."

He quickly retorted, "Apparently, I don't have to."

She quipped, "So wait, weren't *you* there with your family, the matching burgundy and gray clan? Why is it a problem to speak in *we* terms? You were a *we* too."

He snickered snidely, "I wonder if you know what color shoes we were wearing too?"

She gritted her teeth but said nothing else. They quieted down. The server came with the bill and asked if they wanted anything else, which was a welcomed distraction. As John paid the bill with a corporate credit card, Patrice reflected on the conversation. *What exactly are we fussing about?* She made a peace offering.

"My apologies John. I didn't mean to –"

He waved her apology away.

"Let's get back to the office. The meeting about the upcoming trip is starting in another fifteen minutes."

Patrice shifted her attention to the trip, which would include a conference, and three meetings to sure up three major acquisitions that if secured, would expand York & Newton's reach across the east coast.

Later that night, Patrice and Sean were on their way to her place, after a night of Thai food and a movie. Sean popped the trunk and grabbed a package that was wrapped in paper before they headed upstairs.

"What's that?"

He grinned, "Look at you being nosey."

When they got upstairs, he told her to wait in the bedroom while he got things ready. After a few minutes she heard,

"Okay c'mon."

She had heard some banging while she was banished to her room, and now she saw why. She walked up to the painting he had mounted on her wall. He even bought and affixed a lighting fixture above the painting. The painting was a stream of colors flowing like a winding river through mountains with a setting sun as the backdrop. The light reflecting on the painting made it seem alive. The blues, greens, and whites were rippling and flowing.

Patrice and Sean had gone to an art gallery opening a year earlier. Patrice perused the paintings and found herself stuck in front of one that she loved. But she thought spending $300 for it would have busted her budget. Plus the size of it may have been too much for her modest-sized apartment.

She grinned at Sean and hugged him for the gift.

"You remembered! Thank you baby!"

"Of course."

"You know why I liked it? Reminded me of our first trip together!"

During the first year they were dating, Patrice had found a great travel deal for a three-night stay in a Colorado log cabin.

Apparently, prices dropped for such trips in the summer as most people made them in the winter. She loved the idea of staying in a log cabin away from civilization with a good man and a good book. When she first mentioned taking the trip, Sean was skeptical, to say the least.

"What are going to do at a log cabin with no wi-fi? I'm sure we can occupy some time. But, ain't but so much sex that can happen in a day."

Patrice convinced him that hiking in the woods and swimming in a nearby watering hole then having dinner at night would be plenty to keep them busy. And that was just what they did each day. The mountain views were etched in Patrice's memory.

"Babe, this is beautiful. I love it! And I love you!"

She continued to stare at it, looking from end to end, top to bottom. Sean stood behind her with his arms wrapped around her waist. She wrapped her arms around his arms. Then she turned to hug him. Tightly. She kissed him everywhere on his face — cheeks, nose, lips and all.

"One more."

He puckered his lips. She obliged, and they kissed deeply. She stepped backwards as he led her to the bedroom.

18

Lily was in the middle of a psychotherapy session with a client when the phone in her office rang. She had forgotten to turn on the *Do Not Disturb* function. When her session ended ten minutes later, she checked who had called. It was Janelle. She called back as quick as she could punch in the number.

"What's wrong honey?"

"Nothing Ma. Didn't you listen to the message? I said on there that nothing was wrong so you wouldn't worry."

"No. I just saw that you called. And you rarely ever call me at work. So I just called back."

"Oh. Sorry to get you worked up."

"Okay, so what's up?"

"Well, I need advice."

Lily nodded, "Okay, sure."

"Sooo, I have a boyfriend now."

"Oh. Okay. Who is it?"

"Mason."

"Okay, well that makes sense. You've been talking to him a lot lately. And hanging out after school."

"Yeah."

Lily smiled, "Okay honey. Well, we want to meet him."

"I know. Mason *wants* to meet my family too. And I want him to meet you too."

"Okay good. Well let's talk tonight. Maybe he can come over on the weekend. We can have lunch in the sun room if the weather's nice."

The phone fell silent.

"So, honey what was the advice you wanted?"

Janelle spoke hesitantly, "Well. He's white. And I don't know how that's going to go over with dad."

Lily waited for Janelle to say more, but she didn't.

"Okay, honey." Lily paused, then continued, "You like him, right?"

"Yes."

"And he's respectful?"

"Yes."

"And I'm sure your friends have met him and probably gave him the thumbs up."

"Yeah."

"So good. Now we'll meet him, and we can go from there."

Janelle was silent again. Lily inquired,

"Have you two done anything? Have you had sex?"

"No. No. I haven't done that."

"Okay. I'm just checking. Just trying to assess the situation."

"But I have kissed him." She paused. "And -, actually -, I kissed another boy too. But that was just a thing that happened. But anyway, that's not the point."

Lily sounded exasperated, "What? Two boys?"

"No. The other boy wasn't like that. I was nervous about Mason and trying to not be too into him. But the other boy was a huge mistake."

"Okay, well, let's just figure out when Mason can come by to meet your dad and I, and then see how things go from there."

Janelle asked, "So, how do you think dad will take it?"

"Which part? You dating or Mason being white?"

"Both. But mostly the white part."

Lily smiled.

"I don't know. This is all really new. You dating a boy. Bringing him to the house. So, I would say being white isn't the biggest factor to deal with. Your dad has to get used to it all."

Lily continued when Janelle didn't say anything.

"Sweetie, we live in a world with millions of people. And it takes all kinds to make this world turn. You never know who you will like. You just have to figure out what makes you happy."

She paused then added, "I'm going to assume that if you like him that he's not a knuckle head just trying to get in your panties."

Janelle scoffed.

"Ma! Stop trying to talk cool."

"What?!"

They both laughed. Lily spoke with a reassuring tone.

"No point getting yourself worked up and worried about what your dad will think before he's had a chance to meet him. No matter how it goes, we'll have to deal with it anyway."

"You're right. Okay. Well, thanks Ma."

"No problem. Now, what about this other boy you kissed _"

"Oh, that was Trey. That's over. He was an asshole."

"Hey lady. Watch it."

"Sorry. But he was. That's a whole other story though."

"Well, I'll be all ears tonight. Right now, I have another client to meet with."

"Okay. Thanks Ma."

Janelle went to Lily first whenever she wasn't sure what her dad would think about something. Not that he reacted badly to most things. He was good about remembering being a teenager himself. But every now and then, without warning, he became the uncool parent with no wiggle room, two-way discussion or compromise. And when he did, things didn't turn out well. Janelle referred to the last time as the belly ring fiasco. When she asked about getting a piercing in her upper ear, he shot her down with no discussion, saying that she would have to wait until she was eighteen. He then rambled on about why she wanted holes everywhere on her body and that next she would want a belly ring. She couldn't understand what a belly ring had to do with anything because that wasn't even close to what she asked for. *Half my school has piercings all over the place and not to mention tattoos. And he's trippin' off extra ear piercings?* But there was no talking to him after he got worked up.

Lily prided herself on raising her kids differently than what she knew growing up. She had a loving family who had enough money for her to get mostly everything she wanted. Private school education and family trips to Europe. Piano lessons, girl scouts, ballet classes and whatever else she was interested in. But she came from a family who took more pride in upholding an image than in realness. Her parents married and had kids in their early twenties. In the midst of marriage and children, her mother attained a Ph.D. in psychology. Her father went through medical school and became a psychiatrist. Lily's brother Leonard worked his way up the ranks in a mental health agency to become the director, and also married in his early twenties, then had two kids shortly after. Her mother, while believing herself to be liberal, always seemed to place emphasis on traditional ideals as the happiest life option. So, when John came into the picture, her mother was pleased. Lily was already several years past her prime—as her mother often hinted—so she was happy to have a reprieve from remarks about marriage and children. Her mother saw nothing wrong with the Lily and John's six-month transition from dating to engagement.

"He clearly loves you honey! Love doesn't work on a schedule."

That image of perfection, of a perfect family, seemed more important to her mother than the possibility of an unhealthy marriage. Lily had been nervous about getting engaged, but she was in love with John. She hoped the nerves would disappear. So did her mother. So, when Lily mentioned her concerns, her mother quickly waved it off.

"That's natural. You'll adjust once you get into the wedding planning. It'll sink in!"

There was no helping Lily deal with her worries, only dismissive platitudes. The same could be said for several other crossroads Lily faced in life. There was plenty of advice and plowing forward words of encouragement from her mother, but no real empathy.

Once Lily had children, and she considered Janelle to be her child, she wanted to really accept them for who they were. No dismissing of their thoughts and feelings, or expecting them to follow a predestined path. If they never married, or had no children of their own, it would be their choice. Their path. Not hers. And she was not going to judge them for it.

19

Patrice was glad when Friday rolled around, punctuating the end of a week that didn't unfold the way she wanted. She did her first pitch meeting at work and flopped spectacularly. At York & Newton, there was a hierarchy to how new accounts were assigned. Most times seniority mattered for getting assigned larger more lucrative accounts. But the unofficial rule was a new associate could make a request to be on an account if they seriously wanted a shot. And if pitched well to the CEO, then the account was in the bag. When Patrice caught wind of a new account with an all-woman leadership team, who were looking for new company branding after a public scandal, she wanted it. *What better way for me to shine!* With only two days before the account would be assigned to one of the associates, maybe three if it was going to be assigned to more than one associate, she kicked into high gear prepping for the pitch.

On presentation day, things fell apart within minutes. At the finish of her first sentence, sweat beaded on her forehead and back, and moistened her armpits.

"This is the type of account where my talents can shine!"

Patrice quietly gasped. She was winded. The elephant hoof was back securing footing on her chest, closing in on her freedom to breathe. Pitches had to be ten minutes or less. She cut hers short and spoke with a rushed pace and lackluster tone. She wrapped up just in time to make it to a bathroom stall to unravel in private. She emerged from the bathroom with a sweat-soaked blouse under her suit jacket. She left for lunch early that day and stopped by a nearby store to buy a top. Back in her office, she did her best to push the messy morning out of her mind and focus on the upcoming weekend trip to Atlantic City in a couple of days.

Two days later on a Friday afternoon, Patrice sped down the I-495 to Sean's place. She was hoping he'd show some excitement as the trip approached. *He'll get in the spirit once we're on the road.* She knew he had been focused on work, with the Gibson case and the recent robberies. She was curious about if he was any closer to figuring out who killed her. But she knew not to ask. She heard him a couple of days earlier, on a call with an officer, saying that the leads for who could possibly be the father of the unborn baby had whittled down to two. So, she figured there were at least two possible murder suspects. *That had to be the motive. She was probably messing around with a married man who didn't want his wife to find out he got another woman pregnant.*

When she got to Sean's place, he was packed and ready. They jumped on the road within ten minutes. He seemed tense at first but by the time they got on the New Jersey turnpike, he was mumble-singing to the radio. Despite a few patches of traffic, they made it there in three hours. They spent the first night wrapped up in each other, breaking in the hotel bed and hot tub. They slept in the next morning, waking up just in time to catch the tail end of the breakfast in the hotel cafe. Patrice was annoyed that the eggs were gone, but she piled her plate with bacon, sausage, and French toast sticks. And she fixed a bowl of oatmeal for good nutritional measure. Sean grabbed a yogurt, apple, banana, and a coffee. She looked at his hands.

"Is that all you're gonna have?"

Sean nodded.

"Yeah. We're gonna grab a bunch of junk on the board-walk anyway."

"I don't care. This breakfast is paid for, so I'm eating it."

"Uh-huh, and when we go back up to change, you're going to want to nap for two hours before we go out."

She smiled and chomped on a French toast stick. She refused to drink the coffee, fussing that it smelled stale. Instead, she had a coke with breakfast to get her caffeine fix. When they went back upstairs, Sean hopped in the shower, while she picked out what to wear. He came out and found her lying across the bed with heavy eyelids.

"See what I mean? Damn sausages are like lead in your stomach."

Patrice giggled. "Just five minutes babe."

Two hours later, they headed to the boardwalk. They walked through the clusters of people. The path was full and active, with kids running around, families with strollers, and small shops and vendors. Patrice hooked her arm around Sean's and shot him a devilish grin, "You look tired. What were *you* doing last night?"

Sean obliged, "This sexy lady broke into the room last night and stole my virginity."

"Oh? Well how was your first time?"

"Spectacular. Now I want it every day and twice on Sundays, in perpetuity."

She feigned exhaustion and he laughed.

As they walked the boardwalk, they chuckled about the seagulls and pigeons that walked between people, boldly eating everything they could peck on. They saw a stray dog at one point that kept popping up in different places. They nicknamed him Bruno Mars because it looked like he was dancing as he bobbed and weaved through groups of people to get at food on the ground. They had a running joke that he would be at the door of their hotel room when they got back up there and maybe even waiting at the car when they were ready to leave the next day. They had hotdogs, Italian ice, and churros. Patrice's belly was full beyond measure.

They went to one of the neighboring hotels because Sean preferred the game tables at that casino. He had better "Juju" at certain casinos apparently. Sean had told Patrice about his days of monthly trips to Atlantic City when he was younger. How he spent years paying off debt from those days when "things got out of hand." It was hard for her to imagine him back then. All she knew of him was steady and stable.

Patrice had never been to a casino before. Well, not what she'd consider a real one. She had been to the casinos on cruise ships, but she'd only played slot machines and enjoyed the free drinks. She was excited to try her hand at the real deal. He told her blackjack would be a good start. He showed her the ropes, from how to sit, make and avoid eye contact, and the importance of focusing on the dealer's hands. Within twenty minutes she was grinning from ear to ear. She'd won $370.

Sean smiled proudly.

"That ought to buy us some T-bone steaks and drinks for the rest of the weekend!"

She quipped, "Hell no. You're not spending my money. We're having appetizers for meals. Onion rings and potato skins. And just water, no drinks!"

"Wow. Cheap as a dollar menu. Where's my cut? You won that loot with my strategies. See the next time I help you."

She gently looped her arm around his. "My hero!"

They moved over to the poker tables, and this time Sean sat, and she watched. If she liked it, then she would join. But he let her know that it was trickier than blackjack, with different odds and rules for bets. As she watched a few rounds, her nerves got the better of her, and she never joined. Watching Sean had her speechless. He slowly descended into the world of straights, houses, and flushes. It wasn't long before she felt the force field grow around him, and she was on the outside looking in. He was still, tense, and laser-focused. He didn't look up at her once. She could have walked away and came back, and he would have been none the wiser. Now she understood why he was so earnest when he'd asked her to hold onto his wallet and to not give it back to him until they got back to their hotel room, no matter how much he asked her for it. He had taken $500 out of his wallet and seemed to blow through the money like water. He got down to forty dollars at one point, then worked his way back to $230. After an hour passed, Patrice wondered if he was going to come back to reality on his own. She waited another five minutes, and when he didn't budge, she hinted that she was ready to go. Sean seemed not to hear her at first, but when she kissed his cheek and said, "Okay hon, I'll see you upstairs," he came to. He cashed in his chips and they left.

They were back on the boardwalk headed to their hotel. The sky was burnt orange as the sun made its way behind the ocean waters. Patrice motioned for them to sit and watch the sunset.

Sean said, "I thought you were tired and wanted to get to the room."

"I just said that to get you out of there. You were in a zone. I had to do something. I think you might've put up the title on your car or something if you stay longer."

He smiled and leaned back on the bench. He wrapped one arm around her shoulder.

"I guess now you have a *reason* not to move in with me. I might spend the rent money!"

She smiled.

"You'd never!"

They watched couples and families pass by, and birds pick at food wrappers on the boardwalk. Bruno was on the sand in the distance eating spilled French fries. Sean broke the silence.

"You know, I've tried to figure out what the deal is with that. You never want to talk about it."

"About what?"

"Us moving in together. We start but never finish the conversation."

Patrice straightened up.

"We *have* talked about it."

"Okay, then remind me what you've said."

"Well, I just think we should do things organically."

Sean looked ahead at seagulls dipping in the water.

"What exactly does that mean?"

"Moving in together is the thing people do when they've been together and they haven't made any other decisions. It's a default thing almost. We're better than default decisions. We're good. Black love at its best!"

"That's what confuses me though. If we're so good, why wouldn't this be the next step? It would only be a default if it was something we weren't talking through." He paused. "You spend two nights a week at my place, and I'm at your place at least three nights. We're practically together every night. Our families love each other. My son loves you. You even get along with his mother. You have free reign to check my voice mail, email, cell phone, mailbox, and I have access to yours. Our lives are well intertwined, and it all works. We have a good mix of wires connecting rather than tangling."

The thought flashed in her mind, *So then, why haven't you proposed?*

When Sean first brought up moving in together, it was in the worst way from her perspective. An hour after teasing her that her drawers at his place were overstuffed, he had worked out how much money they were wasting on rent by having two separate apartments, and how much they would save by moving in. He had even worked out how much more often he could visit his son and have his son visit him with the increased savings. There wasn't even a remote mention of them getting engaged, married, or having children. Nothing but practicality.

Patrice refocused on the conversation.

"I just think moving in together can only go one of two ways. Stagnating or feeling pressured to keep on the pre-destined track of how couples are supposed to go. To picket fence family-hood." She glanced at him. "I mean, really, what incentive is there to move further if we live together? Living together is grazing heaven."

"I don't think you're a cow Patrice. I'm not trying to get the milk for free or graze for a lifetime."

She said, "I know."

"Okay, then."

Sean grew pensive. Without words, they both stood and headed back to their hotel. Once in the room, they sat on the balcony and continued the conversation.

"If you're struggling with this because of my son, I could understand that. I know that's not something that would be easy to bring up."

Patrice interjected, "Sean, believe me when I tell you, I love Micah. He's a bonus, not an issue. And neither is your ex. Not that it's my situation to dictate, but it's been good seeing how y'all deal with each other and co-parent. Doesn't go that way a lot of the time." She paused and saw his look of relief. "I just think, you know, too many couples move in together, and their relationships get stuck. They stop moving forward. It's like the men start to think, 'Okay then, well, we might as well get married,' or 'No need to get married. We're good.'"

Sean turned to her to ask, "Are you saying you want to get married?"

She thought, *Are you asking? It would be simpler if you were.*

"No. No, that's not it."

Patrice hated having this conversation. *Why do men make it so hard? And they say we're the complicated ones.* She'd thought about marriage. She wanted it. But not like this. Not by a forced hand. If he wanted to get married, really wanted to, he would be asking. He would have already asked. *The real question is what's holding him back.* She only saw the end of the living together road leading to one place: default marriage. She wondered at times how to explain that, without having the power of suggestion come into play.

Sean said, "You know, you think we would get stuck in a rut if we move in together. But truthfully, we're stuck now. In this phase. So, what's the difference?"

Sean's phone rang. He looked at her a few seconds longer before answering the call.

"What's up Dannon?"

Patrice stood and went in the room to grab a bottled water and give him some privacy. Minutes later, he stepped into the room.

She asked, "Everything okay?"

"Yeah. Just an update that couldn't wait. A bit of a complication with the case. But it's being figured out."

He took a deep breath.

"Okay. So what else?"

He waited for her to speak.

"Sean, you've been missing my point."

"Okay, enlighten me. What *is* your point?"

"You act like something's wrong with us. Like we're not working out or something. What are you trying so hard to fix?"

"Something's off about this. You not wanting to even have a conversation about it. It's just off. We're not on the same page about this. I mean, you say you're not holding out for a proposal. And it's not that you think I'm trying to buy the cow for free. But, you still can't seem to come up with a solid reason. You just keep saying these simplistic misgivings. But at this point, we're passed that."

Patrice hated every minute of this conversation.

"I just don't think it's a good idea to default into moving in together because we've been together long enough."

Sean gave up.

"Alright."

He grabbed clothes from his bag and headed to the bathroom for a shower. When he finished, he came out in boxers and slid into bed. Patrice was sitting in a chair in the corner reading. She glanced at him, but he wouldn't look at her.

"See. This is exactly why I don't like talking about this. Somehow it always comes across like I'm saying something bad about our relationship. But I'm not. And you get an attitude."

He focused on flipping TV channels.

"Sean, I just don't want us to take things for granted."

He put the remote down, leaving the TV on an episode of Seinfeld.

She continued, "To be honest, we do some taking each other for granted right now. But that's also how I know we're solid too. Because we always make up for it."

He looked at her expressionless.

"It's all good. I'll be downstairs in the gym."

He popped up out of bed, changed into gym clothes, and left. He returned two hours later, drenched in sweat. Patrice pretended to be asleep when he came back. He showered, slid into bed, and fell asleep within minutes.

The next morning, they headed down early to the cafe for breakfast. They had a large feast of omelets, waffles, fruit, coffee, and danishes. They slowly started talking again, breaking the silence of the night before. They chatted about the sights on the boardwalk they hadn't talked about last night, and laughed about the other men Sean described that were in the gym, trying their best to look cool and not grunt when muscle fatigue kicked in.

He explained, "It's different when you're not at your home gym. Men don't go all out when working out in front of strangers."

When they fell silent again, Patrice stared at Sean.

"Don't be mad babes. We're good."

Sean kept eating.

"I'm not mad. We *are* good."

"I know when you're mad. And now you're going to act shady the rest of the day?"

"No. That's what *you* do when *you're* upset. If I say I'm done with it, I'm done. No petty games."

She cocked her head to the side with mock annoyance.

"Oh, so now I'm petty?"

Sean paused then donned a sly smile with a raised eyebrow.

"Petty *and* pretty."

She smirked.

"That was corny."

He laughed, "Uh huh. And you loved it."

He stared at her lips. She mouthed 'love me?' He mouthed back 'I do.' He reached over the table and kissed her softly. They finished breakfast and headed to the hotel exit to spend the day at the casinos. She walked ahead of him, but he tugged at her waist to slow her down while acting like he was old and couldn't walk too fast. She chuckled. They strolled up the boardwalk.

Sunday night they returned to Patrice's apartment and there were ten messages on her voice mail. Sean listened to a few of the messages then passed her the cordless phone.

"You should listen to these."

She looked up at him worried.

He continued, "Michelle called. All she kept saying was 'Trice pick up, pick up.'"

Patrice's stomach sank.

"Something's wrong. I need to find her, but I don't know where she is."

She figured Michelle had lost her apartment and was probably bouncing from place to place. She didn't need to listen to the messages to know the routine.

"Babe. Can you check the system and see if –"

"See what I mean? You worry about me being a cop but when you're worried about sis being on the run, then you want me to step in."

"Sean, this is *not* the time. Can you help or not?"

He grabbed his phone and made a call to his precinct while she changed into jeans and a sweatshirt. She grabbed her purse, and they were out the door.

20

L ily appreciated that whenever she asked her parents to watch the kids they never hesitated. She didn't ask for babysitting often, so they loved the rare opportunity to spoil their grand kids without anyone around telling them not to. Since her parents agreed to pick the kids up from daycare, Lily was able to head straight from work to McCormick and Schmick's restaurant at National Harbor. It wasn't long after she arrived that Brian came through the door smiling widely.

"Well hey Ms. Lady! Looking gorgeous as always! Like a rainbow after a storm!"

She stood to hug him and smiled.

"Wow, Brian, still got them old tired lines I see."

He grinned slyly, "*Tired*? They were good enough to hook you back in the day."

"So you think. I was in it for your money!"

They laughed. Brian stood six feet two inches tall, in a crisp navy blue shirt and slate gray slacks. He pushed in the chair under her before taking a seat across the table. After placing their orders, they caught up on life.

Brian asked, "So, how's married life treating you?"

"Good. The kids are growing up fast. My daughter, step-daughter, Janelle is fifteen. She's a great girl. Smart and talented and funny. And the twins will be four in a few months. They're all well."

Brian quipped, "Life can't be that good. After all, you're not with me anymore."

She smirked.

He said, "I'm only joking. You're raising wonderful kids, I'm sure. I'm happy for you."

"Well, John has something to do with it. He's a great dad."

They chatted about Brian's divorce, which was surprisingly amicable. He reminisced about his travels overseas, and about giving serious consideration to relocating to France after a job opportunity emerged. Brian and Lily compared notes about travel destinations, which places they loved and the vacation spots that weren't as great as people made them seem. Lily belly laughed as Brian told a story about swimming in a choppy beach in Florida and emerging from the water not realizing that the waves had pulled at his swim shorts. He didn't know his butt was partially on display. It wasn't until a kid yelled, "Butt crack on the loose" that he looked down and yanked his shorts up. He packed his things and headed back to the hotel after that, refusing to go back to the beach for the rest of his trip.

Lily had laughed through most of dinner and enjoyed hearing about someone else's life, that wasn't one of her patients. After eating dinner, they ordered dessert. She ordered peach cobbler, and he got coffee. As she took bites of her cobbler, Brian focused on her lips. He leaned in on the table, his voice low and curious.

"Well. We've come a long way, haven't we. So, are you living the life you wanted?"

Lily took her last bite of cobbler and dabbed at her mouth with a napkin.

"I am. Family life is hard work, but so rewarding. And I enjoy my job, albeit hard work too. I couldn't imagine my life any other way. What about you?"

He nodded slowly.

"I have everything I want in life. Well, almost everything."

His eyes went back and forth from looking into her eyes to peering at her lips. They smiled at each other. He leaned back in his chair.

"Do you ever wonder Lily? About a different life?"

She studied his face. With a confident lilt she said, "No."

He brushed his chin with his hand.

"Have you actually considered it?" He paused. "You don't know until you think about it. Really think about it."

"Well, I know what makes me happy. Life's not a walk in the park. For any of us. It's gritty. It takes a lot of stamina to be in for the long haul. But there's happiness in all of that."

A subtle lift in the corners of his lips showed his amusement.

"Good. I'm glad. That you're happy."

The waiter came, checked if they wanted anything else, then put the check on the table. Brian pulled out his wallet and gave his credit card to cover the bill. Lily put her napkin on the plate, glanced out the window, then at him.

"Thank you for dinner. It was great catching up. Been such a long time."

She adjusted in her seat and crossed her legs under the table.

Brian nodded and finished the last of his coffee.

Lily and Brian had only dated for nine months, many moons before she met John. He was fine, fun and a bit flighty. He changed jobs three times just in the time they dated. He was always ready to try new activities, new foods, or take a day trip to wherever. When a job opportunity came up, he didn't hesitate to suggest that Lily move with him to New York while he was on a year-long contract. He said they would figure it all out, where to set up their life, and if they would stay beyond the contract time if it wasn't extended. He pointed out that, "Your twenties are when you make these kinds of choices. Otherwise, how do you know anything about life, if you haven't lived it?" Lily was excited by the idea, but didn't feel anywhere near ready to give up her life and commit to his. So, he left and she stayed.

After years with no contact, he recently popped up online. It wasn't long before they were connected on Facebook, Instagram, and Twitter. He looked the same except a little grayer and leaner. He was a reminder of life before John. Tonight, he told her that after his divorce he got back into the dating pool but never wanted to settle down with anyone. He told her that whenever he thought he was getting close to someone, Lily came to mind and he hadn't been able to shake the thought.

Lily took one last look out the window over the ripples of the water in the distance. When they stood to leave, she thanked him again for dinner. They strolled to her car. As they neared where she was parked, he reached for her hand and held it as they took the last few steps. She slowed and stood at her car door. He pulled a business card out of his pocket. He flipped it over to show her that his hotel room number was written on the back. Then he slid the card into the front pocket of her purse. He kissed the palm of her hand, then slid her fingers across his lips. He wrapped his lips around one of her fingers and sucked gently. Lily quivered. He reached in to hug her, and they embraced tightly.

"I'll be at the Marriott downtown until Friday at noon, then I head to the airport."

He gave her one last smile then walked away. Lily drove away immediately. She turned on the radio and sang along nervously to every song. She passed her hand over her purse pocket, then made the turn into her neighborhood.

21

Patrice and her friends Jen and Sasha headed to Bus Boys and Poets for poetry night. She felt long overdue for a night with the girls. Preparing for the upcoming presentations at the conference meant a minimum of two days a week of working late at the office or continuing to work for at least an hour when she got home. She spent most other nights with Sean. So, on the rare night when their schedules aligned and the weather was decent, she and her friends jumped on it no matter who was tired and needed rest.

They reminisced on the car ride about their days of nervously getting on stage for poetry nights. Pulling into the parking lot, they hopped out but quickly piled back in. The restaurant was closed to the public due to a private event.

Patrice said indignantly, "Okay, this is not shutting down our night."

Sasha proposed that they head over to Nightingale lounge instead, and that their theme of the night should be having fun no matter what. Everyone was on board. Thirty minutes later they were at the bar on the first floor ordering martinis. They checked out each floor of the club to decide which vibe they wanted. The first floor was blasting 90's hip hop, while everyone one on the second floor was wining and grinding to dancehall. The third floor was thumping with a circle of people taking turns in the center showcasing off their deep house dance moves. Hip hop won the draw and they settled in a corner of the first floor. Three drinks later, Patrice grinned widely as Sean walked up with a couple friends.

She hugged him.

"Hey baby! What are y'all doing here!"

His body was stiff.

"I should be asking you the same thing. I thought you were going to Busboys?"

Within minutes, they were hovering in a back hallway trying to inconspicuously argue. They took turns interrupting the other, each being pissed at the other for interrupting.

"Sean, why are you assuming that I'm being slick? Sometimes plans change."

"I'm just saying it looks shady. Here we go again with you not calling—"

Patrice interrupted,

"Here we go again? You would swear that I never call to tell you what's going on. I mess up one time and-."

"You're acting like I don't have a reason to be irritated."

She retorted, "You keep interrupting and talking over me. And no, this time, you don't have a valid reason to be upset. You're acting like I said I was going to India and ended up in Brazil. It's not that serious."

Sean clarified, "The thing is, I let you know when plans change. Because I wouldn't want you to worry. That's the difference between you and me. I think about how you're feeling and try—"

Patrice sucked her teeth loudly. She leaned her back against a wall, her arms crossed tightly across her chest.

"I really don't get why you're blowing this so far out of proportion. What's really going on? Are you upset about something else?"

He stared past her as if she hadn't spoken. She continued,

"I *did* think about you. And I *did* call. The poetry spot was closed, so Sasha called her boyfriend and he said he could get us in here free. I called your cell phone, but it went straight to voice mail." She paused. "And can we focus on the fact that you're here when you said you were going to play pool at Bedrock?"

He quickly retorted, "I left you a message." He laughed incredulously. "See, this is how I know you didn't bother to call me. Because if you did, you would have looked at your phone and saw my missed call."

She looked confused for a second, then snatched her phone out of her purse to look at the screen.

"No missed call, no message. See? And here, let me show you my call log so you can see that I called you. Because apparently I need to verify my whereabouts."

Sean shook his head. "You're being real extra right now."

She laughed loudly.

"*I'm* being extra?"

After a few seconds of hard taps on her phone screen, she shoved her phone in his face. He pulled his head back so quickly that he bumped into a woman who was passing behind him. He apologized.

"Sorry sweetheart. My bad."

The woman nodded and kept it moving.

Patrice seized the moment.

"Uh-huh. And I thought we talked about you calling random women pet names."

"Really Patrice? You damn near smacked me in my face with your phone, which is how I bumped into her in the first place, and you're going to pick a fight about what I said to apologize. That's all you could come up with to distract from the point?"

She recrossed her arms, stared at the floor and said nothing. He continued,

"Why didn't you leave a message when you called?"

She snarled, "Because I figured you were in a bad area and that I would call back. Then here you were." She paused with exasperation. "Come on Sean, why would I sneak around to go to a damn club? I hardly ever go to clubs anyway. It was just a last-minute change of plans."

Sean glanced around them realizing that the hall was filling with more people. He rubbed his hand over his face.

"Alright. Let's just chill. It's cool."

Sean reached for her shoulder, but she didn't budge.

"No. Hold on. You're making it sound like you caught me doing dirt and you're going to *let it slide*. I told you what the deal was."

Leaning

He shook his head, "That's not what I'm saying. Look, I've had a few drinks. I'm trippin'. I'm just saying I'm not going to bring it up all night. Let's just have a good night."

Sean earnestly rubbed her arms. She finally relaxed. This time when he reached his arm around her, she leaned in, and they made their way through the crowd. By the time they rejoined everyone, it was clear that a few of rounds of drinks had been ordered. Sean ordered a double shot of vodka and after gulping it, he took her by the hand and led her to the middle of the dance floor.

When they got to his place after two in the morning, exhaustion didn't give way to conversation. Patrice undressed and slid into bed. She didn't have the energy to put on a night shirt or take off her makeup. Sean stripped down to his boxers and got in right after her. She leaned over to kiss him goodnight and fell asleep within seconds of her head hitting the pillow.

The next day, Sean called Patrice to apologize as she was driving into work. He went into the precinct that morning, then left by 11:00 a.m., went over to Cake and Cups bakery to pick up her favorite espresso cupcake, then headed to her office to surprise her for lunch. When he got to her office, she had already left.

"Ms. Pearson and Mr. Blackman left for a lunch meeting about a half an hour ago. Would you like to leave a message?"

He shook his head and smiled, "No, thanks."

Sean exited the building and headed back to his car. As he crossed the street he caught a glimpse of himself in a restaurant window. When he peered past his reflection, Patrice came into view. She sat at a table for two in the middle of the restaurant with who Sean assumed was John. Sean slowed his pace and watched intently. John used his fork to eat off Patrice's plate. Then he offered her food from his. *What in the hell.* Sean's eyes widened as Patrice leaned in to eat from John's fork. Sean stood planted on the sidewalk. *This shit is crazy.* Heat was rising in him by the second. Sweat beaded on his forehead. When he got to his car, he paced back and forth on the sidewalk. He contemplated whether to go into the restaurant. *Nah. I could catch a charge if I go in there.* He thought about calling her to say he was there for lunch, to see if she would check her phone and answer. *Nah, I need to bounce.* He handed the cupcake he bought her to a homeless man on the corner. *How do you figure out what someone's really about? Give them space, time, and rope. They'll tie themselves up.* Sean shifted into detective mode as he pulled off.

22

When Lily gave John the rundown on Mason, she let him know that he goes to Janelle's school, lives in a neighborhood near by, and has parents who are together and work in D.C. She emphasized that she thought Mason was probably going to be around for a while. Janelle, up until now, hadn't talked about any boy beyond saying he was cute, far less calling Lily at work for advice. Janelle invited Mason to come over on a day Lily thought would work best, a Friday afternoon. After work, Lily got home with the twins, whipped up sandwiches and ice tea, and had everyone settled in the sun room when John walked through the door. The twins were sitting between Janelle and Mason, messily munching on Cheez-its.

Janelle smiled nervously when John walked in.

"Hey dad!"

"Hey, sugar!"

He walked over to kiss Lily on the cheek then hugged Janelle as the twins bumped into him for their hugs.

"So, dad, this is Mason. Mason this is my dad, John Blackman."

Mason stood and extended his hand.

"Good to meet you, sir."

John shook Mason's hand, quickly looking him up and down.

"Likewise. Have a seat."

John sat and snatched a chip out of Jasmine's hand knowing that she would protest,

"Daddy!"

"Okay, okay."

He gave the chip back to her.

"So, you go to Janelle's school?"

"Yes."

"What grade?"

"Tenth grade."

Mason glimpsed at Janelle, who gave him a nervous but reassuring smile.

"I hear you like football."

Mason looked more relaxed once talking about sports. He answered all of John's questions and jumped up as Janelle stood once the inquisition was over. They were now free to hang out in the basement. They debriefed about how things went. Mason vented his frustration that he fumbled over his words. Janelle comforted him by recapping how impressed her dad was that he plays drums and has a collection of vintage skateboards. After an hour, they headed back upstairs for Mason to head home. John was in the kitchen. He leaned out of the kitchen doorway to watch the two of them say goodbye. Janelle opened the front door, hugged Mason, and kissed his cheek.

A few seconds later, she popped into the kitchen.

"So how long have you two been hanging out?"

"I guess, maybe, for a little while. Not that long."

He grinned at her, signaling he wanted a clearer answer.

"Like two months. But we were really cool, like friends first. So, that whole time might not count as dating."

He squinted, "And what has he been doing to get in your pants? And don't lie to me, Chica. I know when you're lying." He always called her Chica when he wanted to respect for his lie detection skills. He stared intently.

"Dad! Really? No. We just hang out. Laugh. Study. Chill."

He studied her face a few more seconds.

"Okay. Just as long as you know that you're too young to be acting like you're grown."

Then he added,

"Don't forget I was young once too. I know what goes through boys' heads. And definitely Mason's."

"I know dad."

Janelle grabbed an apple juice bottle from the fridge and sat back down. She studied his face. But she didn't say a word. John closed his laptop, pulled the tie off his neck, and got up.

"Janelle, you know, you're a young woman with a lot of things going for you. I just don't want to see that derailed."

"I know."

He gave her a hug then headed upstairs.

Janelle woke up the next morning to the sharp sounds of raised voices coming from the kitchen. She took a few minutes to wake all the way up before getting out of bed. She couldn't make out enough of what was being said to know if the argument was about her and Mason. She brushed her teeth then tiptoed down the hall. She perched on the top step straining to hear. She heard Lily whisking in a glass bowl and her dad flipping pages, of a work report she later figured out.

"Well, the way you're acting right now should provide the full explanation of why I didn't tell you. It's not like she's running around having sex, drinking or doing wild stuff John. She likes a boy. For goodness sake. Where's the crisis?"

"All I'm saying is you should have told me. You could have given me a heads up about him."

"How would that have changed the outcome of meeting him?"

"I'm not saying it necessarily would have. I just would have appreciated knowing. She's my child and –"

John winced.

"Lily, I –, I didn't mean it that way."

Janelle listened quietly. She guessed Lily was whisking up pancake mix. When they were silent for a few minutes, Janelle took the opportunity to make noise coming down the stairs.

"Morning."

She walked in the kitchen and plopped on a stool.

John said good morning and Lily smiled, "Hey honey. Pancakes will be ready in about ten minutes."

The twins came downstairs and bounded into the kitchen. After breakfast when the kitchen was clear of kids again, John and Lily resumed. Lily changed the subject.

"So, I've gotten more info about that trip I saw. It would be nice if we took one soon. It's been forever since we've done something like that as a couple."

John sighed.

"We have a lot of moving parts happening at work. We just took on three large accounts to begin expansion efforts."

She retorted, "Is there ever a good time for you to go on a trip?"

"Don't generalize. I'm talking about right now. Not forever."

"Busy with what? You're a senior executive. You can delegate when needed."

"Of course, but I'm the lead on several accounts. I can't delegate those." He paused, calming his tone. "But you know, just because I can't go, doesn't mean you can't. Make it a girl's trip. When was the last time that happened?"

She scoffed, "I can take a trip with the girls anytime." She pointed at him then herself. "*We* haven't taken a trip since before the twins were born. Matter of fact, they were conceived on the last trip." She paused as if waiting for him to chime in. When he said nothing, she continued, "We really need this. We need to do something different. Change things up."

He closed his laptop.

"Okay. I'll just make it work. But, no longer than three days."

Lily protested, "A weekend trip? You know that's not what I had in mind."

"That's what I can swing right now."

23

Sean was on a call with his brother Ron, who was frustrated with the divorce proceedings. Sean did his best to be supportive but was distracted by his own stress. The image of Patrice and John at lunch crossed his mind multiple times daily. Up until recently, he hadn't done any research on her job. He hadn't had a reason to. Now, he figured out that the man she was having lunch with was John Blackman, the same man who left a message after she interviewed at York & Newton. He knew from John's online profile that he went to Howard University during the same time that Patrice did. He also knew from Facebook pictures, one of which included his family standing in front of a church, that John's home church is Mosaic, the same church Patrice said she wouldn't mind continuing to attend even after the repairs were done at Journey Baptist.

The last surprise was that John was Patrice's ex. He knew she had an ex-boyfriend named John, but he'd never heard her say a last name. He needed to confirm. He went through a photo box she kept in her closet the last time he was at her place. When he came across a handful of pictures of Patrice and John hugged up, there was no more wondering. Their history was clear.

Sean couldn't figure out the angle that she was coming from. *She had to know that it would come out eventually that she's working with him. It's like trying to hide a pregnancy. Eventually, that belly's gonna be too big to hide.* He felt a surge of heat every time he thought about Patrice grinning and eating off John's fork. Sean made a point of asking more about her coworkers now, and she responded casually and openly about all the projects and personalities at work. But she never once mentioned John. Like he didn't exist.

Sean's thoughts pinged from, *I'm trippin'. She wouldn't lie like this,* to the other extreme of, *She really thinks I'm a fool.* He thought about every data point that was relevant. He was rarely wrong about situations like this. *If someone comes into the house and puts their feet up on your couch, something made them think they could. Maybe not in words but in non-words.* Heat surged through his body. *Something's up.* He thought back to when he heard John's voice on Patrice's voice mail all those months ago. He knew John liked Patrice right away. His tone, the tempo of how he talked. With the few words in that message, Sean felt uneasy.

24

After bombing a pitch meeting two weeks earlier, Patrice wasn't sure what her next move should be. John had been good about fairly distributing smaller projects to new associates. So, she was plenty busy and had ample opportunities to show her worth. But she didn't yet feel secure in the firm. She didn't yet have the foothold she was used to, of being clearly seen as an asset. She thought about her options. Should she lick her wounds and be conservative, not asking for any accounts while just taking what came her way? Or should she get back up quickly and pitch for another account. Would pitching again make her look like an overeager rookie rather than a seasoned player?

It wasn't long before the decision was made for her. At the last associates' meeting, Patrice learned that one of the new accounts used to work with her old firm and when they heard she was now at York & Newton, showed an interest in working with her. Patrice was exhilarated at being chosen. *This is it! This is the shot I needed.* She made a priority list for setting up the initial account meeting, and told herself there was no room for error.

New associates at the firm had to give their account presentations in-house first before getting the go-ahead to have an initial account meeting with the account execs. Patrice had a week to prep. But the days flew by fast. Before she knew it was time. The meeting was set for eight o'clock on a Monday morning. She didn't leave the house, not once, during the weekend before. She spent every moment she could, doing as much research as she could, and practicing how she would do her presentation — tempo, intonation, even where she would stand. She had to show she was ready to take the lead. She avoided John as much as she could without seeming ill-mannered. She wasn't sure if he would say something supportive, or something that would shake her confidence. She refused to think about how the meeting could go wrong. She focused on shining.

As Patrice rode into work on the Metro the morning of the meeting, she remembered Cynthia Shaughnessy. Patrice was fifteen when she met her. Cynthia, who insisted that the students call her by her first name, came to speak at a career day at Patrice's high school when she was in the tenth grade. Cynthia had spearheaded an initiative at her public relations firm, one of the largest in the nation, to build a more diverse pipeline for their firm by doing outreach to high schools and colleges. Cynthia was one of five professionals that came, each speaking for ten minutes about their field. She was white, slim, freckled, and had a proud air about her with a slight gawkiness. She was the only speaker who didn't give a bunch of statistics about why going into each respective field was a good choice. All the men, in their dark suits and blue or red neck ties rambled on about the money they made in dentistry, real estate, anesthesiology, and hotel management. All of which fell flat in the auditorium full of bored high school students who couldn't care less about stats, unless the job seemed cool. When it was Cynthia's turn, she was a surprise from the start. She smiled widely when introduced by the vice principal. Then she took off her suit jacket, stepped out of her heels, and did three somersaults to the center of the gym, landing in front of the microphone. Students shifted in their seats and sat up straight from their slumped boredom. When she landed on her feet, she donned a huge ear-to-ear smile while the students applauded.

"Not bad for thirty huh?"

The auditorium ruptured with applause, whistles and cheers. One of the professionals walked Cynthia's heels over to her. She re-donned her suit jacket and ran her fingers through her hair to smooth it out after her acrobatics. She went on to tell two stories, about how she loved being in public relations and how she enjoyed being able to travel and meet new people. She ended by having the students clap to a beat as she recited a rap that she wrote to woo a new client to her company the month before. This meek looking Irish woman with a mild accent and freckles had every student in the auditorium hyped up. It was the first time Patrice saw a woman have that kind of impact, in person. The clincher was Patrice looking out of the classroom window when she went back to class and seeing Cynthia pull off in a shiny black car. She couldn't tell what kind of car it was, but it looked expensive, and she wanted to own it when she grew up. That was the day she decided that she wanted to be in public relations.

Patrice refocused on the meeting as she stepped off the Metro train. When she walked through the firm to her office she thought, *This is my time. I can feel it!* Her presentation lasted twelve minutes, complete with PowerPoint slides that showed the before-scandal company image and her re-imagined vision for the company. Trevor, John, and the associates were nodding along, giving their stamp of approval even before she discussed the research she'd done to prove why her vision would work for the company. She damn near skipped out of the office when she left work that day.

When she got over to Sean's place, she was so excited that she walked in the door talking. She rushed over to him and hugged him tightly.

"Babe, you won't believe how well the presentation went. I killed it! I'm definitely ready to present to the account execs next week!"

She uncorked a bottle of wine while he finished preparing dinner. She went through the play by play of the in-house meeting. Sean congratulated her, and they toasted to her success. She talked all the way through dinner.

An hour later, they laid in bed watching a re-run of Blackish. Patrice realized how much she talked the whole night.

"Geez, I've been rambling all night. I haven't asked you anything about your day. How's work going?"

She tried to engage him in conversation, but he was barely biting.

"It's fine. Same as usual."

"Any updates you're allowed to give on Annabelle's case?"

"We're still working on leads. Always a slow process."

"Any leads that seem like—"

He interrupted, "Yeah, but you know I can't go into it. We're working on some things. There's a chance that something will turn up soon."

Patrice relented. She picked up her book off the nightstand and flipped to the last page she read. After a half an hour, she tried again.

"Seems like things have been going really well for you at work. I mean, if you wanted to take the lieutenant's test soon you would probably be a shoo-in."

He nodded but said nothing.

"Did you change your mind about doing that? I thought you had a five-year plan about moving up to lieutenant?"

"Sure. Thinking about it. But I haven't made any decisions."

"Wouldn't it be a big jump in pay? I just thought you were getting tired of working cases and still feeling like a street cop."

Sean protested, "I never said that. I don't have a problem being a cop."

"I'm just asking about what you've said you wanted before."

He quipped, "I've never asked you to stop doing what you do."

Patrice sat up straighter in the bed.

"Sean, I'm not suggesting that you stop being a cop. Where are you getting that from? We're just talking about moving up the ranks. I thought it was something *you* wanted."

Sean's brows furrowed.

"Being a lieutenant is not just a pay raise. It's a complete role shift. A lot more politics and managing optics than police work. Not a role to take on just for a raise. I didn't realize it was something you wanted me to do so badly."

Patrice retorted, "Well, I didn't realize that asking questions meant that I was pushing you to do something you didn't want to do."

Sean's tone quieted some.

"I was considering it. Never made any firm decisions."

"Okay. You know I really was just asking. I don't like the danger you're in being a cop, but I understand that that's your job and you love what you do. That's what makes you good at it. I wouldn't ask you to leave you job. I don't have a right to do that. It's just, I've heard you talk about moving up the ranks a few times when we've talked about the future. I'm sure the higher salary would allow for putting a few things in place and—"

He interrupted, glaring at her.

"Thing is, I make enough now to comfortably support the both of us. That is, if you ever decided it's *okay* for us to live together. And enough to save for a house, vacations, retirement, and have a college fund for my son. I'm good. And, I'm off the streets as a sergeant. I get involved in cases at that level I think is needed."

"Wow. Okay. I get it. You're happy where you are."

Sean snapped, "I didn't say it was heaven. I still have my complaints. I know there's danger in the work I do. But, I'm not getting shot at every night."

Patrice looked confused.

"Okay, well if you know the job's dangerous, why are you acting like I would be off base if I had concerns about your safety? Not that I'm making that point now. But if I did, I wouldn't be crazy to." She paused. "Our jobs are different. My job isn't life threatening. A PR scandal might ruin my reputation or get me fired, but it won't kill me." She paused again. "You know, that's a part of the reason why I worry about moving in together. I don't want to stay up every night worrying about you."

Sean laughed loudly.

"Wow."

She looked even more confused. "Wow, what?"

"Really? That's the reason?"

He turned off the TV, put the remote on his nightstand, and slid under the covers. He continued with his back turned to her.

"Thing is, you're going to worry regardless of whether we live together or not. It's only natural."

He reached for the lamp to turn it off.

"And *truthfully*, you seem busy enough now that I doubt worrying about me is a high priority. G'nite."

Patrice was caught off guard. She sat staring at his shadow in the darkness, feeling like she needed to say something but not knowing what to say. She had learned that when Sean ended the conversation that way, it was never a good idea to try and continue it. After several minutes of being stunned, she finally scooted down and pulled up the covers. It was hours before she finally drifted off to sleep.

25

L ily paced from the kitchen to the living room while on the phone with her mother.

"Honey, I'm only asking how things are going because I'm worried about you. You just seem so out of it lately. I mean, it's not like you to forget the twins somewhere."

Lily retorted, "I've said this a dozen times already mother. I over-scheduled the day. If I didn't ask you to pick them up, I would've been an hour late getting them myself. If you had such as problem helping out, why didn't you just say so. I would have figured it out."

Her mother spoke calmly, "I love helping. You know that. It just made me realize how stretched thin and stressed you are."

"I am stressed, but aren't we all? It's just life with kids and a job."

"Yeah, and it's that much harder when things are off at home, you know."

"Thanks for that."

"Honey, not talking about it isn't going to help."

Lily cringed. She took a deep breath, four counts in, eight counts out.

"I do talk about it mother. To John. To friends. To Whoopsie. To those who listen without judgment."

After a pause her mother said, "Well, you're probably much less defensive when you talk to them than me."

Lily's tone softened.

"Look mom, I appreciate that you're trying to help. But it doesn't matter how many clients you've had and how many years of experience you've got, John and I have to figure out our own path. You trying to be our therapist is *not* the answer."

Her mother protested, "I wasn't trying to be. I know better. I just want you to be okay and know that I'm here."

Lily relented, "Okay. Well I need to go check on the twins. I'll talk to you on the weekend."

Once off the call, Lily sank into the closest chair. A minute later, she heard the garage door open. She transitioned to sitting in the kitchen and focused on updating their wall calendar. John walked in and plunked down in a chair. He glanced at her.

"They're taking a nap?"

She nodded. She never knew when he would be home late from work. The state of affairs between them was long past calling to say such things unless it would directly affect the children. John headed for the fridge and pulled out what he needed for a ham sandwich.

Lily spoke enthusiastically, "Well, I have some good news. My parents found a great deal and booked it quick. A couples cruise, as an anniversary gift for us!"

She paused as if waiting for his reaction, but he didn't say a word. He just focused with no expression as he spread mayo on bread. She continued,

"They wanted to come over and tell us together, but my mother accidentally spilled the beans. It's going to be four nights and five days in Bermuda. Some days will be on the water and some on land. I was excited because we haven't been there before and—"

John took a bite of his sandwich and spoke with a full mouth. "We haven't been a lot of places."

She nodded. He continued, "Don't you think we should have discussed this first?"

"Well, it was their idea, not mine."

"Lily, we have three kids, full time jobs, and various other obligations. It should be up to us to plan our lives. We can't just pick up and leave any time your parents feel like it. You don't see my mother making such assumptions. I have a big conference coming up and new account meetings. I mean—"

She scowled. She stood and put away everything he had taken out of the fridge for his sandwich.

"John, like I've said, you have enough pull at work to make *this* a priority if you wanted to. My parents were nice enough to think of us and pay for this. I don't see why it's such an issue. There's even an option to take the kids because there's daycare available."

John stared at Lily. He finished off his drink, put the glass in the sink then exited the kitchen without another word.

The next day, Lily's parents took the kids to a children's festival for the day, and John went to a college basketball game with friends. Lily spent the morning running errands and had the rest of the day to herself, an occurrence as rare as a windfall. She headed back to the house after running around most of the morning. She was looking forward to soaking in the tub, without interruption. But at the traffic light, before turning into their neighborhood, she made a left turn instead of a right and was back on the highway driving into D.C. In under an hour, she was parked and walking into the lobby of the downtown Marriott. It was the last day Brian said he would be there. She sat quietly with her eyes planted on the elevator watching as each person got off. After several minutes, Brian appeared when the elevator doors opened. He spotted her immediately as he stepped off with his suitcase rolling behind him. He came over and perched across from her. Lily stared expressionless.

"Did you really expect me to come?"

He studied her face.

"I don't expect anything." His voice was steady. "I hope. Want. Imagine. Fantasize. But, I don't expect."

"I didn't plan to come here."

"And here you are." He adjusted in his seat. "Truth is, people do what they're willing to let themselves do. And the things they won't let happen, they might regret or forget about. You just don't always know in advance. Whether you'll regret or forget."

Lily shook her head slowly.

"You asked me if I was living the life I want to live. And if I wonder about a different life."

He watched her intently as she spoke.

"I realized something after seeing you. I hadn't thought it through before you asked. I don't think I gave myself permission to."

Brian propped his elbows on his knees.

Lily continued, "I'm not living the life I wanted. But that's because we have no clue what an adult life is when we're thinking about it in our teens." She took a breath. "I'm living the life that makes sense for me. Another life wouldn't make sense. Doesn't mean I couldn't choose a different life at any point."

She watched as a family of five walked off the elevator. The mother in front, kids in between, and the father bringing up the rear.

"I've wondered about you. But in the way I wonder about a sexy guy on TV. In a hazy, fantasy way. Not in any way that contends with real life."

She looked into his eyes.

"I hope you find your happiness, Brian."

They looked at each other but neither spoke. Brian checked his watch. Then he stood and reached for her hand to help her stand up. They hugged before he walked her out of the hotel. Then he checked out and headed for the airport.

26

Janelle and Mason met up at the side entrance when the bell rang for school dismissal. It had been weeks since they stopped waiting until they were outside of school to walk together. Janelle grew less worried about what anyone thought and more focused on spending as much time with him as she could. Today, they walked to the park after school. The skies were gray and the air felt heavy. They planned to run home if it drizzled. They shared a bag of Cheetos on top of the monkey bars.

Mason asked, "So, what happened last night? Did your folks stop arguing?"

The night before, Janelle had rushed off the phone. She told Mason that her parents were arguing and getting loud, and she didn't want him to hear them. But they weren't that loud. She just wanted to hear what was going on without distraction.

"Yeah. They got really worked up. My mom wants to go on a trip for like a week, but my dad doesn't want to take too much time off work. So, she told him a bunch of ways to change things around at work so they could take a longer trip. After a while, he didn't know what to say."

"Wow, she's relentless. Y'all are a lot alike."

She poked him.

"I'm *not* like that. What are you talking about?"

He shrugged his shoulder exaggeratedly.

She continued, "I don't know. I think I'm more like my dad about stuff like that. I mean, I don't let stuff bother me until there's something to be bothered about."

"Sometimes. But sometimes you stress out. That's more like your mom."

Janelle looked off into the distance.

"I could be like my real mom. I don't really know."

He glanced at her.

"Do you want to find her?"

"Maybe. I don't know. I feel like it would hurt Ma, you know."

"Nah, she would probably understand. I mean she's a therapist. Plus, it's pretty natural for a kid to want to find her birth mom."

Janelle sometimes wondered about her biological mother. But it wasn't often, and she rarely talked about it when she did.

"I'm a lot like my dad."

She emphasized her words. Mason ate a few more Cheetos then handed the bag to her.

"Do you know where she is?"

Janelle shook her head. He asked, "Do you want to know?"

"We might not like each other. I don't think I want to meet her and then hate her."

"Do you hate her now?"

She shook her head again.

"No, but I don't know what she's like. And she doesn't know me."

Mason looked up to the sky.

"I just felt a drop. Let's go."

Janelle climbed down the side of the monkey bars while Mason jumped down. They walked toward her neighborhood. She picked up her pace as she felt more raindrops spatter. They got to her house just before the rain began to pour.

As they said goodbye, she added, "I like my life the way it is. I don't think it really matters if I meet her. There's nothing she's going to add to my life."

He nodded.

"Do you want to come in and wait until the rain stops?"

"Nah. There's already tension at your house. I'm not getting in that mix."

She smiled.

"Okay, well run."

"It's fine. I can just change clothes when I get home."

He turned and ran. Janelle went inside, quickly ate a snack then went to her room. She had two tests to study for.

Every now and then she thought about asking her dad questions about her real mother. She hadn't asked anything since she was a kid. He'd always answer her questions, but he never brought up Janelle's mother himself. As she laid on her bed with her books out to study, she remembered the dream she had last week. It was a replay of Mason coming over and meeting her family. But in the dream version, her real mom came over and joined the family on the deck.

27

After the other day's argument, Patrice steered clear of asking about Sean's job. She wasn't sure what to make of his edginess. He usually snapped out of whatever mood he was in fairly quickly, with the exception of a handful of times when a full workout and a couple days apart was needed to clear his head. But now, it had been days of him responding to her with a slightly sharp to flat out biting tone. And no amount of her asking what's going on yielded any clear answers. She knew it had been awhile since his son visited and that usually had him ill at ease. But this was different. He seemed disconnected. Only mildly interested in anything she brought up, and didn't bring up much himself. Her biggest worry was that they hadn't made love in two weeks. And for that not to be on his mind was shocking and made her nervous. She felt uneasy every time she thought about it. Lately, they had been spending the beginning of the week at her place and the end of the week at his. His kiss and hug before they left on mornings felt obligatory, and there was no snuggling up when watching TV. If her arm or leg even touched him while they were on the couch, he maneuvered so that they weren't touching anymore.

When the weekend rolled around, Patrice was happy to have a couple of days together uninterrupted. She had looked up weekend activities happening in the area, and found a beer festival that she knew he would love to check out. But when she brought it up, all she got in response was,

"Nah, I've got research to do on some cases. Let's just stay in."

Sean stayed on his computer most of the day on Saturday and Sunday. Whenever he put his laptop down, he'd swiftly change clothes and head to the gym. Once back, he would shower then take a nap. Sunday night rolled around, and they had only said a handful of words to each other. As they lay in bed after dinner, Patrice reached over to rub his leg and felt him tense ever so slightly when she touched him. He didn't drop his gaze from the TV.

She spoke softly, "Babes, you okay?"

"Yeah."

She waited for him to say more, but he didn't. She continued,

"I know work has been a lot lately."

He nodded slowly.

"Is there anything else going on though?" She paused and looked at him. "You just seem—"

Sean glanced at her, "Seem what?"

"In your head a lot."

He offered, "Yeah, well work has definitely been all-consuming."

She was happy to hear a more relaxed tone, so she didn't push.

"Well, I'm hoping things settle down soon."

She reached for her book on the nightstand. She got through two paragraphs of the book when Sean surprised her with sudden interest.

"I'm sure there's no character in there more interesting than me."

She giggled, "Nope. Not one."

He reached for her book and put it back on the nightstand. Then he kissed her. He slid over her and nuzzled at her neck. She wrapped her arms around his neck and arched her body into his. She let her legs fall open. They didn't waste time slipping out of their clothes and into lovemaking.

But it wasn't long before the hope Patrice had that things were back on track was shattered into a million shards. Her eyes were closed as they moved rhythmically until the moment where everything changed. It was only a second. Her eyes popped open with shock. Confused, she paused when she heard him whisper,

"Mya, baby."

Patrice's body stiffened as she more fully registered what was just said. Time seemed to stop ticking. She blinked like her eyes were taking quick snap shots. She focused on his face. The heat rose through her body, up her spine, and into her head. *I couldn't have heard him right.* But the boiling inside her served as confirmation that her hearing was fine.

"What the *HELL* did you just say?"

Her stilted, grating words pushed through gritted teeth. She shoved him up and scooted out from under him.

"What *did* you just call me?"

Sean sat up in bed, the light from the TV glimmered off the sweat on his nose. He looked earnest. Patrice stood at the foot of the bed, her hands clasping her naked hips.

"You just called me *Mya*?"

Sean said indignantly, "No. No. I said baby."

She reached across the bed for her clothes.

"No, you said 'Mya, baby.'"

"I don't even know a Mya."

She shook her head.

"Well, *you're* the one who just said it. So, apparently you do."

Patrice roughly pulled at the covers trying to find her underwear.

"I was just saying baby. I think I stuttered a little."

He stood up and walked toward the bathroom. She ran and blocked the bathroom doorway.

"No, that wasn't a stutter. It was clear as day."

He shook his head and opened his mouth, but she interjected before he could say a word.

"So I'm hearing things? Or are you calling me a liar? Which one is it?"

"I didn't call you a liar. Come on Patrice. You're —"

"Oh no, Sergeant Robinson. You don't get to act like I'm being dramatic right now? Not after you call me by some random bitch's name." She shook her head vigorously. "That's not how this goes."

With a look of frustration, he wordlessly leaned his back against the wall by the bathroom.

"Oh, you don't have anything to say now?"

"You're jumpin' on top of everything I say. So -" He shrugged indignantly.

"Is there something I need to know?"

She stood in front of him, her arms crossed tightly. Her voice shrill.

"Let's put it all out on the table right now. You've been acting off for weeks now. We need to be real about whatever is happening. No turtling on this one. What's going on?"

Sean stared at her as she paced in front of him. He adjusted his stance. And with steady words he retorted,

"I've been wondering the same thing."

He moved with slow decisive steps into her way and she stopped pacing.

"There's nobody else in my life. And up until recently I thought that was our deal. But here's what I know now. That wasn't me you were having lunch with the other day, now was it?"

Patrice pulled her head back to get a better look at his face. She uncrossed her arms then crossed them again.

"What?" Her voice lowered.

Sean laughed.

"Oh a second ago you had sonar powered ears, now you're hard of hearing?"

He planted his feet and stood square with her.

Patrice's voice cracked. "You're really trying to flip this right now? You just called me by another chick's name, and you're asking me about a business lunch? I was having lunch with John. He's one of the senior execs. A colleague. That's it. Colleagues do have lunch you know. It's allowed." She paused. "Why didn't you say something that day?"

Sean laughed loudly.

"So who's turtling now?" He shook his head. "You know Patrice, I never realized how full of shit you really are, until now. Right in this moment."

Sean moved to the corner of the room. He grabbed his sweats that were hanging on the chair in front of the desk and slid them on.

Patrice looked confused.

"Sean, what the hell is up with you?"

His jaw was clenched. His voice ripped through the air.

"What's up with me is that you've been working with your ex-boyfriend for months. And not once, NOT ONCE, did you say anything about it."

Her eyes widened.

"So, you've been investigating me now?"

"Yes. After I realized how shady you were."

"Shady? Because I work with my ex, you automatically think something is going on?"

Sean shook his head vigorously.

"It's the fact that you *hid* working with your ex. That's the problem."

"Okay, but—"

He cut her off, "I saw that shit. Your so-called *business lunch*. Y'all were grinning in each others' face. He was reaching over and picking shit off your plate. I even watched you eat food off his fucking fork. *Business* lunch? That's how y'all do at York & Newton? Taking turns eating off each others' forks? What comes after that, eating off laps? And who goes first?" He glared at her, his eyes like laser beams searing through her skin. "Yeah okay." He grabbed a t-shirt out of a drawer.

Patrice's hands grew clammy. She watched as he laced up his tennis shoes. She searched for what to say. *What can I say to prove there's nothing going on? That we're just coworkers? Shoot, if I didn't know the truth, I'm not sure I would be convinced if the situation were reversed.* She inhaled as deeply as her lungs allowed, steadied herself on her feet and opened her mouth hoping she would find the words as she went along.

"Sean, I know you're pissed. I would be too. I'm sorry I did things this way. Not saying that—"

Sean shook his head and shot his hand out, halting her words.

"What I really want to know is when did it start. Right away, or was there a slow build? I need to know just how trifling this shit was. And don't lie at this juncture. It's pointless. For all the sneaking around you've been doing, you're really not good at lying."

Patrice's voice was exasperated, "I know it looks bad. But there is nothing, I mean *nothing*, going on. We're cool, but not beyond friends and colleagues. He's married—"

Sean grabbed his wallet and shoved it in one of his pockets. Her breath was stilted. Her chest tightened.

"Sean, you're blowing this way out of—"

He scoffed.

"And by the way, I know that you were at lunch with him when the fire happened. I know you called your mom that day. And that he texted you that night to see if you were doing okay. So, that bullshit you told me about not calling anybody, was just that. Bullshit. The only person you didn't call was me."

Patrice's knees buckled a bit and she leaned on the dresser.

"Sean, it's not like I set out to keep anything from you. It just felt like if I told you, we would have argued about it and that would have affected if I took the job. I wanted to—"

Sean looked at her with disgust in his eyes as he shook his head.

"Okay. Then tell me what the actual situation is. Let's get specific. What is the nature of your relationship with John Blackman?"

Patrice was stumped. So many thoughts swirled in her head, and she couldn't settle on where to start. What to say to sort this out. She had told herself so many times that she would tell him about her past with John, but she never started the conversation. And after a while, it didn't make sense to bring it up. It would make it even more suspicious that she waited so long to say anything.

She didn't realize how long she sat there silently until Sean darted out of the bedroom into the living room. She trailed behind him.

"Sean? *Sean?* You're leaving?"

He stopped and stood in the middle of the living room. He turned and stared at her, his voice calm.

"Am *I* the rebound? Or is *he?*"

"W-What?"

He glared at her.

"The dude looks just like me. Or maybe I look like him. So, who's the rebound at this point?"

Her stomach sank to her toes. Vomit pushed at the back of her throat. She swallowed vigorously and steeled herself. Her mouth watered and the back of her throat tickled. She ignored the sensation and focused on pushing her words off the cliff of her lips.

"We dated at Howard. But that was over a long, long time ago. We hadn't been in contact at all. For like seven years. On social media or anything. Never ran into each other, nothing."

She paused to catch her breath.

"When I interviewed there, that was the first time I saw him in years. And somehow, I didn't know he worked there. I don't know how I missed that."

A headache pressed at the back of her eyes. "But, working together hasn't been a problem. Our conversations are very professional. No reminiscing about the past, no flirting. We just talk about work. We're cool. Not cool where I talk about my life outside of work. But cool like we can laugh about co-workers and work stuff. And we grab lunch sometimes. And sometimes with other colleagues. Everybody has good vibes, so we all get along pretty well. When you've known someone before, it's hard not to be friends."

She finally took a full breath.

"I wish I knew you came down to my office that day. I could have told you all this then."

He scoffed. "You could have told me months ago. When I first asked you who he was. You could have told me any one of the days between then and now."

She stood quietly, the weight of his words pressing on her shoulders.

He spoke in a low voice, "So, I'm the rebound. I'm the idiot. Got it."

He shook his head. She felt a bulbous knot lodge in her throat. Her stomach tightened.

He glared at her. "I could have jumped through that storefront that day and snapped you both in two. You have no idea."

Sean abruptly turned and went back to the bedroom. He snatched two drawers of his dresser open and yanked out clothes, dumping them on the bed. Patrice came into the bedroom and watched helplessly. He charged into the bathroom and came back with a handful of her makeup, shampoo, conditioner, and a toothbrush, dumping all of it on the bed on top of her clothes. He dug around in the closet and tossed her shoes out. She jerked back as they skidded across the floor. She didn't know what to do to stop what was happening. It was all moving so fast. All she could do was command herself to keep breathing. She pleaded,

"I can't believe you're really doing this?"

She stared at him with tears streaming down her face and plunking onto her t-shirt.

"We can't leave things like this. That's not us. That's not how we do."

Sean stopped, smiled stiffly, then calmly walked over to her.

"Is he going on the business trip you have coming up? The one you haven't told me about?"

His eyes narrowed on her.

"Well yes, several of us are –"

He shook his head.

"Sean I, I know this looks bad –"

"*Looks bad*? That's what you think? This *looks bad*?"

Patrice cried uncontrollably. Her body shook so much she felt like a seizure was coming on. Or a panic attack. He was unfazed by her tears as he headed to the front door. Just before walking out he turned and glared.

"Whatever you don't take with you tonight will be in the garbage tomorrow. Leave the key on the counter. Bye Mya."

He slammed the door behind him.

Patrice cried until every muscle ached in her body. Her head was pounding by the time the tears stopped flowing, leaving her weak and numb. After washing her face, she gathered her strength to fill two trash bags with her belongings.

28

L ily slipped into a red silk bra and panty set, then slid into bed like it was something she wore all the time. She and John were two days into the Bermuda cruise, and she'd gone out of her way to be sweet. The first night, she massaged his back, taking her time to work out all the knots. Tonight, she'd been snuggled under him watching TV until he fell asleep. She woke him by sliding on top of him. She kissed his neck first, then slowly worked her way down his chest. After sucking on his nipple, she nibbled on it.

"Ouch!" he said.

"Shh honey, you know the walls are thin."

They made love for the first time in months. It was awkward, but they found their way.

They slept in the next morning and had another lovemaking session before showering and leaving the room. They went to breakfast smiling. Even though Lily's parents were on the cruise, they only joined John and Lily at dinner. There was also another couple, friends of Lily's, on the cruise. They met up with the couple at the pool and for lunch. Otherwise, each couple moved around in their own spheres. At dinner, Lily's mother beamed at her and John the way a homeowner proudly looked at the blooming flowers in their garden. When Lily called her parents a month earlier, asking them to act as though the cruise was their idea, her mother quickly chimed in that, "This is just the type of thing I've been suggesting you do anyway."

When Lily and John returned from the cruise, John's mother welcomed them back with a four-course meal of bruschetta, chicken parmigiana, tomato soup, and Mediterranean salad. She and the kids had been busy the past few days, taking horse riding lessons, go-cart racing, and going to the movies. She jumped at the chance to make the trip to Maryland from Florida to watch the kids. She loved being "Grandma-in-charge."

As John and Lily settled back into daily life, it wasn't long before status quo returned. Within a couple of days, John was back talking about his upcoming business trip and fussing about Janelle not being focused on school because she was too caught up with Mason. Her grades hadn't been slipping, but he insisted that she was studying less and would have bad grades on upcoming tests.

After several conversations, he and Lily couldn't agree about what he was proposing. And when that happened, he usually found a way to pull biological rank. Janelle was *his* daughter, and he knew her best. Lily conceded, which is to say she quieted and accepted his wishes. A week later, they sat Janelle down and talked with her about switching to a new high school that had a newly implemented International

Baccalaureate program that would give her an advantage for getting into college. She had another year before she would need to start applying to colleges, and two years before graduating high school.

John pointed out, "It's excellent timing to make this change."

Janelle protested as much as she could, making every case she could that it was actually poor timing and a bad idea. She said it would destroy her confidence because she would lose the friends she had, which would make her severely depressed. She made the point that changing schools would be a big adjustment midway through high school. That she would have to get used to new teachers and that her grades would drop at first, as she got used to things, which wouldn't look good on her transcripts.

John assured her, "We're not going to let that happen. I've already looked into getting you a tutor."

He said she would have a more diverse student body to choose friends from, which would create great connections for life. He told her that she was gifted and needed a school that was more challenging. That she could easily keep in touch with old friends in this day and age of texting, Snapchat, and FaceTime. And that new friends would come easily because she was so easy to get along with.

Janelle looked at Lily imploringly, every few minutes, as if hoping for a lifeline. But she saw defeat in Lily's eyes. She knew Lily had probably fought a losing battle on her behalf. Janelle sat on the edge of a chair in the living room, her shoulders dropping more and more as defeat sunk in. After a half-hour of talking that seemed like six hours, she knew she wasn't going to convince her father otherwise. Abruptly, Janelle stood and decidedly moved to the stairs bounding up to her room.

"This is some bullshit."

Janelle's voice trailed off to a barely audible whisper.

John swung around and stared.

"Excuse me? What was that?"

John daringly asked her to repeat herself.

"Nothing."

She paused midway up the steps.

He cautioned her, "Watch your mouth young lady."

She turned and came back down the stairs,

"This is so unfair. How can you make a decision like this about my life without including me in it? I'm closer to eighteen than eight. It's just not right."

John shook his head.

"Yeah, old enough to think you know everything, and young enough not to know what's best for you."

Her eyes were bloodshot from crying. She wiped at her tears.

"You don't want me to change schools because I'm not being challenged enough. It's because you don't like Mason. That's what this is about, and you know it. You're just pretending to have some big agenda to better my college chances. How come you've never said anything like this before now? Never. Not once."

John watched her intently.

"Janelle, sometimes you can't see the full picture. We're looking at what's best for you. Mason is the least of my concerns."

She steeled herself, crossing her arms.

"It's fine. You get to run my life. I have to deal with it, until I'm out of here. But who knows, maybe I'll have even more white boyfriends there. You know, that more diverse student body and all. You never know."

Without missing a beat, John moved in a few inches from her face with a clenched jaw. Lily pushed forward to the edge of her seat nervously.

"Who in the *HELL* do you think you are talking to?"

He gritted his teeth, "Make no mistake, I am not one of your friends. The tone, the attitude, the flippant remarks. I'm not having it. You *BETTER* not *EVER* use that tone with me *EVER* again. *EVER*. Do you understand me?"

John was breathing heavily, his breath causing stray hairs around her face to wave.

Janelle uncrossed her arms as she shakily said, "Yes sir."

He straightened up then took a step back. Janelle made one more plea.

"Daddy, I'm sorry. I, I was just saying that –, all I'm saying is that why can't I have some say in my life? I'm almost sixteen. I'm old enough to learn to drive soon. In a few years I can vote. I do everything I'm supposed to and take care of all my responsibilities. I do my work in school and get all my homework done and—"

He retorted, "Not lately. You haven't been studying and that's going to catch up with you."

"Daddy, I have been studying. Just because you don't see me do it doesn't mean it's not happening. My grades are good. I don't have a single C. You can look on Parent Connect and see for yourself."

Her voice quivered as she pleaded. John didn't speak. He just stared at her.

Janelle continued, "I'm going to break up with Mason."

"Honey, that's fine if that's what you want to do. But it's not going to change anything. This is happening."

"Oh my God, this is just so wrong."

He offered, "You can't see it yet, but you will one day. We want what's best for you." He paused. "And whatever you decide with Mason, well, if he's a good kid, he'll understand. The new school is not far away. And it's not like we're moving neighborhoods. One thing you'll learn one day is that boys who think you're worth it will treat you that way. Trust me."

Janelle scowled. She couldn't stifle her words before they tumbled out of her mouth,

"Like you treat ma?"

Janelle lowered her tear-filled eyes, and glanced at Lily before she looked at the floor. Lily sat still as a weathered rock. John stood still as a tree stump. He took a step toward Janelle again. He opened his mouth to speak, but remained quiet. Then he walked around her and headed up the stairs.

29

"What's up with you and Wilson? What was going on out there?"

Dannon was in Sean's office providing an update. Sean wondered what he walked into when he arrived in the precinct parking lot hours earlier to find Dannon and Wilson in their squad car with a heated exchange going. They waved and pulled off as soon as they noticed Sean.

Dannon spoke with an even voice.

"Nothing. It's been handled."

"What's been handled?" Sean asked, straightening the papers on his desk.

Dannon said, "I just think we need to broaden our search. Check with Mrs. Gibson's friends again about anyone else who could be the father."

"That's already been done."

Dannon nodded. Sean continued, "What do you think we're missing?"

"Not sure. Just feels like there's something right in our face. Another run through of questioning might reveal something, anything, that's been missed."

Sean searched Dannon's face.

"Fair enough. I'll reach out to another precinct. I'll get us fresh eyes for the case."

Dannon nodded.

Sean got a call from Hodges later that day asking for updates. He asked about expanding the search, which Sean confirmed was already happening. Hodges had it in for Mitch. This wasn't going to turn out well for Mitch whether he was his wife's killer or not. Sean seemed confident when he talked to Hodges, but he knew the Gibson case had stalled. He wasn't sure what other direction to go in. It wasn't a bad idea to have some cops from another precinct involved, but he was more hesitant about doing so than he let on in front of Dannon. For one, he didn't like having other cops be the savior for his squad. Didn't look good. Made them look incompetent. For two, when you bring other guys in, it means there's a problem within the team. It wasn't that unusual to bring in new guys when a case involved a police officer, but it still casts a shadow on the team. And three, more guys meant more room for error. On the one hand they could pick up things that hadn't been noticed before, but they could also make mistakes.

But Sean's frustration with having no leads was getting to him. Trying to find out who Annabelle could have been pregnant by was about the same as a Missed Connection ad in the personals being seen by the person who was missed. No one had seen her with a guy. She hadn't told anyone anything about a guy. The kids hadn't seen anything meaningful to the case. There was no paper trail or records indicating anything useful.

Sean got a couple cops from another precinct and had them re-interview Annabelle's friends. Then he had one of them talk with people in local places near Annabelle's house and her job. Cashiers at stores and gas stations, postal staff, and library staff. Maybe someone saw her meeting someone in one of those places. Clearly, Annabelle was careful not to have the guy come to her house before the night she was knocked unconscious. *But nobody was 100 percent careful.* There was the slim chance that the baby was a result of a random hook up. But that seemed unlikely. She was too careful to not use condoms with a stranger. *It had to be someone she knew,* he thought. So, he kept digging.

Sean pored his focus into work. At nights, when he got home after work, he studied online for a certification he decided to get and prepared to take the exam in another week. He would study until he was exhausted enough to sleep. When he wasn't doing that, he was at the gym on evenings. And when those options weren't enough, he planned for his son's next visit, looking for flights and kid friendly activities. This was how he didn't dwell on Patrice. For the most part, it worked.

30

Patrice felt like a zombie for days. The night of the breakup, her head swirled driving from Sean's place to hers. As she walked in the door, she saw Sean's keys on her counter, and her chest stung. She immediately went to the hallway closet, knowing but not wanting to accept, that the spaces where his shoes used to be, would be empty. She knew the two dresser drawers in her bedroom would be cleared out too.

She couldn't wrap her mind around how quickly everything imploded. Flashes of the scene at Sean's place kept sprinting through her mind, with her trying to figure out what she was missing. *How does that happen?* she thought, *Where you're moving along, and life's good, and your boyfriend's amazing, and you're happy with work and then BOOM.* She stripped out of her clothes and crawled into bed that night. Other than to use the bathroom, she stayed on the covers for days. As far as work was concerned, she had the flu and was too sick to even work from home.

Thinking about calling Sean sucked up a lot of her mind. She struggled with deciding whether to call Sean, then she would actually call. Then there was deciding whether to leave a message, and actually leaving a message. Sometimes she would hang up before the call could ring, sometimes her message was rambling, other times just a few words. Each time, she said some version of wanting them to take the "time to talk and sort things out," and that "this really wasn't enough to end things." Sometimes she scolded him for not valuing their relationship enough, because, "how dare you just drop everything we have like that, with no chance to talk it through? How is that adult? Or respectful? That's not who we are." Sometimes she simply said, "I'm sorry babe." She sent several texts and instant messages. The read receipt check mark didn't turn green for any of them. She knew he was purposely not checking the messages. Somehow, that realization hurt worse than if he read it and didn't respond. She felt scalded by the deep, searing line he had drawn in the sand between them.

On the third day, Patrice sent an inspirational meme to him by text message. It was her only effort to connect that day. The chance that Sean was just angry and would cool down was thinning with every passing day. The more likely reality was that he had, in fact, reached a breaking point, and he wasn't going to reply. But she couldn't accept that reality. Not just yet. She decided to type an email to him. Maybe she would send it at some later time. When she was more accepting of every-thing. Maybe she wouldn't send it at all. Either way, it would help her say everything she wanted to say. Sort out what was in her head.

Patrice got out of bed, only to grab her laptop and climb right back in. She started the email with what she was thinking. *Where do I start?* She typed a few sentences, then deleted them and started again. After an hour, she put the laptop on the floor, and laid down. She fell asleep and woke up when it was dark outside again.

By day four, Patrice got her first break from the hollowness she'd been swallowed by. She woke up without hesitation. Her eyes were puffy, but tears weren't constantly escaping without her permission. She didn't feel a swirl of thoughts in her head. The gnawing sensation in her stomach and the steady ache in her head had dissipated, enough to stand straight without wanting to coil-over again. She looked at the clock on her nightstand, suddenly back in the world of being mindful of time. It was four o'clock in the morning. She could hear the faint chirp of birds outside her window. *Have they been out there every morning?*

She sat on the edge of the bed.

"An object in motion stays in motion," she said aloud.

She lifted off the bed with the intention, for the first time in several days, of not getting back in as quickly as she could. She walked into the living room, peering around. *Looks so strange.* She had lived there for four years with the same furniture, and after four days of not seeing it, she was surprised by the sense of unfamiliarity. She perused her bookshelf. Once, maybe twice a year, she would reread one of the books on her shelf instead of a new book. She decided the winner this time would be Michelle Obama's *Becoming*. She had just read it a few months ago, but it was definitely worth revisiting. She needed wholesomeness to nurse her back to life. Immersing

herself in Michelle Obama's upbringing in Chicago and dis-
covery of deep love with her boyfriend, before he became the
leader of the free world, would be a good start. She sat in
her living room in the hammock chair that was in the far-left
corner, where the sun would pour in once it rose shortly.

Patrice wasn't ready to tell any of her friends about what
happened. She couldn't even bring herself to fully accept
that it was a breakup. *We just need time to figure things out,*
she thought. *He's just too pissed to think straight and talk this
through.* She would vacillate from that position to one of
looming doom every few hours. She checked the text messages and voice messages from the last few days. Sasha had sent
several texts. Jen had sent one as well. Her mother had left her
a voice message, then texted her when she hadn't called back.
If she couldn't tell her friends, her mother was nowhere near
an option to call. Not right now. Not yet. Patrice knew that
she would feel better if she were holed up at her mom's place,
knowing that she would have tea and hot chocolate and soup
brought to her as she curled up in her mom's bed, but she
couldn't yet bare the empty platitudes that her mother would
give and the asking for details, all with good intentions but
awful timing. Ultimately, Patrice knew she would get through
this, but right now her world was just blown to shredded bits
of nothingness, and she wasn't ready to hear anybody say,
"It's going to be okay."

About two pages in to reading, the odors emanating from
Patrice's body unexpectedly assaulted her. After hibernating
in bed for days, the smells of her various body parts that had
been wrapped up under bedsheets and a comforter — roasting,
broiling, and boiling — were aggressively and deftly aiming at

her nostrils causing her nose hairs to prickle. She wandered into the bathroom and paused in front of the shower, looking with heaviness. She tried to will herself to turn the shower knob. The whole production of undressing, stepping in the shower, washing her body, shampooing her hair, drying off, hanging her towel back up, lotioning, figuring out what to wear, and dressing, felt like it would be equal to fighting off a bear. Painful, strenuous work. After what seemed like an hour, but was more like five minutes, she turned in defeat and walked out of the bathroom.

Patrice picked up her laptop from the bedroom floor and took it to the kitchen island. She tried again to write the email to Sean. Maybe writing, she thought, would get her motivated to shower. Maybe Sean would be willing to talk if she waited a few days and then sent the email. Maybe he would have missed her enough to break the code of silence he'd been holding to. Maybe not. He could think she was lying no matter what she said. Maybe if she said the right thing, he would believe her. Maybe she *was* cheating, emotionally. *Is it cheating if nothing but friendship, not even flirting, happened? Would it be cheating if it were Sean doing the same thing?* After several rounds of typing, and erasing whole paragraphs, she closed her laptop again feeling assaulted a second time by her stench. She hurried to the bathroom. "Object in motion," she said aloud. She turned the shower on quickly, stripped off everything and hopped in. She didn't wash her hair but lathered up her body twice. She decided to wear whatever she first saw in the closet and not worry about matching. She kept the momentum going by making a cup of coffee and having a slice of toast with peanut butter. It was now 6:34 a.m. She figured, *time to check email.* By the time she pored through over a hundred emails, she thought, *it's time to go back to work.* She would go in tomorrow. She wouldn't even have to fake being sick for the past few days. She felt and looked beat down as though she *had* been flu-stricken.

The next morning, exhaustion enveloped her as soon as she left her front door. Just getting ready for work took most of her energy. Before she had even stepped in the door at York & Newton, she knew she would have to conserve her energy throughout the day, to make it to the end. It was going to take every ounce of fuel she had on reserve to be productive. She had two projects with approaching deadlines, and she need-ed to make up for her four days out of the office. She might as well have had the flu for the past week, because by noon, she wanted to lie down and sleep right there on her desk. She grabbed a yogurt out of her office mini fridge for a little fuel. She focused on only having to get through the second half of the day before the weekend would begin. *Just hold it together for a little bit longer.*

John popped up in her doorway at around 9:40 a.m., right when she had decided to give up on trying to answer the backlog of emails in her inbox in one fell swoop. She made a plan. She would scan for the emails that were priorities, deal with those first, then come back for a second round closer to the end of her workday. John came in his usual manner, smiling lightly, checking in about the agenda for the day. He asked about having a working lunch. What usually happened from there — Patrice running through her day's itinerary and picking where they would go for lunch — wasn't anywhere near the surface of her thoughts. Instead she said curtly,

"Can't. Days of work to catch up on, and I'm still getting over the flu."

As Patrice took the Metro home that day, she wondered about social media. Sean had blocked her from all his accounts. She could only see two pictures, profile pictures at that, on his accounts. Only what the public could see. He even went so far as to block her on a picture sharing website. Now, she wished she had downloaded the shared pictures from their trips. Never thought she had to. She wondered if he took down all their pictures together. *Geez, I hope not. Then everyone would know something was up,* she thought. On her end of things, she kept up pretenses. She posted an update that could still be interpreted as though nothing had changed.

"Glad to be heading home from a long day. Looking forward to dinner!"

She steered clear of their mutual friends online. She decided that was best after she saw a mutual friend's Instagram post with a pic of an elephant and a dog hugging with the caption, "Being there for a friend is the best gift you can give and receive!" Patrice was certain that was about her and that the friend had been consoling Sean. When she saw it, she was going to reach out to the friend and fish around to see what was out there about the breakup. Then she figured, *No one cares. They've got their own lives to live.* She finally settled on avoiding those mutual friends, for her own sanity. By the time she walked through her apartment door at 6:30 p.m., all she could do was crash, fully clothed, on her bed. She fell asleep within minutes and didn't wake up until 5:00 a.m. the next day.

Patrice woke up Saturday morning thinking she actually wanted to do something with the day. To make some attempt to rejoin society for something other than work. She called Jen and Sasha to make plans. Jen was busy until evening but could come over. Sasha was free but would have to leave early because she had to help another friend move early the next day. Patrice knew she would have to tell them what happened, and she felt ready to do it now. Maybe having a girl's night — a good movie with wine and sushi — was just what she needed.

Patrice got out of bed and instead of poring over the details of the breakup dozens of times, she cleaned while listening to Ledisi's *Let Love Rule* album on iTunes. After an hour of scrubbing, sweeping, wiping, and dusting, she showered and dressed, then had some fruit, oatmeal and coffee for breakfast. Her appetite wasn't back, but she knew she couldn't continue going whole days subsisting on coffee and yogurt. She was out the door in time to be one of the first customers walking in at Bed Bath and Beyond. She had it in mind to grab different size storage containers and shelving she could install herself to make added use of space in her bedroom closet and linen closet. She also wanted a spice rack. She found what she needed, plus a few other items, in about twenty minutes, and stood in line with just two people ahead of her.

When her phone buzzed, she looked at it, and somehow Sasha's name looked like Sean's. It took only a couple seconds to refocus and realize who was actually calling. She answered knowing that Sasha would be asking what kind of wine would be best to pick up for tonight. They chatted briefly, then Patrice left the line to grab a pack of nails for hanging the shelving. As she returned to the line, there were now three people in it. She stood pushing her large containers on the floor in front of her, every time the line moved forward.

As she stood behind a young man, Patrice felt sweat forming on her forehead and trailing down her back. Her clothes stuck to her skin from perspiration. She shifted uncomfortably. Before she knew what was happening, her breath was slipping away. She sipped at the air then held her breath hoping to somehow control her airflow. As she focused on her breathing she was forgetting to move up in line. The woman behind her cleared her throat, which sounded as loud as a boulder rumbling down a hill. Her chest was tightening, the weight of an elephant hoof pressed on her sternum. The lights overhead seemed to be strobbing.

Patrice tried with all her might to keep her grip on the hangers, Lysol wipes, nails, and coffee filters balancing in the crook of her arm and her hands, but her fingers grew numb, and her palms moistened with sweat. She was losing the battle and succumbing. With a thud and tumble, everything dropped out of her hands. She gasped for air, but felt like only 10 percent was getting in. She heard the woman behind her say something, and saw the cashier shoot a concerned glance her way, but it all seemed hazy. She willed her legs to move. She wobbled toward the exit, leaving all her items on the floor in the line where she had stood. She made it a few steps toward the exit. For the next few minutes, moments happened in flickers, like a movie montage.

When Patrice was fully alert again, she was sitting in a back room with a paramedic asking her to say her full name.

"Patrice. Patrice Pearson."

"Ms. Pearson. Can you count to five for me?"

"One, two, three, four, five."

"Okay good Ms. Pearson. Do you know what happened to you?"

"I think I, I passed out."

"Yes, you did. For a couple minutes. The security guard helped you. Then the staff called 911 and we came. Do you have any health conditions that could cause this?"

Patrice shook her head, which worsened the headache that pressed on the back of her eyes.

"Ms. Pearson. Has this happened before?"

"No. Well, yes. I, I had a panic attack, I think. Once before. Maybe twice."

She thought back to that day in the parking lot, after getting the job offer from York & Newton. And to her meltdown in the bathroom after her flopped pitch.

"Okay. Well your vitals are back to normal. But you could need additional medical care. Would you like us to transport you to the hospital?"

She answered quickly.

"No. I want to follow up with my doctor. She knows my history, and I'd feel better with someone I know, not just going to the ER." Patrice had no intention of spending the day in a hospital waiting room for hours, just for them to confirm that she had a panic attack. *Damn.* She was annoyed that it was back. After the first one happened, she had thought about going to her doctor, but when weeks passed and she didn't have another one—well, at least not another full on attack—she figured the worst of it was behind her.

The paramedic asked, "Are you sure?"

"Yes, yes, I'm sure. I'm feeling better. If I just sit here for a little while longer, I'll be okay."

"Okay. Do you have someone that can come drive you home? It wouldn't be safe to drive in your condition."

"Yes. I'll call one of my girlfriends. They'll come pick me up, and we can come back later to get my car. Or maybe take an Uber."

"Okay Ms. Pearson."

Patrice watched as the paramedics packed up to leave. She was irritated and embarrassed over the whole fiasco. *Geez, an hour of the day lost.*

31

Mason and Janelle were a team. They both always wore the black corded bracelets Janelle made for them. Mason's smirk quickly became a wide smile the day she came to the park with a black pouch, and gave him the bracelet. It was the day they made their relationship official. Once they decided they were together, Janelle didn't much care anymore what anybody thought or who was looking. Most mornings, he would wait for her at the corner of her street, and they would walk to school together. They would walk into school holding hands and laughing about whatever inside joke they had going. Rainy days were the only time they wouldn't arrive together, each getting rides from their parents or friends' parents to school.

Mason and Janelle were standing in front of her locker at school, and he looked at her with surprise.

"You sure?"

"Yeah. I told you, I don't like all that mushy stuff."

She'd told him she didn't want a bunch of balloons for her birthday. She didn't want to feel like everyone was looking at her, just when she finally felt like they weren't anymore. She was genuinely surprised when she opened her locker, and there was a little black box, with a little silver ring and a red rose with a card. Her face lit up, and her façade melted. The card had two teddy bears on the front, walking into the sunset while holding hands and hearts floating up to the sky above them. She hugged Mason's neck so tight, he faked choking sounds.

After school that day, they sat on a bench in the park. She sat in his lap and tugged at his collar as he kissed her neck. She usually made soft sounds, but today she was quiet.

"You good?" Mason said curiously.

"Yeah."

She slid down off his lap onto the bench to sit next to him.

"My dad is serious about this school thing. He hasn't budged. At all."

She shook her head.

"Can't believe this is happening."

Mason quietly listened.

"It's like, I should be excited about my sixteenth birthday. Instead, I'm all stressed out about whether I'm going to a new school next year. Gotta start all over making friends, figuring the teachers out. It's so irritating. And whack. I should be chillin'."

Mason picked up and threw pebbles one by one into the grass.

"I know. It really sucks. I can't believe he just sprung it on you like that."

Janelle sat quietly as he continued,

"But you know, it might not be a bad thing."

She glared at him.

"You're seriously taking his side?"

"No. C'mon. I'm just saying that it's a good school. Have you looked it up?"

"No. What for? I don't want to go there."

"Okay. But you might not have a choice."

Janelle abruptly stood, snatching her backpack off the bench and walked in the direction of home. He rushed to catch up.

"Come on, Apple. I don't want you to go to another school."

"Are you sure? Because it sure sounds like you would be fine if I left right now. In the middle of the school year. Good riddance to bad rubbish."

Mason jerked his head back.

"Wow. I didn't say anything like that."

She shrugged and slowed down. They walked the rest of the way in silence.

32

Sean banged repeatedly on his brother's apartment door. He finally heard shuffling, and then the door swung open.

"Slow as molasses."

Sean bee-lined to the bathroom. When he returned to the living room, he looked around.

"I thought you finished unpacking," Sean said as he leaned to look in one of the boxes.

"Almost. Just a few boxes left."

Sean plopped on Ron's living room couch and scrolled on his phone. Ron sat across from him in a chair.

"So, what's going on with Patrice? Y'all really done?"

"Yeah."

Sean didn't look up from his phone.

Ron shook his head, "I really thought she was the one for you."

Sean furrowed his brows, "Based on what?"

Ron shrugged.

"I don't know man. Y'all were happy. And she's a good girl. She's fine, focused and driven. All the things you want in a woman."

Sean leaned back on the couch.

"Yeah, well, things change. Anyway, how come you didn't call me back? I've been sitting around all funky and sweating waiting to take a shower. You know my landlord had the nerve to tell me that it would be forty-eight hours before the pipes are fixed. Ridiculous. I'm supposed to *not* take a shower for two days?"

Ron got up and headed to his kitchen.

"Oh, I, I haven't checked my messages."

Sean got up and headed to Ron's hallway closet to grab a towel.

"Usually I would go to Patrice's to take a shower when crap like this happens."

As Sean closed the closet door, Ron hurried out of the kitchen and nodded toward the bedroom.

"Hey, um, I have company."

Sean smiled.

"Oh man, didn't mean to intrude." He paused. "Can I take the shower though and change in the bathroom?"

Ron nodded.

Sean took his gym bag into the bathroom, took his shower, and changed clothes. When he came out, he rounded the corner of the hallway and paused as he stepped into the living room.

Ron was sitting with a guy on the couch. Dressed in a white polo shirt, blue jeans and Vans, the guy sat comfortably with a beer in hand. Ron smiled at his companion, then at Sean.

"Sean, this is Tyrone. Ty this is my brother Sean."

Sean momentarily hesitated then stepped forward and extended his hand for a shake.

Tyrone stood.

"Good to meet you. I've heard good things."

Sean glanced at Ron, then at Tyrone, then at Ron again.

"Alright, well, I'm going to get going."

Sean didn't waste time getting out the door.

33

Time moved fast and simultaneously slow for Patrice. Sean was constantly on her mind, and after three weeks she still had moments of thinking the breakup wasn't true. She hoped he would calm down enough for a conversation. She felt the finality of how the break up went down. But she just wasn't ready to let go yet. *If I could just tell him my perspective while everything's calm between us, he would get that I should have said something, but that nothing was going on.*

Her chance came unexpectedly. After weeks of no responses to her calls, texts, and IMs, Sean randomly responded to one of her texts with a simple, "I'm home. Come at six to talk?" She stared at the message for minutes before it sunk in that the conversation she'd imagined for weeks was going to happen. It was 4:50 p.m. so she didn't have much time to think about what to wear or to redo her hair. She kept it simple because she had to be on time. She headed over to his place with no idea what vibe she was going to find. What he was going to say. How it would go. But she felt like a rainbow was in the sky after weeks of rain.

At 6:02 p.m., Patrice sat in Sean's living room on the edge of her seat, afraid to sit back and get too comfortable. She was standing on a weak tree limb, and she wasn't going to pretend otherwise. When he had opened the door, he looked at her for a few seconds, expressionless, then opened the door wider for her to step inside. She walked in tentatively scanning the room. He gestured for her to sit in the living room while he went to the kitchen. He came in a few seconds later and handed her a bottled water. He opened his and took a sip. He sat on the armrest of the chair across from her and stared at her from head to toe. She wore a black sweater over a t-shirt and jeans, with her hair in a ponytail and barely any makeup.

"You look good Patrice."

She focused on breathing. Then she smiled.

"Thanks babe—uh, thanks."

It was hard not to fall into usual routines even after weeks apart. She looked around the room, somehow expecting that it would look different. It didn't. She felt the awkwardness of sitting there with what was ahead of them to discuss. She didn't want to waste any time. This was the opportunity she'd been wishing for. She inhaled and spoke as she released her breath.

"Sean, I've thought so much about what to say if I ever had the chance. And I just first want you to know that I didn't have some plan to hide things from you or to make you feel stupid."

She glanced up to see if he was receptive to what she was saying.

"I want you to know for sure, as sure as I can communicate it, that nothing happened with John and I that was cheating."

He looked at her intently, unflinchingly, patiently.

"I absolutely know that I should have told you that he was my ex. You have every right to be angry and feel like you can't trust me or believe what I say. Hidden things are shady, simply because they're hidden. I know that, and I'm so sorry that I made the selfish choice not to have the conversation just because it was going to be uncomfortable."

She was relieved to get through those words. Even if he didn't respond. She took a breath hoping to conserve what felt like a limited amount of energy.

"Babe. Sean, I was so happy with us. I mean really happy. We weren't just going through the motions. We were good."

Her throat tightened. She pushed through. *It's now or never.*

"To me, John's a friend. We hadn't spoken in years. Not since we broke up seven years ago." She stared at him earnestly. "York & Newton is one of the best Public Relations firm in D.C. There is a lot of room for growth. They gave me the best offer and I definitely wanted the job. But I didn't take the job because of him." *Breathe girl, breathe.* "We do have lunch. Sometimes we plan for upcoming meetings. Sometimes we decompress from a busy morning or week. He functions in a supervisory and mentor role. Despite the years of not being in contact, we have known each other for a long time. We're friends."

Sean moved from the arm of the chair to the seat of it. Patrice took a sip of her water.

"I get now that we were too comfortable with each other. I haven't gone to lunch with him since three weeks ago. I keep a different level of boundaries now. Not because anything happened. But because I can see it now. Why it was impossibly uncomfortable for you to see us acting like that. But, nothing happened. No lingering hug, no flirtation, no kiss. And never ever sex." She paused. "And I just hope you understand, no matter what happens between you and I, that you meant everything to me. I'm so sorry that I jeopardized what we had."

Sean never looked away as she spoke. He sat silently, then he spoke.

"Well. Thank you. For clarifying."

Patrice waited. For more. But he said nothing else. He just stared at her.

"I'm telling you everything because I want to be as real as possible. I didn't really think that through before. Now, I get it. So, I just wanted you to know everything." Tears pricked at her lids. "Sean, I feel like we need to talk things through more. Everything just happened so fast. And I understand why. But, I just wish we could talk it through. I just want us to have the chance to do that."

They sat in silence for several moments. His voice was low and pensive.

"You know the thing is, once an idea grows, it ricochets through your mind, getting in all the cracks and crevices. And it's hard to get rid of it."

He leaned forward and put his water bottle on the floor in front of him.

"For a man. For me. Once it's in my head, any idea that my lady is with another guy, I can't shake it. It's seared in there. That's why women forgive cheating easier than men do." He watched a tear roll down her cheek. "Women think of all the reasons to forgive their man. Men, we think of all the ways to kill that guy their girl was with." He shook his head. "I can see that day in my head like it just happened two minutes ago." He stared at her. "The thing is Patrice, you don't eat food off of a friend's fork. Not your girlfriends, not even your mother. That's not friend territory. What I *saw* was sex. Maybe it hadn't happened yet, but it was going to."

She shook her head profusely, "Sean —"

"Listen. Just listen. I know what you told me. And I believe you. I know you think what you told me is true. I know. But you're not looking past what's happened to where it was going."

Patrice wiped at her tears and blinked to clear her vision. He continued.

"You're not being real with yourself. It was going there. And you weren't turning away from it. And, had I not seen you and said something, then what?"

Patrice shook her head slowly, but no words came out. Pain ripped through her. She leaned over with her arms crossed and stared at the floor.

"We didn't flirt Sean. That's how things get started is with flirting, and that's not what we do or did. Not even joking about it."

He quietly took a drink from his water bottle. Then he spoke with peaceful resignation, "What does it matter at this point? We're not together anymore. You can do or not do whatever you want at this point."

The image of Sean tossing her shoes out of the closet flashed through her mind. The breakup was happening all over again. She sniffled.

"You're so cold. It's like you just turned everything off like a light switch. This just hurts."

The damn burst. She cried with a heaving force that hurled her body forward. He didn't move from his chair. When she calmed enough to speak, she tried a different angle.

"Sean, have you considered that it might not have gone wherever you think things were going? I mean, I know you're really perceptive, but predicting things is another ball game. The future isn't written in stone. It changes. It could have gone differently than you think."

Sean replied, "Maybe. But I'm not living with that possibility hanging over my head. That image ricocheting through my mind all the time."

Patrice blinked to clear her vision. She stared at him, a mixture of disbelief, pain, and defeat on her face. They sat in silence while she cried. Eventually her crying subsided, and she took sips from her water bottle. It was strange, sitting across from him like this. At no point in their relationship had she ever cried with him in the room, and he not try to comfort her. The cold stiffness was strange. She sighed. *Oh my God, we're really done.* She jumped when Sean spoke, his voice disturbing the silence.

"Did you realize that he looks like me before I said it? Or actually, more accurately, that I look like him?"

Patrice stared at the floor then at Sean. She tried to form her thoughts into words,

"I, I don't think so. I mean—" Sean waited patiently. She blew her nose and again tried to settle herself. "I can see why you think that. Same bald head and complexion, about the same height."

Sean took a deep breath.

"It's more than that Patrice. And by this point you know that." He shook his head. "You still haven't taken stock in that."

She dabbed a tissue at her tears. He spoke in a low tone.

"Trice, I have nothing against you. I'm fine with us being friends. And if that's not cool, I'm okay with that too. I've come to terms with this. I'm just ready to move on."

She stilled herself to respond as steadily as she could.

"What if I'm not?"

Patrice stood and walked over to Sean. She sat near him. She lifted his hand and put it on her chest. She put her hand over his.

"Babe, we need time to work through this. To talk about it. Maybe you think I have subconscious feelings for John. Maybe you think I was using you to get over him. But that's not the way the timing of all this worked. John and I were over and out of contact long before I even met you. And I had another relationship after John, and before I met you. It just isn't the way you're putting things together in your head. Not at all."

Sean lifted his hand from her chest. He looked at her with a kind smile. But no words. After a moment of silence, Patrice slowly stood. She picked up her purse and coat, and headed to the door. She heard Sean stand and walk behind her. As she walked through the threshold of the door, she turned and asked, "Were you serious about us being friends?"

He nodded. Slightly at first, then with more emphasis. She smiled dimly as tears brimmed again. Then she left.

Part 3
Sunset

34

Lily yawned repeatedly while chatting with her mother on the drive home from work. After a long week of the twins refusing to eat anything that was green, brown or orange, daily cluster headaches that Advil couldn't touch, and two new patients with overbearing families, she was breathing a sigh of relief at the one good outcome of the week.

"John finally let go of this bone he's been tugging on. So Janelle won't have to transfer schools."

Her mother said, "Well good. At least that's over with. It was creating such a mess."

"Yeah, it was so much more grief than it was worth. It's not as though Janelle is at an impoverished school getting sub par education. She's been consistently doing well in her classes and testing above average on statewide assessments. Her scores are higher than the averages of the school he wanted her to go to."

Janelle made her unhappiness known about not wanting to transfer and hadn't softened over time. She refused to do anything with the family for her birthday, insisting on no gifts, no party, no special dinner. She stayed out most of that day, going to school then hanging out with Mason and friends until late evening. When she came home, she sat with the family for a few minutes as they gave her gifts despite her wishes.

"Thank you everyone. I think I'll open them in my room."

She hugged the twins for their homemade cards and said a quiet, polite "Thank you" to John and Lily for their gifts before heading upstairs. The next evening, Lily sat John down to reason with him.

"John this isn't going away. I know you want her to accept it, move on, and be grateful. But we're nowhere close to that. This is lingering."

She did her best to reason with him.

"And yes, she was disrespectful and shouldn't have been. But the truth is her tone was wrong but her message was right. Her grades and study habits aren't the issue. You know she's a stellar student. The AP and honors classes that she takes are equivalent to the IB program, just without the title. Are you really sure the gains are worth the losses here?"

John shifted in his seat but said nothing. After a minute or so, he said he wanted what was best for Janelle, and he didn't understand why she was being so stubborn. Lily dropped the issue at that point. They left the topic alone for a few days. Then after dinner a few nights later, John told Janelle they wanted to talk with her. He said that they still believed the new school could be a positive educational move, but that she needed to have a say in such a big decision. That if she wasn't comfortable with the transfer, they wouldn't force the issue.

Surprisingly, Janelle didn't jump for joy. Instead she let them know what had been percolating behind the scenes.

"I've been doing some research to compare the new school to my school. I just need a couple more days. I have a PowerPoint presentation that I want to do so that you can see everything I found."

On Saturday morning with her laptop on the kitchen island and dressed in slacks and a crisply-ironed dress shirt, Janelle showed them all the ways that her current school fared as well as, and in some ways better than, the new school. John listened without interrupting and Lily quietly beamed. Later that day, John told Lily,

"I just want her to have every chance she can get, you know. But I know I really need to see her for the adult she's becoming not the child she still is."

When Janelle left the kitchen after her presentation, that was the last mention of transferring.

35

Sean had been at the precinct since 6:00 a.m. poring over the Gibson case file, and the new reports from each of the officers on the case. He called Dannon and Wilson into his office when they arrived to brainstorm and debrief.

Dannon offered, "Forensics just came back on the bag of clothes, and the Coke can from her car. No useful fingerprints."

Wilson spoke next.

"Her kids have been interviewed twice. Their stories and memories were fairly consistent."

Sean provided what he knew.

"Okay. None of the DNA in the system matched the baby's DNA. And none of the four leads Mitch came up with are likely our guy. Three gave a DNA sample. Two already came back and don't match. Still waiting for the third to come back. The fourth guy is holding out, worrying about how it's going to look to his wife that cops are asking for his DNA. I've got a warrant coming to get his sample."

Sean flipped through a few pages of the file. He homed in on Wilson's reports on the Gibson neighbors.

He asked, "These reports were from three days after she was knocked unconscious. Did you talk to all the neighbors? Usually takes longer than that to talk to everyone."

Wilson nodded, "Yeah I did. I went back day and night because we needed leads as soon as possible. But no one saw anything useful."

Sean scanned a page and pointed to a section.

"Any follow up with the neighbor that saw a car in front of the Gibson house the day before the incident?"

Wilson shook his head, "She couldn't remember anything about the car. It was nighttime when she saw it while walking her dog. Couldn't even say what color it was. And no one else noticed a car."

Sean glanced at Dannon.

"What about Annabelle's friends and coworkers? I need updated reports on those interviews."

Dannon said, "I'm almost done with a second round of interviews on her coworkers. She was close-lipped at work. No one mentioned anything worthwhile."

Wilson stepped in.

"I'm finishing the report shortly on the friend interviews. The one friend that was suspicious that Annabelle had hooked up with someone didn't know anything concrete. I'll come back around to her to see if she remembered anything else."

Sean asked, "What about the bar? Anyone see Mitch leave, act strange, or anything?"

Dannon shook his head.

"The times customers saw him are all over the place. But the bartender remembers him throughout the night until around the time he got the call from his daughter."

Sean flipped through the file again.

"What about phone records?"

Dannon responded, "Yeah, all numbers checked out. She didn't make calls to anyone she didn't have established friendships with. Mitch's calls checked out too. Same for text messages."

Sean leaned back in his chair.

"I've got reports from my guys from fourth precinct. They've been doing a broader search to see if there's anyone that Annabelle's been seen with. They checked out the establishments near her job, home, grocery, and her hair and nail salons."

Wilson asked, "Can we take a look at their reports? They could have leads that we can follow up on."

Sean nodded.

"Right. I'll get 'em to you today. So listen, keep expanding from the inner to the outer layers of Annabelle's life. She couldn't possibly be screwing a guy and no one saw or knew anything unless it was a one time deal. It just doesn't work that way."

Dannon and Wilson nodded.

Dannon asked, "What about the kids' schools? No one's looked at the staff. It's not that crazy for a mom and a teacher to have something going on."

Sean pointed to Dannon then Wilson.

"Good. You check out the oldest kid's school, and you take the youngest one. And while you're at it, figure out if she was close to any of the other students' parents."

Sean wondered what quieted Hodges down. He hadn't heard from him in a week. He wondered if there was a new bone to chew on. There had been some newspaper coverage about a recent police shooting of a black teenager who was now in the hospital in critical condition. *Maybe he's busy cleaning up that mess.*

36

Patrice had spent the past couple weeks tirelessly prepping for the new acquisition meetings that were scheduled for the conference in the next week. She was glad for the distraction from her personal woes and poured herself into work. Now she needed a distraction from that distraction. After weeks of sulking, she vowed to shake off the funk. Sasha suggested that a night out was in order, and she agreed. She and Sasha were having dinner at the DC Harvest restaurant on H Street, waiting for Jen to join them before going to a lounge.

While getting dressed for the night, she thought about how she wanted the night to go. *I'm not talking about Sean, not once tonight.* But she had already brought him up twice during appetizers.

"You know, I told myself I wouldn't talk about him. Geez."

Sasha gave her a sympathetic look.

"It's only natural girl. Y'all were together for a long time."

Patrice nodded.

"The thing that gets me most is how done he was so quickly. Based on nothing really. He just turned off, like a shower knob."

Sasha shook her head.

"Did he turn off, or did he shut down?"

Patrice asked, "What's the difference?"

"Well, men act like things don't bother them and like they don't get emotional, but they're just as emotional as us. They just have more practice not showing what they feel."

Patrice sighed.

"Either way, felt like a slap in the face. Still stings."

She fiddled with food on her plate.

Sasha questioned, "Hon, have you thought about this from the positive end of things? If he can't handle the going getting tough, it's better to know now than later, you know. Better he show his colors now than after marriage, two kids, and a mortgage."

Patrice nodded.

"Yeah. I mean, what's for you is for you, right? And if he walked away, he wasn't for me."

"Right, exactly. And, really, y'all might not have been compatible. Maybe that's why you never wanted to move in with him."

Patrice reflected, "But that's the thing. We were compatible. I mean, not that finish-each-others-sentences type of compatible. But the, hardly-ever-argue, families-get-along, love-the-same-activities compatible."

Sasha tilted her head, "Okay. But were you really truly happy with that?"

Patrice leaned back in her seat. Sasha continued, "All that compatibility is cool and all. But it sounds boring. Maybe you didn't want that. Maybe deep down, you wanted something more." Sasha smiled slyly. "Maybe you were tired of the same old cucumber, and needed some spicy pickle in your life."

Sasha curled her pinky finger next to her mouth. They burst out laughing.

Just then, Jen walked up to the table, plopping down with a thud and a breathy hello.

"Heyyy ladies! Sorry I'm running late. Jeremy would *not* go to bed. It's like he senses when I have plans and makes plans of his own for me. But Tim took over so I could get outta there. So, what are we drinking?"

Jen always had a bustling energy about her. She talked like her words were running a race. And she always had an inconvenient amount of stuff with her. She often left something behind when they went places together. Winters were the worst time for her trail of crap, because she was always cold and carried every winter accessory possible — scarf, gloves, hat, travel mug, and usually a CVS or Safeway plastic bag because she'd stop to "grab a few things" before they met up. Patrice and Sasha made it a habit whenever they met up to look around the area before they all left to be sure Jen didn't leave anything behind that they'd have to go back to get.

The three ladies got to the Ultrabar lounge just before midnight. Patrice felt herself aging ten years as they walked in the door. The stream of ladies in too tight, too short dresses with seemingly airbrushed makeup were painful reminders of being past her prime. In the wake of a break-up, feeling washed up and old was a part of the package. After a while, she shifted from "I'm too old to be here" mode to "Fine wine gets better with age" mode. It happened around her second glass of wine.

By the end of the night, a happy exhaustion washed over Patrice. She, Jen, and Sasha laughed all night at the montage of cute to gaudy outfits, drunk idiots that were one step away from starting a fight, and men with pitiful pick-up lines. It took everything out of them to wait until guys walked away before snickering. By two in the morning, they'd had their fill of the night's foolishness and made their way to the coat check. As they retrieved their coats and headed out the door, Jen abruptly stopped.

"Oh damn, didn't I have a scarf? Where's my scarf?"

Patrice and Sasha rolled their eyes in unison. Patrice said,

"Really Jen? We're tired. I can buy you a new scarf."

Jen protested, "No. It was a birthday gift from my sister. I can't just leave it."

Sasha corrected her, "Um, hon, you already left it."

"Let me just run back up and see if it's where we were sitting. I'll be back in a sec."

They sighed and turned to walk back upstairs. The bouncer let Jen back in to look for her scarf but said Patrice and Sasha could stand just inside the door and wait for Jen.

Jen flew up the steps past a couple on their way down. Patrice glanced at the couple, then did a double take. Her heart raced and palms moistened. As they neared the bottom

of the stairs where she and Sasha stood, her fear was actual-
ized. She couldn't help but stare.

"Hey lady."

Sean nodded at Patrice as he handed two tickets to the
woman in coat check. The woman by his side smiled at
Patrice. Sean introduced them.

"This is Sienna. Sienna, Patrice."

Both ladies looked at each other with knowing smiles.
Fumbling for words, Patrice hoped to sound calm and col-
lected, but struggled to pull it off.

"Hi –, hey Sienna!"

Sean glanced back and forth between the two of them.

"You know each other?"

Six degrees of separation is crap. It's really two.

Sienna glanced at Sean.

"She comes to the salon. Hey girl! Tiffany's your hairdresser, right?"

Patrice nodded and shifted her weight from one leg to the
next.

"Yup. Hope business is doing well."

"It is, thank you! What do you do for a living?" Sienna
asked.

"I'm in public relations. And work is good."

"Good."

Sean received Sienna's coat from the coat checker and
held it out for her to slide her arms in the sleeves. Patrice's
chest stung. She glanced at Sasha, helpless fear in her eyes.
Sasha stepped forward.

"Hey Sean."

She hugged him and shook Sienna's hand. After an awkward silence, Sean led Sienna forward to the door.

"Alright, take care ladies."

Patrice watched as Sean and Sienna walked out the door and down the sidewalk. Tears welled up. *He thinks she's girlfriend material? Really?* She felt bad for herself for all her pining over spilled milk. She felt bad for him settling for pretty and available. She didn't care enough to feel bad for Sienna.

That night, Patrice tossed, flipped, and turned in bed. Sleep was as elusive as a mermaid. In her mind she replayed the scene from earlier. She thought about all the things she could have said. His words repeated in her head. "Hey lady." *Such an asshole. Like we hardly know each other. Please. I know where every mole exists on your body.*

After a few winks of sleep, Patrice got up, did some reading, then looked for yoga discounts on Groupon. Eventually her mind drifted to Sean insisting on how much he and John resembled. *Yeah, in general, I guess. They're so different though. Personalities are like night and day.* Beyond broad similarities she couldn't see the resemblance. *So what if they're the same height and complexion? So are thousands of other men.* She thought back on their conversation when she was last at his place. She was still confused about Sean ending things so quickly. *How could it not count that I didn't cheat, no matter how it looked?* She thought about calling him, then decided against it. *What could we possibly say to each other at this point?*

37

Sean glanced at his phone and saw that it was Ron calling. "Hey man. How's it going?"

Ron sounded surprise, "I was wondering how long you were going to dodge me?"

Sean chuckled.

"Nah man, just busy. You know how it goes. Everything good on your end?"

"No, you were dodging. But okay. Let's just say you were busy."

"No really. There's a lot happening right now. A lot of eyes on me looking for the next step, you know. But, it'll slow down at some point. Anyway, how about some ball this weekend?"

Ron said, "Yeah, that's cool. But, so, are we going to talk about it?"

Sean said, "Sure."

They quieted for a beat. Ron said, "It's just not an easy thing to talk about. If I was straight it would be a non-issue. I think it would been easier if I just showed up to the next holiday dinner with a date and kissed him while the sweet potatoes were being passed around. Then it's just out there. No major coming out conversations."

"Why not? That sounds like a plan."

"I don't know. You just never know how people are going to react."

"Even me?"

"Yeah, even you. Look how you've been dodging me since you were here."

Sean hesitated. Then he asked, "So when did you know?"

"Long time. Since I was a kid. Since Mike."

"Mike? Mike who?"

"Miksey."

Sean thought back to their friends from high school and college. "From high school? Mike was –. Damn."

They talked for the next half-hour. Ron talked about a few high school moments of experimentation, and of not knowing for sure until after getting married. He lamented about being so unhappy. And hating himself for not fully testing the waters before marriage. For hurting his wife by testing the waters after marriage.

"I know it was a shitty way to do things. But, I'll tell you, it was the happiest I felt since I was a kid."

Sean listened intently as Ron continued, "The thing is, I was so attracted to Rita that I thought something had changed in me."

Sean asked, "So that's what happened between y'all? Did you finally tell her?"

"She found out. She heard me on the phone with someone. I was saying goodbye. She said that my voice sounded so flirty that she thought I was cheating. She started following me."

Sean said, "Well listen, I'm your brother. I might have to adjust, but I mean, who you're with and how you're with them is your business. Unless somebody needs their ass kicked. Then I got your back."

They moved on to talk about Sean's life.

Ron asked, "So how's the new chick?"

Sean chuckled.

"Sienna doesn't quite qualify for new chick status. She's sweet. And the sex is -, sweet too. But right now, I'm just chillin'."

"I hear that." Ron laughed. "Really, I think you're waiting things out, and you and Patrice are getting back together. You just want to make sure she gets the point, that what she was doing wasn't cool."

Sean shook his head, "Nah. That's over. Way over."

Ron asked, "Is anything ever *that* over?"

Sean sighed. "I don't know man. You never know. But I've moved on. I'm just appreciating dating. See who I want to see. Nothing more. I'm good."

38

Patrice couldn't help but wonder how serious things were between Sean and Sienna. She ping-ponged between opposite thoughts. Sometimes she figured Sienna was just sympathy sex. *He probably never lets her spend the night or takes her out on dates during the day.* Other times, she imagined that Sienna's stuff was already housed in the drawers that used to be for her clothes. She sometimes imagined that Sean refused to introduce Sienna to his son because he didn't plan on seriously dating her, but then it switched to her imaging them, all three, playing in a park. *She's probably already trying to suck up to Micah.* She couldn't stand how much she thought about Sean. *He probably doesn't give me a second thought.* But then there were moments when she just knew that he was missing her and wishing he could take back his rash decision. She knew it was time to move on, and she felt like she was on her way to that, until she saw him with Sienna at the club.

Patrice spent the rest of her day cleaning her apartment from top to bottom to keep her mind busy. Going through her closet for clothes to donate, she found some of Sean's clothes. A pair of pants and two polo shirts. She put them in a bag by the front door and kept cleaning. When she was done, she showered and plopped on her couch. She stared at the bag of Sean's clothes. *I'll mail it to him.* Later that night while laying in bed, unable to sleep yet again, anger swelled in her. She thought about the pain she felt when he tossed out their relationship so flippantly. How he sat and watched her cry, never budging to even offer a tissue. All because of what he thought *could* happen. *All our years together. In the trash like leftovers.*

Early the next morning, Patrice stopped at Walmart. She bought men's cologne and a couple t-shirts that weren't Sean's style. Once back home, she ripped open the bag with Sean's clothes and laid them on the floor along with the new t-shirts. She tore the tags off then sprayed everything with cologne. Then she got her rain boots out of the hall closet, wet the bottoms, then stomped on the clothes, smearing dirt across them. *Sweet and shitty.* She chipped the tip of a mug he had forgotten and added that to the mix for good measure. Then she boxed everything up and went to the post office.

Once back home, Patrice sang aloud to keep her mind busy.

"I bust the windows out your car."

She paced her living room, refusing to sit and over-think. *No stewing. Move on.* She cooked lasagna for dinner and focused the new problem at hand. Needing a new hair salon. Finding a hairdresser that she could trust, that was good, and that knew exactly how she liked her hair done was going to be a process. One which had gone awry before, ending in bad haircuts and breakage. It took a few visits for Tiffany to learn what Patrice liked, but that was quicker than any of her past hairdressers. She knew how to color Patrice's hair too. She concocted a hair color that Patrice had stuck with for years, combining three dyes that were different shades of brown from golden to auburn. Knowing that Patrice didn't like being under the dryer more than fifteen minutes, she'd use a blow dryer on low heat to do the rest of the drying. She knew Patrice always preferred the red rollers, and that she only wanted her hair ends trimmed — and only a centimeter or two trimmed off — once every other salon visit.

Patrice wondered if she could stomach going back to Tiffany. *This is not the time to have to train a new stylist on how to do my hair.* But, as much as she didn't want to start over with a new stylist, the idea of seeing Sienna even for a second made her cringe. She wanted to strut in there like she didn't give a damn, but it would take all her might to do so. If she didn't go back she could look like she was running with her tail tucked between her legs. But if she went back, she might throw up right in Tiffany's chair.

She decided that going back was the better option, and that she could time things out to avoid Sienna. With the work conference and acquisition meetings coming, she wasn't ready to chance going to a new salon and coming out with embarrassing hairstyling. Of course, she could style it on her own, but self-styling never lasted as long as salon-styling. *Buck up buttercup, grab the horse by the mane and bite the bullet.*

Patrice called ahead and made an appointment for as early as possible on the upcoming Wednesday, hoping the salon would be fairly empty. She remembered mostly seeing Sienna there when going to afternoon appointments. Patrice arrived that morning at 7:28 a.m., a couple of minutes before the salon was due to open. Tiffany was already there along with one other hairdresser, and the front desk girl.

"Hola Ms. Patrice. Come on in!"

"Hey Gabriela!"

"You getting the usual wash and set today?"

Patrice took her coat off and hung it on the coat rack at the front entrance.

"Yeah, I need a style that will last through a four-day business trip with little maintenance."

"Well, Tiffany's back there already. She'll hook you up! Did you want to pay now while she's getting the chair ready?"

Patrice nodded. Once paid, she went back, hugged Tiffany then sat in her chair. She loved that Tiffany was quick and wasn't chatty. Patrice could read a few book chapters while her hair was getting done without interruption. Today though, she kept losing focus and re-reading sentences. Every time the front door chimed, she forced herself not to look up but wondered if it was Sienna. She kept reading, but none of the words registered.

Tiffany was done washing, setting, drying, and styling Patrice's hair in an hour and fifteen minutes, record time for a salon. *Whew, I might make it out of here with no sighting of her! I'll be in my office by 9:30!* She hugged Tiffany and headed to the front. As she waved goodbye to Gabriela and put on her coat, she heard the door chime.

"Hey Patrice. Long time no see."

Patrice looked up to see Sienna with a plastic smile.

"Hey lady. I was just heading out."

With that, Patrice left, summoning as much calm as she could to walk out not looking flustered. Once in her car, she pulled off within seconds of clicking her seat belt. Her chest tightened. *Just make it around the corner.* She made it through two traffic lights, then pulled over on the side of the road when hyperventilating kicked in. It was twenty minutes later before she calmed down enough to start the car again.

Up until that moment, she had refused to think of the panic attacks as an ongoing problem. More of a fluke. Now she knew they weren't going away. She called the office to say she was running late, then headed home to change, given that she sweated through her blouse. Staring at her image in the bathroom mirror with flopped over, sweated out hair, she sighed. *Wasted money.* Tiffany's work of art was now a sopping, droopy mess. Patrice called work again and said she wouldn't make it in due to car troubles. She knew John would be irritated because this was their last day to prep for the meetings at the conference, but there was way too much happening for her to be any good in the office. *And what good would it do if I'm prepped for a killer presentation but then had a panic attack in the middle of it?*

Patrice called her doctor's office hoping she could come in that day. When she was told no appointments were available, she went to the urgent care center near her house. On her way in, she called back to her doctor's office to ask to be called if any cancellations occurred. The assistant told her then that there had just been one. The last appointment of the day was now available. She was happy that she lucked out.

Once in with her doctor, Patrice explained when her panic attacks started, how long they last when they happen, and how exhausted she'd be after. Her doctor reviewed her chart and noted that Patrice's last physical was only seven months ago. She said there were a few tests she wanted to run, but it was likely that there was no underlying medical cause for her symptoms and that she was likely triggered to have a panic attack by psychological distress. She prescribed a low dose of Xanax to be taken as needed. Her doctor recommended that she seek counseling, and do meditative activities such as yoga. Patrice listened to all the recommendations while thinking, *Counseling? My sister needs counseling. What I need is a good vacation.*

Once Patrice left the doctor's office, she felt relieved because now she was armed to deal with any attacks that might come. She turned her attention to figuring out what she was going to do with her hair on the trip. She had it pulled into a ponytail. She shook her head as she caught sight of her frizzy hairline from sweating earlier. She could call Tiffany and see if she could go back in before the salon closed, but there was no way she was going to chance seeing Sienna again. She could have a bun for the whole trip, but that's what she did on weekends when she didn't want to deal with her hair while running errands. She could wash her hair again then curl it herself, but her hair just wouldn't look the way she wanted, and she would be self-conscious about her hair the whole damn trip. As she checked her watch, she saw her window of time was closing to make a decision. She needed a worry-free hair option for the trip not to become an exercise in how to pretend you feel confident when you don't.

Once back home, Patrice made a pot of coffee. She checked her phone and saw that John had texted her earlier asking what was going on and saying that they needed today for last minute prep for the meetings. She didn't bother to respond. She saw a missed call from a number that looked vaguely familiar. She wondered if it was Michelle.

Patrice got halfway through her mug of coffee when the solution to her hair problem dawned on her. She grabbed her keys and headed back out the door. In forty-five minutes she was sitting in a salon chair at Sister Kati's African Hair Braiding salon getting goddess braids done. She hadn't had braids in years. She used to love having them for the gift of low-maintenance hair for weeks. She could get up on mornings and spend five minutes styling her braids, spraying hair oil for shine, then she was all set for the day. But she hated the hassle of having to take braids out. It was a whole day affair, removing over a hundred braids one by one then combing through her hair, one small section at a time, to get the knots out before washing and deep conditioning. The next day she would be at the hair salon getting a relaxer done then styling, all of which led to a sore scalp for days. Eventually, the weeks of hassle-free hair stopped feeling worth that awful weekend of suffering. That mindset change occurred somewhere around the time that she lost a quarter-sized chunk of hair that was so knotted after braiding it had to be cut out. Despite her history with braiding, getting eight large goddess braids styled into a swirl coiled to the crown of her head felt like the perfect solution right now given the day's circumstances.

Patrice had packed her suitcase a little each day for the past week. When she returned home from the braiding salon, she put the last items she needed for her trip in her suitcase and zipped it up. She was in bed by 10:00 p.m. She sighed with relief as she laid her head on her pillow, albeit with a sore scalp from the braiding. She drifted off quickly, but when she got up at four o'clock in the morning, to catch her seven o'clock flight, it felt like she hadn't slept for more than an hour. Nonetheless, she was dressed and out the door, on time, to get to Reagan National Airport and grab a large cup of coffee before boarding her flight to Louis Armstrong New Orleans Airport.

39

Janelle and Mason sat on the monkey bars at the playground after a long day of AP tests at school. She was knee-deep in complaining about her teachers not letting up on giving homework.

"Come on, they know we have these tests. Do we really need to be stressing about getting homework done right now too? Geez."

Mason nodded.

"I know right. I just skipped a couple homework assignments. I'll try to make them up before the end of the quarter."

She shook her head, "They might not let you. Trying to prove a point about us being responsible."

He chuckled.

"Nah, I know how to make it happen. You just have to seem quiet and pensive in class for a couple days. Then the good teachers will ask if you're okay. That's the time to say you're stressed out about failing AP tests and failing in class too. Then you say how you messed up on getting homework done, and it's probably too late to turn things around. That's when they say you can turn a couple assignments in late for partial credit."

Janelle teased, "Look at you. Shady."

"Hi, my name is, huh, my name is, who, my name is, Slim Shady!"

They laughed out loud.

"But c'mon. I'm figuring out ways to turn in homework. That ain't shady. Shady would be me breaking into the school to steal AP test answers."

They jumped off the bars to head home. Mason asked, "How do you think you did on the tests? I think I did okay."

Janelle said, "Yeah, me too. I got caught up in the free response section and took too much time. But I still finished everything."

They cracked jokes about breaking into school and leaving *Bad Teacher* DVDs on all the teachers' desks. Janelle pulled out her phone and scrolled through her pictures. Then she said,

"You're probably gonna think I'm making this up, but I saw this lady the other day. I really, really thought she could be my mom."

"Really? Where'd you see her?"

"She was standing by a tree at the gates of the soccer field last week when I went to practice. We were getting our shin guards on and coach was fussing about last week's game saying that we need to tighten up defense. I looked up and she was looking at me."

"Why'd you think it was her?"

"I don't know. She kinda smiled a little bit. And it was like a proud kinda smile. I couldn't see her face good though. But, I don't know. I just felt like she knew me."

Janelle passed him her phone. He scrolled through two blurry pictures of a woman in the distance.

She asked, "What do you think?"

Mason pondered, "It could've been her. I don't know. It's hard to see her face."

He gave her phone back. As she looked back and forth at the two pictures, he asked, "Did you show your dad?"

She shook her head. "No. It might not even be her."

"Yeah, but he knows what she looks like. He could tell better if it's her."

She chuckled.

"For all I know, she could just be a homeless woman looking for food. I'm giving her a whole identity, and she just wants some leftover fries and cigarette money."

They laughed.

Mason said, "Well, she might pop up again. Take a zoomed in picture next time. By the way, are we still doing the movie thing this weekend?"

"I don't know, I didn't set anything up."

Mason started a group text with their mutual friends. Within a few minutes a group date was set up to go see the new Avengers movie on Saturday.

40

Patrice hunkered into her airplane seat, set up her inflatable footrest, laid out a couple magazines, and pulled out a pashmina to wrap up in during the flight to take a nap. Her breath was a tad shaky as the plane took off. But then she remembered that she always loved flying, which settled her. As a kid, her parents let her sit in the window seat and make a fort around herself with coats. Michelle usually fell asleep as soon as the plane took off, but Patrice would be up for the whole flight. Her dad told her booger bandits were looking to snatch her up any chance they got. When she would peek out of her fort for a few seconds, her mother would say, "Better stay down in the hole before the booger bandits get you." She would quickly duck her head back in the coat fort and peer out the window at the clouds.

Once the plane landed in New Orleans, Patrice turned on her phone and saw a couple texts from John that he had landed an hour earlier and wanted to do a final presentation run through before tomorrow. She hadn't responded to his text yesterday and was tempted not to respond to this one. She knew it could help to practice more to polish and sync up their parts, and the transitions between PowerPoint slides and video, but she didn't want to chance getting freaked out. Like not picking an outfit the day before an interview. She couldn't bring herself to jinx it. So, she responded saying she had made plans to meet up with a friend and wouldn't have time, but that she was confident that they were ready and would hit it out of the park. She wasn't as confident as she sounded, but for now, she felt better saying the words. She spent the day walking the streets near the hotel and buying trinkets and food from street vendors. She'd been to New Orleans once before and was curious how things changed post-Hurricane Katrina. She had crawfish and French wine, then beignets for dessert.

The next day Patrice woke up three hours early. The meetings were set to happen one after the next and wrap up at 1:00 p.m. She traveled with five suits so that she had options. She went with a burgundy pant suit and black pumps. When she left her hotel room, she felt ready for however the day would unfold. For the first meeting, John had her take the lead. As she set up for the presentation, nerves bubbled in her stomach. She pushed them down with the promise to herself that she would not let herself crumble. She would leave the room before letting that happen. She reminded herself that Xanax was an option if she absolutely needed it. And with a deep breath, she started the presentation strong.

"York & Newton is the premiere public relations company not just of the east coast, but of the U.S. We've specialized in taking companies from good to great by our multi-layered strategy of public performance recognition. Because publicity is prosperity!"

When she fumbled five minutes in, she made a joke of it.

"We flopped — I mean flipped two companies in the last two months through changing their social media approach and presence." She paused. "So we turned a flop to a hop! A hopping success!"

She made some changes to the presentation on the fly, based on questions and feedback from the executives. By the end of it, she was pleased with how the meeting unfolded and was ready for the next one.

Patrice beamed when she saw that the three executives in the second meeting were all female. And they took to her with ease. She and John were a duo for this one, working in sync like a well-oiled machine. They stuck to the script though, as she saw the side-eye John gave her when she diverted from script in the first meeting. The third meeting, John did with Richard, one of the other associates that started at York & Newton around the time Patrice did. By the end of the meetings, she felt energized and on top of the world. They had prepped for weeks, and when meeting day arrived, there was nothing left to do but deliver.

After meetings wrapped, there were two more conference days. While attending conference sessions, she met a few associates from competing firms, and firms in surrounding states. She had worked out a plan to reach out to each of her connections, once back at the office in D.C. to discuss any possible partnerships that could be mutually beneficial. By the last day of the conference, Patrice thought the trip was a success. The closing reception finished at 5:30 p.m. and she planned to have one last local meal on her last night in the city. She headed to her hotel, picking up some gumbo and crab cakes from a local hole-in-the-wall diner on the way. The concierge had told her that diner had "the best crab cakes in N'orlins!"

Patrice took her food up to her room, showered, and slipped into a green silk camisole set. She kept the temperature in her room toasty and settled in at the table in her room to feast. She had bought a bottle of wine the day she arrived, so she could unwind at nights without paying hotel bar prices. For dessert she savored every bite of a beignet. She felt satisfied in every sense of the word by the time she laid back in bed to watch *Best Man Holiday*. When her cell phone rang twenty minutes later it woke her from dozing.

"Hey!" John's voice wafted through the phone, light and relaxed.

Patrice sat up in bed.

"Hey. How was your last day?"

"Good. I think I got to every conference session I wanted to catch. Glad it's all done though. You know how these conferences can be. After the first couple of days, it gets old quick."

She agreed.

"I know. I felt done after the first day. I really only cared about our meetings. Once those were done, I was set. The rest of the time was just about the food!"

They both laughed.

John asked, "So, you all set over there?"

The hotel rooms of all the York & Newton associates were all next to each other. She and John's room were adjacent.

"Yeah, I'm watching movies. I'll probably be asleep in—"

She was interrupted by his laughter.

"Turn to channel 25. Quick."

Patrice flipped channels.

"Better yet," he said between laughs, "Come quick before the scene ends."

"Well—"

He hung up before she could object. She hesitated for a few seconds. Then she grabbed her robe and slippers. She heard his side of the adjoining door between their rooms unlock. When she walked in his room, he was still laughing heartily.

"Did you see this episode?"

John stood in front of the TV waving her over. He pointed at the chair in his room near the window. An episode of *Insecure* was on. It was a rerun of the third season premiere episode where Issa started driving for Lyft to make extra money so she could move out of her ex's apartment. There were two customers in the backseat in mid-tussle. Then one of the guys bolted out of the car and left the other one bruised up. Issa and her best friend Molly, who happened to be Issa's riding partner for the night, were stuck figuring out what happened and what to do about the maimed customer. John and Patrice laughed aloud. After a few minutes, her laughter stirred up her full bladder.

"Where's the bathroom?"

He shot her an 'are you serious' look.

"It's a hotel room. Ain't but so many doors in here. Where do you think it is?"

Patrice playfully shoved him as she hurried past to the bathroom. While in there, she saw that his toiletry bag was on the counter. After washing her hands, she couldn't help but peek inside. Nothing surprising in it though. Toothbrush, cologne, aftershave. She looked at herself in the mirror, and as she saw her nipples making their presence known under her robe, it dawned on her that she was bra-less. She straightened her robe then went back into the room. When she sat back down, she crossed her arms over her chest.

She asked, "How does this episode end? I don't remember how it went?"

"The guy Nate that ran off ended up leaving Issa a tip in the Lyft app."

"Oh yeah, I remember now."

She had seen the episode when is first aired. She watched as John walked over to the mini bar. He untucked his dress shirt from his slacks and was barefoot. He hadn't changed from the conference.

He poured a rum and coke then turned to her.

"You want something to drink?"

"Yeah. My wine is wearing off."

He fixed another drink and handed it to her. She took it, sipped, and crossed her arms again, feeling her nipples tighten.

They watched another episode. Issa was now mired in the muddiness of staying temporarily with her ex. The sexual tension and mixed up feelings were unfolding messily. Patrice finished her drink, got up and grabbed one of the bottles of water sitting on the counter. She glanced at John, silently asking if she could have a bottle, to which he nodded. He stood and walked over to the bar himself, topping off his drink. Patrice took a sip of her water. They both turned and leaned against the hotel desk side by side.

John offered, "You worked your magic at those meetings! When these deals close, it will be mostly because of you."

She smiled, basking in the compliment. She of course didn't mention needing to pop a Xanax just before they started presenting to make sure her nerves didn't morph into a full-on, collapse-on-the-floor, call-the-paramedics, attack.

"Well, I know you could've pulled rank at any point. I really appreciated having the time to shine."

He smiled, "You shine all the time."

She chuckled, "Wow, a line straight out of a movie."

They laughed.

She asked, "So what's next?"

"Well, we just keep following up until the deals close. Usually you head the account you took the lead in presenting. So, the Jewel account would be your baby."

They chatted about what would be entailed in setting the course for the new accounts and a tentative plan for turnaround regarding the new account's public image. She stood straight and stretched. Then she took a step toward the chair she was sitting in.

Patrice felt the warmth of John's hand as he touched her wrist then held her hand. He took a sip of his drink then put it on the counter. He moved in front of her. His eyes traveled slowly from her eyes, down to the edges of her camisole slightly visible under her robe.

"Green looks good on you!"

His words were soft. His eyes lingered on her nipples that were pushing against her robe. He stepped closer, and she felt his thighs against hers. He reached down to nuzzle her ear and neck. His hands slid onto the small of her back. Patrice felt the heat rise in the room and warmth enveloped her body. Her eyes closed as she moaned. She felt naked. Bare and exposed. They locked eyes. And there it was. The moment. She never considered this scenario happening. Never felt that he had flirted with her, or her with him. She never fantasized about them hooking up since working together. She never thought of them as a possibility again. Yet here they were, and the moment felt as familiar as a favorite meal.

41

L ily sat stiffly in the black leather seats of a divorce attorney's office, fending off the shakiness of her voice by
repeatedly clearing her throat. This was their second meeting.
She quickly scheduled to meet within an hour of finding out,
through sorting out an old box of mail, that John had com-
municated with a divorce attorney a year ago. She also found
emails about a condominium application when she fished
through his personal email account. After further searching,
she found the Facebook page of a woman who tagged John on
a work photo. The woman was his ex-girlfriend and they work
together. She dug around on York and Newton's website and
figured out, from the Current Happenings section, that the ex
was one of the new, up and coming associates who was going
on the conference trip. He hadn't said a word about any of it.
She felt blindsided by the secrecy and wondered what else
had been going on behind her back.

Lily channeled her outrage into action. At the first meeting, the attorney gave an overview of the divorce process and

time frames, potential custody issues, and the financial cost estimate based on the different ways to proceed. At the meeting today, he focused on what documents would be needed throughout the process and particularly what was needed to get started. He wrapped up the meeting with a last piece of info.

"You may need a forensic accountant, and if so, I can make recommendations."

Lily dabbed at her eyes and nose with a soggy tissue throughout the meeting, hoping to keep her face from being a snotty, mascara-smeared mess. She blinked to clear her vision.

"A forensic accountant?"

"It sounds more ominous than it is. It's a specialized accountant who can research to reveal essential financial information. This becomes important for accurate division of assets and deciding about child and spousal support. They'll let us know if there are any hidden monies in undisclosed or off-shore accounts, or IRAs that you're not listed as a beneficiary for."

Lily smiled painfully, "Not necessary."

The attorney was disapproving.

"Don't be so sure. Things aren't always what they seem. And if he started talking to an attorney a year ago—"

Lily interrupted, "Money isn't something he would hide. John would never leave his kids without, which means he wouldn't leave me without. If anything, I'd have to worry about him wanting custody of the kids."

The attorney relented.

"Well, let's just see how it all goes. As soon as you get me the initial documents and retainer we can get started."

She stiffly smiled.

"Thank you for your time."

No sooner did the words come out of her mouth did tears burst through the dam. She cried with vigor and volume. The attorney pushed a tissue box across the table.

He calmly reassured,

"This is a difficult and serious step to take. Maybe take some time to wrap your head around all this. You really want to be sure before proceeding."

She nodded, blew her nose, dabbed at her eyes, then stood to leave.

As she stepped out of his office, she pulled out her compact from her purse to clean up her smudged makeup.

Lily's mother called shortly after she walked through the door at home, after picking up the twins from daycare. Her mother asked about how the kids were doing, recapped the cruise for the umpteenth time, then arranged a weekend for the kids to sleepover. Then she turned her attention to Lily and John.

"So, is it feeling like you two are getting back on track since the cruise?"

Lily sighed, "We're fine."

Her mother pressed on. "It just seemed like you two were connecting again on the cruise. Changing up the routine can really be a launching pad to rekindle the fire."

Lily said tersely, "Sure."

"What's wrong? You're upset with me again?"

"Well, it's the way you say things." Lily paused. "I'm not the one getting in the way of my own marriage. I've tried. You know, it's easy to look from the outside and assume and judge. I appreciate the concern, but it feels condescending. You're basically saying I'm the failure because I'm not trying enough."

Lily's eyes blurred from tears. Her mother sighed exasperatedly.

"I'm not saying that. At all. Why do you always think I'm putting you down? I'm not saying anything about you being a failure. I just know that when things are rough it can be easier to turn away from each other instead of towards each other."

Lily laughed through her tears.

"Well, evidently you should've been giving that advice to John because he's on his way back from shacking up with a work skank, while I have this ridiculous conversation with you."

Her mother gasped, "What? Are you sure that's—"

"No, I'm not sure. But I'm sure. And at this point, I don't really know how much it matters whether I'm sure. Everything's so screwed up. I just don't know."

"Oh honey. I know it's hard right now. But it takes time to —"

Lily screamed into the phone, "Oh dear God, Dr. Redford, stop with the therapy sound bites. I'm not your GODDAMN patient. Just stop trying to help. It's *not* helping."

Lily ended the call and pelted her phone across the room as her tears unleashed.

Later that evening, since Jasper and Jasmine had been asking all week to FaceTime with Whoopsie, they got their wish. They loved it because she usually made it a point to answer the video call wearing a mask. This tickled the twins to no end. Lily set it up so that they could call after dinner and TV time, just before their bath and bedtime. Janelle volunteered to help with bathing the twins and putting them to bed after the call, knowing that Lily liked having a few minutes to herself to chat with Whoopsie.

On the call, the twins excitedly showed pictures from the new books they got through their reading program, and the new glitter shoes they made at craft hour at the Funky Farm children's festival they went to over the weekend.

Janelle came in to take the twins upstairs for their bath. As they headed up the steps, Lily said,

"I put their toys in the tub already, and their pajamas on the bed. You just have to run the water. Don't forget to check the water temperature really good before you let them get in. And don't let them stay in past fifteen minutes, okay?"

Janelle tilted her head. "Ma, don't worry. I've done this before, quite a few times. I got it!"

They smiled at each other. Lily turned back to the screen and asked Whoopsie, "How many masks do you have? I've seen three different ones already."

Whoopsie laughed.

"Well, you know kids get bored real quick. Gotta keep it interesting. I caught a sale at Party City over the summer and just bought a bag full. I don't even know how many are in there."

They laughed. Lily told Whoopsie about the cruise, leaving out the tough parts in favor of focusing on the fun parts. Whoopsie listened carefully, then she leaned into the screen.

"Honey, you look tired. You okay?"

Lily's tears gushed at the sound of Whoopsie's words.

"Oh lily-pad, whatever it is, you're going to be okay."

Whoopsie blew kisses to Lily as she watched her cry. Lily finally cleared her throat enough for words to form.

"Whoopsie, I, I just –."

Her grandmother patiently listened as Lily spoke in spurts about her troubles with John and that their marriage could be over. She shared her suspicions that he was having an affair. That she never thought she would be divorcing and having to raise kids without their father in their daily lives. That she worried about what would happen to her relationship with Janelle after divorcing.

Whoopsie smiled, "You know, I think you're brave. It's not easy figuring out if you have enough to stay in a marriage, and to know what's best for your kids. And for you. It's just so tough."

Lily sniffled then blew her nose. She gave an appreciative smile.

"Thanks. I wish I knew what's best. I just don't know." She paused. "Even if we do stay together and work through it, I don't know if I'll ever be in love with him again. Right now, I can't imagine getting there. And I don't know if he was ever truly in love with me. It's been rough for so long. It just feels like so much to deal with. Sometimes, it feels like we've been trying long enough. Sometimes, I feel like I'm the only one trying. Other times, it feels like I'm checked out."

"Well, are you?"

"Maybe. In some ways. I just –. I can't keep feeling like I'm carry the weight for both of us. Why do I have to be the one to fix everything? I didn't make this a mess."

Lily wiped her face on her sleeves. Whoopsie sighed.

Lily continued, "And I think about, you know, if we end it. I don't know if he would fight for custody of the twins." She whispered the rest of her words. "I probably wouldn't get to see Janelle anymore. I've been in her life since she was a kid. She's my daughter too."

Whoopsie nodded as she listened. They sat silently for a few moments.

Whoopsie offered,

"You know what, you'll know when you've had enough. When you've done enough. When it's time to press eject. But you can't know that until you've tried everything. You have to do all the leaning you can do before you know when it's time."

Lily looked intently, "Leaning?"

"Leaning is everything Lily-pad. In life, in marriage, in friendship, in education. You have to put your time in learning how and when to lean. Leaning on people for support and letting them support you. Leaning into whatever needs you to put in the extra effort. Leaning back when you need to let things be and accept what is. And definitely leaning sideways to dodge bullcrap!"

They erupted in laughter.

Whoopsie continued, "Leaning is everything. When you've put in all the leaning you can, then you'll know. If you don't know, you're not done leaning."

Lily smiled. A lone tear trickled down her cheek.

"I love you Whoopsie."

"Yes honey, send the love my way. I always need it. I love you back!"

She blew kisses at Lily.

"Now, I gotta go. I've got a garden club meeting first thing in the morning. We're picking the flowers for our spring showcase. You would never believe it. These old biddies argue to the hills and back about flowers, soil, and planters. I need my rest to compete!"

Lily laughed heartily.

"Okay. Well, sleep well."

"Yes. And you sleep deep!"

42

Sean sat with a small black notepad at the kitchen table in Shauna Reeves's home. She was one of Annabelle Gibson's close friends and had been interviewed twice previously by officers. After pouring over all the reports for Annabelle's case for months, Sean still wondered what wasn't in the report. Most interviews weren't recorded, so what made it into the report was based on memory, notes taken, and what was considered important enough to include by the officer. That meant a certain amount of important information was lost in every case. And then there was information that was intentionally left out.

Sean opted for a mystery shopper approach to figure out what wasn't written in reports. He'd show up without notice at interviews, or talked directly to a witness or person of interest on occasion. It helped him to have his finger on the pulse of each case and not rely 100 percent on what cops chose to say. Once he read the newest reports on this case, he decided he needed to talk with Shauna Reeves directly. He noticed that each time she was interviewed she gave more information. And given how close she was to Annabelle, what Shauna knew, no matter how insignificant, could make a difference. He needed to talk with her to make sure every drop of information had been gathered.

Sean offered to come to her home for the interview, which she was grateful for, so she didn't need to find a babysitter. She opened the front door within seconds of him knocking. Then she sent her six and nine-year-old boys upstairs. She motioned for Sean to sit at the kitchen table then she took a seat. She already had juice boxes in the center of the table.

"Would you like a juice?" She smiled sheepishly. "We haven't had time for adult grocery shopping in awhile."

Sean shook his head.

"No thanks I'm fine. I don't want to take up too much of your time. You've been gracious enough agreeing to be interviewed for a third time. I appreciate that. We want to be as thorough as possible in this investigation."

"Sure, sure. Anything I can do to help, I'm glad to do it. I mean, she would have done the same for me."

She teared up as she spoke. Sean gave an empathetic smile. He reviewed the notes he jotted down at the office after reading through her previous interviews.

"I just have a few more questions. So as I understand, you and Mrs. Gibson were pretty close."

She nodded as he continued.

"Did she ever complain about her marriage?"

"Of course. And I complained about mine. But nothing out of the ordinary."

"Did she ever talk about divorce?"

"Only out of anger. She never seemed serious about it because a day or two later she was onto something else and they were fine."

"Did she ever mention any male friends to you?"

"Well, I've told the other officers this too. We have friends we know from working together. Donald and Sam. But she didn't hang out with them outside of work or anything. Just more keeping in contact on Facebook and Instagram you know. I know she and Mitch had mutual friends too. I would hear about Sean and Will sometimes."

Sean smiled, realizing that he was the Sean that was mentioned.

"Any other friends?"

Shauna shook her head.

"Tell me about Will? What was the nature of their association?"

"She never came out and said anything, but I used to think maybe something was up between the two of them maybe about a year ago."

"Can you describe him?"

She shook her head.

"No, I never met him. She just mentioned him like when they went on double dates and stuff."

"What made you think they messed around?"

"I don't know. Just a feeling. She just had that secretly-happy, inside-joke look about her once or twice when she talked about the double dates. And she seemed nervous or something when they were going on double dates with him.

I'm not sure. You know, it almost feels –, almost like I'm making things up in my head at this point because I'm talking about stuff from a year ago."

"I understand. And she never mentioned any details about him?"

She shook her head, "No, not really."

Sean put down his pen and pad.

"You know, one thing I've learned doing this work is that there is a lot of space between 'no' and 'not really.' Every detail matters. Any information, no matter how small, is important. It could be things like mentioning something he said, or did, or something Mitch said about the guy. Can you think of anything?"

Shauna shook her head.

"Did she ever mention where he lived?"

"No. Oh actually, I think he lived in Southeast. She and Mitch were late once meeting the guy and his wife, and she said that they were on MLK Ave stuck in traffic because of construction."

Sean jotted down a note.

"Anything else? Any other guys that she mentioned in her life. Maybe someone she met briefly at a grocery store or at the gym?"

Shauna stared at Sean for a bit. Then a curious look came over her face.

"Yeah. She would go to the gym on and off. And I think there were a few times when she got personal training sessions." She paused. "She talked about a trainer once. She thought he was cute. He had a birthmark on his stomach. She said it was sexy. Looked like a tattoo. She said it look like a panther walking down –," she pointed down her body, "You know."

Sean glanced at her and he nodded.

"Did she ever mention anything else about him?"

"Not that I can remember, no."

Sean continued, "Okay. Do you think she was involved with him?"

Shauna looked pensive.

"I don't know. That was the only time she mentioned him. I don't think so."

"Ms. Reeves, this was helpful. Appreciate your time."

Once Sean left, he made three more stops. The last stop clenched the case. Finished with interviews, he raced back to the precinct in record time to make the calls needed to get a search warrant. Within hours, the search was executed and evidence was sent to the lab for expedited results. When he returned to the precinct his anger boiled so high that he was sweating like he'd played full-court basketball, with no breaks. He entered the precinct and on his way back to his office, he signaled to Wilson.

"I've got some new info on the Gibson case. In my office."

He didn't slow his pace as he spoke. Wilson looked at Dannon, then fell in tow. Wilson stepped into the office behind Sean and closed the door.

Sean grabbed him by the collar, slammed him face first against the door, and jammed his elbow deep in Wilson's back. Then he took one of Wilson's arms and pinned it to his back. Wilson screeched in pain. His temple was pressed so hard against the door frame that his face lost color. Sean's voice was gritty as he spoke through a tight jaw.

"You're such a *fucking* bastard."

Wilson tried to lift his head off the door frame. Sean didn't back off.

"And here I thought you were trying not to be a snitch. But really, you were covering your own ass."

Wilson screeched again as Sean buried his elbow deeper, "SARG? What the —"

Sean growled, "You know what they say about what's done in the dark —"

Wilson's words were muffled as Sean pressed his head into the door frame more,

"What are you talking about, Sarg?"

"Oh, you don't know what I'm talking 'bout?"

Wilson pleaded, "I don't know what Dannon told you. But he's probably lying to save his own ass."

"That's the thing *Will*, Dannon didn't say a word." Sean paused. "Your problem is not realizing after all these years on the force that you can't kill someone without leaving some proof behind. It's impossible."

Sean drew back his elbow and slammed it into Wilson's back, which banged his body against the door frame. He winced in pain.

"AHH! Back up off me Sarg."

Sean foamed at the mouth, spit welling up at the corners.

"I ain't backing off shit. But here's what I'm about to do –"

Sean banged Wilson's head against the door a few times then pinned him up again. He released Wilson's collar, reached for his cuffs, and snapped them onto Wilson's wrists.

"You're under arrest for the murder of Annabelle Gibson. Anything you say can and will be held against you in a court of law."

Sean read Wilson his Miranda rights, then finally released him to stand on his own now that he was cuffed. Wilson spun around and glared at Sean.

The voices of other cops outside Sean's door grew louder.

"Sarg? What's going on? Do you need back up?"

Sean shoved Wilson to the side and unlocked the door. Three officers, including Dannon, rushed into the office with hands resting on their holstered guns. They saw Wilson's handcuffs and looked to Sean for answers. He launched in.

"The officers from the other precinct that I've had on the Gibson case re-interviewed several people. For each person Wilson interviewed, information was left out. I personally re-interviewed a few people and found out info that led to suspicion that Wilson was was a suspect. A search warrant was executed and blood splatter was found on some clothes that he was likely wearing the night he attacked her. It was sent to the lab for rushed testing. It matched Mrs. Gibson's DNA." Sean paused. "DNA from his toothbrush is being compared to the DNA sample of Mrs. Gibson's unborn fetus. If, or when, that matches, that's a motive for murder. On top of that, he left out of his report details that a neighbor gave. The neighbor was out in front of her house, letting her dog out and saw a black Lexus parked in front of the Gibson's house that night. She thought Mitch had gotten a new car. She remembered the first letters of the license plate because it started with BEV, which were the first three letters of her name. Those letters match Wilson's plate number, which places him at the scene of the crime. He was also seen with Annabelle at her gym as well."

Mitch walked in just then. He looked around, saw Wilson in handcuffs, looked briefly confused before anger took over. He lunged. The other officers grabbed at him, but not before he got a punch off.

"You FUCKING fuck! I'll take your life. That was my wife. My kids' mother."

Mitch crumpled into one of the chairs in Sean's office, as Dannon and the other officers led Wilson out.

Three days later, Sean knocked on the door at Mitch's house. They sat and talked about the case wrapping up. When he walked in, Mitch's daughter smiled widely sitting in the kitchen eating a sandwich.

"Hi Uncle Sean!"

"Hey, little lady!"

He gave her a hug then he and Mitch went down to the basement to Mitch's office.

Sean nodded to Mitch as they sat down.

"I know you're glad this is over."

Mitch nodded. He glanced at Sean.

"How did you know that it was Wilson? I mean, you had to have a haunch to follow up like you did."

"Not everything makes it into reports. In cases like this, when there's nothing but dead ends, my gut starts churning to find out what didn't make it into reports. One of the officers I had on the case from another precinct found out that Wilson had left out of his reports that the neighbor remembered the license plate letters. So, I re-interviewed everyone he did. I started with Shauna. Apparently, Annabelle didn't directly tell her about the affair. But she mentioned things and acted like it was someone else. Annabelle mentioned that she once trained with a personal trainer at her gym with a birthmark on his stomach that looked like a panther."

Mitch shot him a look. Sean nodded.

"Yeah, exactly. How many jokes have we cracked at Wilson about that birthmark when we were changing in the locker room after a workout." Mitch gave a knowing nod. Sean continued, "From there, the pieces came together."

Mitch shook his head. Sean asked, "Did you know she was messing around?"

"No. She just was never like that. At least that's what I thought. To be honest, as much as I was doing, I never stopped to think I needed to check up on her."

Sean and Mitch talked for a few more minutes then Sean left after he apologized for not believing Mitch. As he headed home, he thought about how this case could change things for him. He was already talking with some of the police brass about opportunities for mobility. With the way this case went — no media leaks or scandals — he knew this was a solid stepping-stone. He felt good about the possibilities, but regretful that it had to be as a result of Annabelle's death. *I hope I did her justice.* Mitch was cleared of suspicion, but having been a murder suspect and banging a lieutenant's wife wasn't going to lead to much beyond being a cop on the beat.

43

Patrice hadn't thought through the possibility of John and her — not this many years after they were together. She was irritated with Sean when he brought it up. *How dare he accuse me of something I didn't do,* she thought. While she readily admitted that it didn't look good for them to be eating off each others' plate, that wasn't a surefire sign that they were cheating, because the fact was that they weren't. Not only had nothing happened, but she hadn't even *thought* about anything happening. She and John were over. He was married with kids. She was with Sean. There was nothing to think about.

But as she stood pressed against John in his hotel room in nothing but a camisole set and thin robe, feeling the heat of his body and the warmth emanating from her own, now she felt like it was a moment destined to happen. In his eyes, she saw all that she remembered about being with him when they were together in college. It suddenly felt like all that time apart had melted away, like butter on popcorn soaking in and making for an all the more delicious treat.

They kissed sensuously, John's hands gliding over all parts of her. His hands felt firm and warm. He held her with a strength that made her feel secure within his arms. She wrapped her arms around his neck. She ran her hand over the back of his head, feeling the waves of his hair.

He whispered,

"You're sweating Mami."

Her lips parted and she sighed with pleasure before words came out.

"Am I?"

He softly brushed sweat from her temple with one hand, while the other snuggled in around her waist. He slowly shifted his weight backwards, creating room for his eyes to travel downwards. He pulled at the sash of her robe. As it loosened, he watched the imprint of her nipples pressed against her silk camisole. He traced around her left nipple with his finger and whispered, "Beautiful."

John pulled her closer. She felt the sensation of his hand gliding down her spine. He reached down her leg then slid his hand up the back of her leg until he squeezed the roundness of her butt. They kissed deeply.

A commercial came on TV with an oldies song playing.

John whispered,

"That's one of your favorite songs, isn't it?"

Lyrics crooned from the TV, "Come bring me your sweetness, now there's you there is no weakness."

She nodded and they kissed again. She felt his tongue and longed for more. Their kisses were soft, firm, then soft again. She uttered a moan of pleasure. The rhythm of their bodies felt like rippling ocean waves, ebbing and flowing. The slight rustling sound of their clothes as they embraced was like the distant sound of waves against a shoreline. He gently slid the straps of her camisole off her shoulder then let it drop to her waist. She unbuckled his pants. They both let out a breath of relief when they returned to an embracing kiss. She was soft with desire. He was firm with anticipation. John reached down and enveloped one of her breasts in his mouth. As he did so, Patrice opened her eyes and caught sight of their reflection in the balcony glass door.

She felt a jolt. She watched for a few seconds as they were intertwined, and felt like she was watching herself on a video. Her body shuddered as a chill ran through her. She tensed up. John stopped and pulled back from her. His hands dropped from her waist. They stood for a few awkward moments.

Patrice felt self-conscious. She slid the straps of her camisole back over her shoulders and picked up her robe. John buckled his belt. He sat on the edge of the bed. Patrice slowly stepped back and sat in the chair. After some moments of silence, John walked over to the balcony door and stepped out. Patrice put her robe back on. Still feeling exposed, she went into his closet and pulled out one of the hotel bathrobes. As she wrapped herself in the white terry cloth, she felt more secure. She walked out onto the balcony and leaned on the railing next to John. They watched the people five stories below walking near the pool and outdoor bar.

Patrice broke the silence,

"What now?"

John shook his head.

"I don't know."

Patrice nodded, happy that she grabbed the hotel robe as a night breeze blew.

She sighed.

"Feels like a forty-eight-hour day."

He stared at her for a few seconds.

"Yeah." He paused. "I'm actually glad we didn't."

She agreed, "I am too."

He lamented, "I should've been the one to stop."

She waved his words away, "What does it matter? It didn't happen."

John smiled, "Haven't smoked in years, but I could use a cigarette right now."

Patrice grinned, "I thought the cigarette was for *after* sex!"

They laughed. Then silence settled between them as the hum of the people below mixed with the sound of breeze. After a while, John spoke.

"You know, Janelle's sixteen now."

"Wow, that's amazing. I bet she's a beauty too! I didn't really see her face well at church."

John pulled his wallet out of his back pocket and showed her pictures of Janelle, and the twins.

"Aww, look at these beauties! These little ones look like trouble."

"They are! Always getting into stuff. They're a lot like—," He paused, "their mother."

Patrice glanced at him. She studied the pics a bit longer then asked, "So, where are the rest of your pictures?"

He stared at her. She gave him a reassuring look. He pulled out another picture from his wallet. When he handed it to her, he leaned against the balcony railing and watched silently as people passed.

"Very pretty."

He nodded. Patrice had seen Lily in the distance at church, but a close up picture really showed her beauty so much more.

She handed all the pics back to him. She abruptly stood straight, headed into the room and strutted toward the adjoining room door. As she reached for the doorknob, she said,

"I'll meet you at the bar downstairs in fifteen minutes."

The door was closed before there was any sound of objection.

Patrice cried as soon as she shut the door in her room. She took a shower, washing off the feeling of what almost happened. She wondered what his wife would feel if she knew what happened in his room a few minutes ago. She wondered if he would tell her. Mostly, she wondered how to feel about fooling around with a married man.

44

The bar was on the first floor of the hotel. It had a renaissance theme with lighting that had a slightly bluish hue. The walls were peppered with oversized 17th century paintings that sparked curiosity about if they were real or knock offs. There were a few couples dining at tables, and a few men sitting on the stools at the bar. Patrice looked around when she walked in to see if John was there yet. She sat on a stool at the corner of the bar near the storefront windows. She ordered a cosmopolitan and ordered John a Hennessy on the rocks. She was glad she threw on a sweater over her t-shirt because the temperature was dropping as night took hold. John finally popped up at the entrance. She wondered what took him so long, then assumed he had called home. He straddled the stool next to her and studied the drink she had ordered him before taking a sip.

"You made it down here quick. I had to call the kids. Caught them just before bedtime."

Patrice took a sip of her drink. She avoided the small talk he was starting. She turned to look at him squarely.

"John, why didn't we work out all those years ago?"

He took a swig.

"I don't know." He glanced at her then continued as if pondering out loud,

"We were young. And arrogant. Both wanted what we wanted. Being selfish and not really communicating. Life takes you in different directions. You never know what—"

She grew impatient and faked pulling money out of her pocket and putting it on the bar.

"Okay, here's five hundred bucks. Thanks for the couples retreat generic crap. Come on John. What happened?"

She wasn't in the mood for hearing how communication was their problem. Or existential fluff about the different directions life can take.

He scoffed.

"*Actually*, I don't know why you're looking at me for answers. As I recall, you ended it, not me. I should be asking *you* why we didn't work out. I still remember your voice on that message." He took another swig. "I wasn't even worth a real face to face conversation." He finished his drink and slammed the empty glass on the bar counter, seemingly harder than he intended because he glanced sheepishly at the bartender who looked irritated as he asked,

"Another drink?"

"Sure. Thanks," John said.

Patrice sunk into her seat and leaned on the bar. She pensively stared at a couple walking by outside.

"John, I tried to talk in person, but we were arguing so much we weren't getting anywhere. Plus, it seemed like you didn't want to be bothered. You acted like I was in the way of your new life. Seemed like you couldn't wait to graduate and leave everything behind." She shrugged. "And what did it matter anyway? You moved and didn't even tell me."

John scoffed again and adjusted his position on the bar stool. He spoke using air quotes,

"*Your message* said we weren't working out and that it was best for us to end things. Then neither one of us called each other. We hadn't talked for three weeks before I left."

"Don't play games. You knew you were moving. You've been with York & Newton for seven years, so you started at the Atlanta office right after we broke up. Clearly, things would have ended anyway."

He grunted, "Games? I'm not the one who plays games."

She straightened her back, and crossed her arms over her chest.

"All I'm saying is you could have told me that you were moving. I never knew what happened. Yeah, I ended it, but I didn't think we would never speak again. Couples break up and get back together all the time. We did before too."

John sipped his second drink.

"Patrice, every time I tried to talk to you about anything, you couldn't say anything positive. Negativity left and right. It's a wonder you didn't try to sabotage my interviews, staining my ties and suits or something."

She huffed, "What? Are you serious? So I had it in for you? I was masterminding a way for you not to succeed? Please, you sound absurd."

"When I interviewed at the Atlanta office, I wasn't sure if I wanted the job. If I wanted to uproot Janelle. She hadn't moved since she was a baby. Plus, they were just getting off the ground. Still fledgling. They barely offered me anything for a salary. All they offered was a title that would look good on my resume, and a chance at upward mobility, if the company took off. I had interviewed at Anderson & Smith PR in Virginia too, and they were offering a better compensation package. So, I really was considering staying here. But when I got back from the interview, I heard your message that it was over. That made me really consider the move. And when I found a neighborhood with a good school for Janelle, I mean, what reason did I have to stay? Why not take the job and have a fresh start? I didn't make that decision until *after* you broke it off."

Their relationship replayed in her mind. Her memories now seemed one-sided. Lacking in perspective. Him taking off and leaving her behind. Him not caring about their relationship. Him cutting things off like she didn't matter. She hadn't factored in her role in all of it.

She stared at her glass. The shininess of his watch caught her eye when he lifted his glass.

She asked, "Is it engraved?"

John followed her eyes to his watch then said.

"I will love you for a lifetime."

She peered pensively at people walking by outside.

She offered, "I always wondered if we were right for each other. I don't know. How much should you have to work at love? We were easy at first, but then it was hard. Is that because we were young, or just not right for each other? I don't know."

John listened quietly. Then offered, "I don't know. Love and relationships. Two different things. You know, you could love someone all you want. Doesn't mean they're right for you. I don't think being right for each other is predestined. Being right is being willing to work things out."

He took a sip.

"We had the love. It was the rest that didn't fall into place. Neither one of us ever wanted to be wrong, always had to be right. Not enough give and take."

Patrice nodded and sipped the last of her drink, eating the cherry that remained in her glass. After a long silence, they stood and hugged before heading to their respective rooms. They didn't say that they would never speak of that night again to each other, but they never did.

When Patrice got back to her room, she made sure the door between their rooms was locked, then undressed and slid into bed. She didn't want to put on the camisole set from earlier, so she slept naked. When she woke the next morning, she felt like she was waking up from a hibernation. She was energized. She worked out in the hotel gym for an hour before packing to catch her flight.

45

John went to Janelle's championship soccer match right after hopping off the plane in Maryland. He made it within the first fifteen minutes of the game starting. He sat in his usual spot and texted Lily to let her know he was back, and that he would be home with Janelle after her game. He scanned the stands. As he looked to his left, he watched as a woman shifted uncomfortably in the back row with her face covered by the shadows of the baseball cap pulled low. Then he looked to his right, and there was Mason approaching tentatively from two rows down the bleachers.

"Hey, Mr. Blackman."

Mason smiled respectfully as he sat next to John.

They shook hands.

"Mason! How's it going?

"Good. Just came out to support Janelle."

"Good. I'm sure she appreciates that."

"Yes sir."

"Well how's school going for you? And football?"

"Um, good sir. I'm doing well in school. I didn't make the football team, but I'm playing with a community center team instead. I'll try out again next year."

"That's good."

They watched a few minutes of the match. Then John studied Mason.

"Let's be real here son. I'm going to assume that you understand Janelle is a sweet, smart girl with a good head on her shoulders."

Mason nodded as John continued.

"She's always been focused. Doesn't let things distract her, which isn't easy nowadays."

John stared at Mason square on.

Mason said, "Yes sir. I know she is."

"Good. So, the thing is, I don't want to hear anything at any point that remotely suggests that you are pressuring her into anything that she's not ready for. You understand what I mean?"

Mason nodded but didn't speak. John continued,

"I'm going to need you to verbally acknowledge what I'm saying. You understand?"

"Sir, we're not doing anything inappropriate. I respect her. And she respects me. We care about each other. I want her to be successful and she wants the same for me. We bring out the best in each other." He cleared his throat. "I don't want a girl distracting me from my goals either. I plan to become an engineer and I'm going on college tours next summer."

John exhaled.

"Okay, well good. Then we're on the same page."

They were silent. Mason stood up.

"Well, my little brother's over there."

He motioned to a boy two rows down.

"I don't want to leave him alone too long. He gets into stuff quickly."

John smiled, "Good thinking."

Mason nodded and walked away. John settled in to enjoy the match. He heard Mason cheer at the same time that he cheered for Janelle.

"Go Janelle"/ "Go Apple."

Although Janelle's team struggled throughout the match, they won the championship. At the end of the match John waited at the bottom of the bleachers near the exit of the field. Mason walked over. He introduced his brother, then asked if they could wait with him for Janelle. John nodded.

"Hey, why do you call her Apple?"

Mason chuckled, "It's her nickname. Her friends gave it to her when she..."

He explained how the name came about and all three of them laughed. Janelle walked up and smiled.

"Hey! What's funny?"

"You!" Los said giggling at her.

She playfully grabbed him by the shoulder.

John beamed proudly.

"Looking like Pele! You did your thing out there!"

Janelle grinned, "Um, how about I look like Mia Hamm! You *do* know there're famous female soccer players too right?"

"Yes, I know. Women's rights and all that!"

John gave Mason a 'she thinks she's a hotshot now' look. Mason grinned.

They all walked to the parking lot. Janelle walked next to Mason and filled him in on the on-the-field details.

"Did you see my signature move? I was on fire!"

Meanwhile, Los chatted John's ear off about Mason teaching him how to play the drums.

"I be killing it! I can play four songs already!"

Janelle interrupted,

"Dad? Can Mason and Los ride home with us and stay for dinner? His mom can pick them up after."

John shot her a playful look, then pulled out his phone and dialed Lily. He said, "Honey! Guess who's coming to dinner?"

They erupted in laughter.

46

Patrice spent most of her flight home from New Orleans immersed in thoughts about revamping the decor of her apartment. She wanted a new color scheme, new stain-free rugs, a new dish set, and no dust collecting baubles. Time for more wall art and less cluttered shelves. When the plane landed in Atlanta, she efficiently got to the next gate for her connecting flight to Washington D.C. No sooner had she sat on the second flight did annoyance kick in. The pilot came over the loudspeaker saying that there was a problem with the electrical system. They were going to have to deplane. Her travel time ended up being two hours longer than planned. She occupied her time between deplaning, boarding another plane, and waiting for takeoff, by texting friends.

Patrice: *Flight delays. Sigh. Had a good trip. I killed at the presentations.*

Sasha: *Nice! I knew you would! So, did you "sample" everything in N'orlins?*

Patrice heard another announcement come over the loudspeaker to turn off phones. So, she quickly checked her email, then returned to Sasha's text before turning her phone off.

Patricia: *Gurl, sort of. Hard to explain on text. But it was enough for me to get over Sean's tired a$$. Matter of fact Sean who? More details later.*

She sent the last text then shut off her phone.

Once the plane landed in D.C., she couldn't wait to get to her apartment and have the rest of the evening to soak in the tub and read. When she turned her phone back on, she was surprised to see a text from Sean.

Sean: *Wow. SMH*

That's when she realized that she had mistakenly sent her last text to him instead of Sasha. She gasped, mortified. She couldn't bring herself to respond. *Shit, it's done now. Can't fix it.*

When Patrice entered her apartment building, she sighed with relief to be almost home. She took the elevator to her floor and rounded the corner to her apartment. When she put the key in the door, she realized it was unlocked. She thought back to when she'd left days before. *Maybe I left it unlocked,* she thought. Once in her apartment, she saw dark shadows on the floor. She flipped on the light switch and gasped at the disarray. Pillows and cabinet drawers scattered on the floor. She stepped in further and heard the crunch of glass underfoot from a broken lamp.

Patrice noticed that the painting Sean had given her was on the floor, face down with glass shards around it. Then she noticed two dresses on the floor that Sean had given her. They looked ripped. *That fucking bastard. This is in no way on the same level as me stomping on his damn clothes. Cops think they can get away with anything.* Her blood boiled at scorch status. She dialed Sean's number while walking back out of her apartment, leaving her suitcase at the front door. She left a seething message. "You are truly a freakin' bastard. This was a punk ass move. You come up in here and tear my shit up. What the hell is wrong with you? You're the one who ended things. Not me. So, what the hell is this about? I didn't say shit to you, and your new piece of ass that night at the club. Didn't bother y'all. But I promise you I've got a lot to say now..."

Her words poured out like lava, hot and searing with no end in sight. She was shaking with anger and exasperation. When she finally hung up, she sank to the floor and sat at the entrance of her living room. She felt drained and defeated.

As she quieted, silence didn't take over the apartment. She heard sounds coming from her bedroom. She gathered her strength, stood, and hustled to the bedroom, not clearly thinking of the potential danger. She entered her room and found Michelle slumped on the floor.

"Michelle? Oh my God. What are you doing here? What happened?"

Patrice's sister was stretched out in front of the bedroom closet. Her eyes were glazed and barely open, only the bottom rims of her pupils visible. One of her breasts was hanging out from a ripped tank top. Her jeans and underwear were pulled down to her ankles. Her legs were bent at odd angles. Patrice squinted, staring at Michelle's leg. She saw a needle in the crease between her right thigh and groin.

"Oh God, Michelle."

Patrice got down on the floor. She pulled the needle out of her sister's leg. Then she slid behind Michelle and pulled her up, propping her sister's upper body on hers. Her body was warm but close to limp. She covered Michelle's breast and grabbed one of the sweaters that was nearby on the floor to cover her up more. They laid still. Patrice felt her sister's heartbeat and listened to her breathing. She wrapped her arms around Michelle. Tears leaked from Patrice's eyes.

"Why do you do this to yourself?"

She felt Michelle's breath on the crook of the arm. Michelle sobbed. Patrice softly rocked back and forth, remembering when they were kids that she could get Michelle to stop crying by rocking her. She wished now that she could rock away the pain as she could back then. Michelle's tears dripped onto Patrice's arm. She wiped away her sister's tears and her own.

Michelle's voice was scratchy and low.

"Dre's gone, Tricey."

"What? Where?"

Michelle shook her head, "He's dead."

Her tears seeped.

"He was in rehab for two weeks. He was getting cleaned up. I was too. I was going to my program everyday. We were good."

Patrice stayed silent. She felt Michelle shiver, so she reached over and pulled the blanket off the bed to cover her.

"We were celebrating being clean, you know. Just some drinks. A couple drinks."

Michelle explained that they celebrated at a bar, and were driving home when Dre swerved to avoid a big piece of metal the road and hit an oncoming car, dying instantly and killing the two children in the other car. Patrice thought she would feel a sense of relief if she were to ever hear that Dre was out of Michelle's life. But relief was far from what she felt now.

"I'm so sorry Michelle. I know you loved him."

Patrice took a deep breath and listened to the sound of a siren going by outside.

Michelle whispered, "I'm sorry about your place." She sniffed and wiped her nose. "I owed this guy money and he followed me here. If I didn't give him something, he wasn't gonna leave me alone. He didn't take much though."

Patrice shook her head.

"It's okay. I get it."

Michelle sighed.

"I'm tired, Tricey. I'm just so, so tired."

They sat in silence. Michelle chuckled.

"Remember how daddy used to say, 'If you can say you're tired, you ain't *that* tired.'"

They laughed in unison. Patrice gently squeezed Michelle's hand.

"Shellie, I'm going to get you help. And this time, I'm going to come visit everyday. Everyday, okay?"

Michelle slowly wrapped one arm around Patrice's arm, and they embraced tighter. Patrice felt her sister's body shake as her sobs gained momentum. When she quieted down, her voice was a whisper.

"I saw her today Trice. She was beautiful. She's sixteen now. Sixteen."

"Who is?"

"My baby. She's all grown up."

"Your what? Shellie, honey, you don't have a child. Your baby –, your baby died. Remember?"

Michelle shook her head slowly.

"She didn't die. I know where she lives."

Patrice pushed herself up to sit straighter. Michelle moved over to sit next to her. Patrice's mind whirled through the past. She stared at Michelle.

"Wait a minute. She's been alive all this time? Why did you say she died then? How could you keep something like that a secret?"

Michelle leaned her head back.

"She's with her father. I knew he would take care of her."

"Michelle, what are you talking about?"

"I went to her soccer game. I sat in the back. They didn't see me."

Patrice was so flabbergasted she could hardly think straight.

"So you have a daughter? I have a niece? My God. I can't believe this." Patrice paused. "So you've seen her?"

Michelle nodded.

"Just from a distance. John would never have me coming in and out of her life. He wouldn't stand for that."

Patrice's eyes bulged. She stared at Michelle. The puzzle pieces were falling into place.

"Janelle?"

Michelle's eyes lit up at the mention of her daughter's name. She nodded.

Just then Patrice heard a voice and footsteps coming from the living room.

"Patrice? Where are you?"

Sean appeared at the bedroom door. He walked over and knelt down in front of them.

"What happened?"

Patrice stood.

"It was a misunderstanding. I, I'm so sorry I called you like that. I was way out of line."

Sean gave an empathetic nod.

"You okay? You hurt?"

"No, we're okay."

Like the team they used to be, Patrice and Sean got Michelle properly dressed and took her to the closest hospital emergency room. After filling out paperwork, and waiting for hours, she was admitted to the hospital and set to be transferred in the next three days to a rehabilitation program in Virginia for a six-month stay.

By the time Sean took Patrice back home, it was after midnight. He waited for her to get into her apartment, said goodbye, then turned to leave.

"Sean?"

He turned back to her.

"I really appreciate everything you've done. And I'm sorry. So sorry for what I said. For even thinking you would've done this."

He stared quietly.

"Get some rest."

47

After dinner at the Blackmans, Mason and his brother left when their mother came to pick them up. Janelle went to her room and listened to music while doing her homework. Lily had put the twins down to sleep then she ventured back down to the kitchen, where John was sitting at the counter on his computer. Lily walked into the kitchen and uttered her words with the same nonchalance as saying, "How was your day?"

She said, "When were you going to tell me you wanted a divorce?"

She glanced at John then busied herself unloading the dishwasher. John responded.

"My *trip* was fine in case you cared."

He pulled out containers from the cabinet and scooped the leftovers from dinner into containers to put in the fridge.

Lily continued, "I didn't ask you about your trip."

She put the kettle on the stove. She reached in a cabinet for a cup and pulled the sugar bowl from the tray on the kitchen island. John remained quiet. When he packed and put away all the leftovers, he sat at his computer again.

"I saw Janelle's mother today."

She glanced at him. He continued, "She was at the soccer match."

Lily hesitated.

"How did she seem? Did Janelle see her?"

"No, she had no clue. I think Michelle probably saw me, but we didn't make eye contact or speak." He paused. "She didn't look good."

Lily asked cautiously, "Are you going to tell Janelle about it?

John tilted his head.

"Maybe. Sometimes I think every child should know their mother and their father. And other times, I think she's better off not knowing that her mother's an addict. I mean, what good would it do her?"

Lily took a long breath then said, "Janelle asked about her mother last year."

Surprise spread over John's face.

"Why didn't you tell me?"

"She didn't want me to. She didn't want to hurt your feelings, or for you to think that she wasn't happy."

John stared blankly at his computer.

"I would've been worried that her asking about her mother was hurtful for you."

Lily turned to the sink and kitchen window. She looked over her shoulder in John's direction then out of the window again. The kettle whistled. She poured hot water, added a tea bag, and stirred in sugar. She sat, quietly blowing on her tea. She glanced at John.

"Do you want something hot?"

"No. Thanks."

Lily's next words raced out of her mouth.

"I saw a divorce lawyer."

John flinched, his eyes squeezing shut for a few seconds as though her words stung. He adjusted in his seat. He shut his laptop and leaned on the counter.

In a barely audible voice he asked, "Did you start the paperwork?"

She shook her head.

"Lily –, we –"

Lily didn't bother to wipe at the tears that fell.

"We what John? We what?"

John continued, "I know things have been rough."

Lily gave a pained smile.

"*Rough?*"

She glared at him.

"That's how you describe the last few years? John, we haven't been okay for a long time." She paused. "I'm tired of paying silent penance."

John scoffed.

"No one asked you to pay penance."

"And yet I've been paying it. You *make* me pay for your decision to marry me. Like I made you do it. Like you were dragged into it." She sipped on her tea, and he shifted the coasters on the counter, rearranging them from left to right, then right to left. She sipped the last of her tea and got up to wash the cup. She dried her hands on a kitchen towel, then leaned with her back on the sink's edge. John finally spoke.

"I know we have a lot to work on. I haven't handled things well. At all. There's so much we need to sort out. But I think we're worth saving."

Lily glared at him.

"Yet you looked into a divorce attorney a year ago. Were we worth saving then?"

John explained, "Lily, it's not what you think. I saw an ad that said something about making sure you don't screw yourself out of a future after divorce. When I clicked on it, there was info about how to make sure divorce is fair. Then I started getting mail from the website. That's all there was to that. I wasn't seriously looking into it."

Lily shook her head.

"But you started looking for a condo too. What was that?"

"That wasn't for me, that was for Ron. That was when Rita asked him for a divorce and he had to be out of the house quick."

Lily crossed her arms over her chest.

"And the fact that you work with your ex? Is that a happenstance too."

John paled.

"I didn't –, I just didn't want to make it a thing. Seems like everything I say lately is a problem and I didn't want to –"

Lily snickered snidely, "An answer for everything. No wonder you work in PR."

John quieted. Then he said, "I know we have problems but I don't want to give up."

She bristled.

"Do you know today is the anniversary of the day we met?"

John shook his head then smirked.

"When I stalked you."

They smiled painfully at each other. She continued, "You know what I was thinking that day?"

He sat still, staring at her.

"I wanted to see your house." She continued. "Your kitchen, bathroom, and bedroom."

He tilted his head as she spoke.

"If you had clean towels, and a decent brand of toilet paper."

She sighed and continued, "That's the crap women think about. We think stuff like that matters. Like that's how you can tell what a man is really all about." She smiled. "When I saw your house, everything checked out. Clean towels, plush toilet paper. Really nice dishes. You were the real deal."

John asked, "What did that prove?"

"At the time, it meant that you cared enough to have a decent house. You weren't just for show in public, and a filth pig at home. That matters to women."

He nodded slowly.

Lily said, "And how you were with Janelle, how you were raising her. That was the most amazing part."

She wiped at a tear.

"I didn't just jump in blindly. I thought we had everything together."

She dabbed at her eyes.

She added, "You know, I saw it on our wedding day. In your eyes. You looked like a trapped animal."

John glanced at her briefly then turned away. He rubbed his hands over his face.

Lily's voice was shaky,

"I don't know when trapped turned to hating me. But it happened."

"It didn't –, I don't hate you."

Lily shrugged.

"I need to stop feeling shitty all the time. That's how this feels. Painful and shitty."

She adjusted her shoe on the kitchen rug beneath her feet.

"The other day, I was thinking about what to do for the twins upcoming birthday. I remembered their second birthday party. Like it happened yesterday. You hardly looked at me in the eyes that whole day. Your eyes never made it past my neck." Tears streamed down her face. "You have no idea what it feels like to be married to someone, to love someone, to build a family and a life with someone who hates you and can't look at you. He has so much disgust that he can't even look you in the eyes because it would be obvious."

She took a deep breath.

"You never wanted to be married. Or maybe you just didn't want to be married to me. Either way, why did you propose? Why'd you create this mess if you didn't want it? Maybe you felt you had to. For Janelle. But I never pressured you into this."

John opened his mouth to speak, but she put her hand up to stop him.

"Somewhere along the way I made it my mission to overcome it. Me, Ms. Therapist, trying my best to therapize us." She laughed mockingly at herself. "But now, I get it. I can't *make you* love me."

John spoke before she could stop him, "Lily I do love you. You're the mother of my children. All my children. You've done everything I could want."

Lily stared at him, shaking her head.

"John, I don't know if I want you to love me anymore. When I start living again, when I figure out how to after so many years of trying, it won't matter if you love me. There'll be nothing for me to prove anymore."

John's eyes brimmed with tears. Lily turned back toward the sink and looked out the kitchen window. Deep sobs released from her body. Her tears were soaking wet with her pain. Her shoulders shook. She leaned hard on the counter.

John stood and walked to her. He stood behind her, close enough for the warmth of their bodies to mingle in the space between them. He saw her look up at his reflection in the window. Her body tensed. She leaned more firmly onto the sink's edge. John's breathing was deliberate and steady. He moved closer. He lifted his hands and placed them on either side of her body on the sink. She stiffened and turned her head to the side. John moved his face towards hers, brushing his lips against her skin.

Their breaths began to sync. He shifted his hands from the sink edge to envelop her waist. And she wrapped her arms around his. He finally released words into air.

"I'm sorry, Lily. We didn't need to rush to get married. I should have waited. Until I was man enough to feel good about getting married. Until I had worked through unfinished past relationships. Not just doing it because it was the next thing on the list to get done. You deserved more."

He inhaled deeply and hugged her waist tighter. And she leaned into him.

48

Each time Patrice thought about the connection between Michelle, John, and Janelle, disbelief smacked her in the face. She never knew who the boy was that Michelle was pregnant by. It was so hush-hush in their family. Their mother had worked on convincing Michelle to have an abortion. But she refused. One night, Michelle told Patrice that she could never get rid of a baby.

"I could never. My baby's going to love me without judging me."

Michelle had been living with their paternal step grandmother and refused to come back home. She only sporadically visited but never brought the baby with her. After the baby was born, Michelle came over one day and said the baby died in her crib.

Patrice was certain John didn't know that Michelle was her sister. It was a conversation she didn't look forward to having. Patrice called John the day after they returned from the conference and told him the parts of Michelle's life that he didn't know. He was shocked, to say the least. Two days after everything was out in the open, Michelle went into rehab. He asked about her treatment, and offered to help defray some of the cost.

Patrice had been thinking about Sean more than she had at any point since they broke up. Seeing him the other night, reminded her of why she fell in love with him in the first place. But she couldn't tell if he just helped her out of obligation. He always talked about how a cop was a cop, even when he wasn't on duty. In fact, she convinced herself not to read anything into him helping her and Michelle. Because what good would that do to open the door of false hope again. But when Sean texted her two days after the ER visit, asking how she was feeling, she couldn't help but wonder if there was hope. They texted back and forth for the rest of that day. He sent her a picture of his son making funny faces. She sent a picture of the teapot she made at a pottery class. By the end of the day, she was ready to risk it. She asked him if they could have breakfast soon, no strings attached. He surprised her when he responded saying, *"How about Wicked Waffles tomorrow?"*

They met up at nine-thirty the next morning, and the line was already looping out of the door. After getting their food, they were lucky enough to catch a couple as they were getting up from an outdoor table. They sat, chatted, and savored their chicken and waffles.

Sean teased her,

"Hey, is that the Obamas over there?"

Patrice whipped her head around in the direction he was looking. Then she sucked her teeth and shot him a playfully annoyed look.

"Don't play with me, boy. You 'bout to make me have a panic attack."

She grabbed at her chest, looking like she actually was working to calm herself down.

Sean smiled then said somberly,

"Have you had an attack before?"

"A few actually." She licked syrup off her lips. "It's been better lately. I started doing meditation most mornings. And my doctor gave me a script, for back up in case I need it."

Patrice was surprised at how easily she talked about it, but it felt good to finally tell someone about it. After they ate, they strolled to a nearby park. As they walked, she built up her courage to say what was on her mind. She didn't want the opportunity to pass without trying. No matter how remote the possibility was.

"Sean, I've really thought about what you said about John. How you two look alike."

She launched into details about her and John, how long ago their relationship was, how it ended, how she never knew what happened to him. That Michelle was his daughter's mother, and that now she knows John's daughter is her niece. She ended by letting him know why she never wanted to move in. It was the one thing she knew he wanted an answer for that she never gave him.

"I loved our relationship. But moving in would've made it a reality that we were never going to have a pretty marriage."

Sean stared at Patrice as if she was speaking another language.

"What?"

"See, this is what's so hard about this. It not easy to explain it without feeling like an idiot." She sighed. "Men know when they want to marry a girl. It doesn't matter if he's broke, young, or whether or not he's achieved a certain status. Doesn't matter if he has her dad's approval. Once he knows, he knows."

"So, you think I didn't want to marry you?"

"I know you didn't. I mean, not of your own free will."

He continued to look perplexed.

"But we talked about it before. I asked you about marriage, and it seemed like you weren't concerned about it. You kept saying you like things the way they were."

She smiled.

"That's all I could think to say. I wasn't going to say 'Well, you haven't asked me to get married so you must not want to.'"

Sean asked, "Why didn't you tell me?"

She looked at him intently.

"Tell you what? That I want you to want to marry me without me ever having to bring it up. So that I know for sure that it's what you want?"

Sean looked at her silently as she continued.

"You know what would have happened? I would have moved in. We would have lived together for a year, maybe two, then you would have proposed."

Sean chimed in, "Wow, sounds awful."

She smirked.

"We would have had a default marriage because it would have been like, 'well we might as well.' I would have had that question in the back of my mind the whole time, trying to ignore that it was there. Did you really want to? Was it a practical decision because, hey, we love each other and we're good together, so why not?"

Sean listened quietly. She smiled widely.

"I wanted a pretty marriage. Clean and completely of your own free will. Marriage is hard enough without dealing with a man who didn't really want to get married."

She took a breath.

"It's such a tricky thing. How do you ever know that someone wanted something for themselves if you had to plant the seed for them?"

They sat on a park bench. They watched people walk by, watched birds peck at food on the ground. Sean put his arm around Patrice's shoulder. After a while, he looked at his watch and said he needed to head home. As they stood, he hugged her tightly. Then he softly kissed her forehead. He looked into her eyes, his words almost a whisper,

"There's no such thing as a pretty marriage Patrice. Just real, raw love, and two people working to keep it alive."

He smiled. She leaned into him and squeezed. Then he walked away.

Epilogue

Patrice woke up as the sun edged into the sky. She was eager to get started hunting for patio furniture. Happy with her interior décor for her new house, outdoor living was the next focus. It was new for her. She never had a yard and patio to decorate. She'd found a couple patio sets that she loved online, but wasn't sure if they'd look good in person. *How can you buy furniture without sitting your butt in it first*, she thought.

She was at her third furniture store of the day and had sat in more than a dozen patio sets. She switched back and forth between sitting in a hunter green set with flecks of sunset orange, and a brown wicker set. She was sitting in the green set, moving around to make sure it felt comfortable when she heard a familiar voice.

"I'd go with the green one."

Startled, she spun her head around toward the voice. She smiled widely.

"Think so?"

Sean nodded.

"Yeah, the rattan is going to start creaking after a few weeks and definitely after a good heavy rainfall."

They simultaneously stepped in for a hug, which to Patrice felt as warm and sweet as pecan pie. For a split second, it didn't feel like four years had passed, since they last saw each other.

"Well, I see you're still in one piece, so the job hasn't taken you out yet. How's life?"

He chuckled.

"I'm retired from the force actually."

She dropped her jaw open dramatically.

"Yeah, I made Lieutenant and did that for a year and a half before it fully sunk in that I hated it. I couldn't stand being a political cop. I don't care about optics. It wasn't for me."

"Wow. I can't believe it. So, what are you up to now?"

"I went back to school for IT. I own a company that services the IT needs of small businesses."

"Oh my goodness! That's great! I'm so happy for you. That must've been a real change. Do you miss the pace?"

He shook his head. "Not. At. All. When I'm done, I'm done. I was ready."

"That's great!"

They sat on the green patio set.

Sean asked, "So, what about you? Still at York & Newton?"

"I'm good. Really good. I left them two years ago. I partnered up with an old colleague, and we started a PR firm that focuses on women-owned businesses."

"Oh, so now you really running *thangs*!"

She grinned, "Well!"

"Yeah, I'm not surprised."

Sean asked, "So, how's your sister?"

She spoke in a low voice. "She's better. She's able to see her daughter pretty regularly now. I think that gave her a purpose to stay clean. She still relapsed a couple times, but only for a day or two, not like how she used to disappear for months."

Patrice reflected with pride on Michelle's progress.

"I think it makes her proud knowing she has such as smart, amazing daughter. It's like she wants to be like Janelle."

Sean chimed in,

"That's a hell of a lot of progress. She's beating the odds."

Patrice nodded. They were quiet for a few moments.

She asked, "I thought you might have moved out of state because we never run into each other."

Sean smiled. "Not out of state, but I did move. I'm in Rockville now."

She pulled back her head with surprise, "Oh. Way across town. Moved on up to the *Eastside*?"

Sean glanced at the furniture.

"Looks like you moved as well."

"Yeah, I bought a house. I'm gonna be house poor for the next five years, but at least it's my little piece of the world."

"Congrats!"

She grinned.

He asked, "So what's next after patio furniture?"

"Well, I'm going to get a fire pit and a few potted plants for the patio. Also, I need to create an office space in the basement, which will take some doing because there are still a ton of boxes down there."

Sean grinned.

"That sounds great. But I meant literally. What are you doing after patio shopping? If you have a little time, how about we grab a late lunch?"

Patrice hesitated for a moment. *Does that make me look lonely and thirsty if I have time to go with him with such short notice?*

Sean slyly glanced at her.

"I know how you do it. You probably got up early this morning, had a cup of coffee, caught up on some work, did some cleaning, then started on your errands for the day at around ten or so. And if I'm right, you've been at it ever since, which means you haven't eaten yet. So, I *know* you're hungry."

Patrice smiled sheepishly.

"Damn, am I *that* predictable?"

Sean continued,

"And whoever is in your life is probably just as busy as you, so you probably don't have plans with him until later, so I'm sure you're free for a late lunch."

He grinned confidently. She laughed.

"Still a cocky cop underneath! Think you know *everything*."

Sean motioned for them to head out of the store. Once outside, he asked where she was parked and walked her to her car.

She said, "Actually, there's a Japanese steakhouse three blocks up, and the food's great. Really good sushi!"

They walked into the restaurant, and there was no wait to be seated. They had a leisurely lunch while catching up on life. They talked about their relationships for the past few years, how Sean's son is now starting high school, and how Patrice got lost in Nebraska on a cross-country drive that her friends convinced her would be a good trip. She cracked up laughing as he told her about how he wiped out in a mudhole during a Fun Run marathon. When Patrice looked at the time and realized three hours had passed, she couldn't believe it. Within a few minutes, they left the restaurant and walked to Patrice's car.

"So, how does this theory of yours work? Can the clock reset to have a pretty marriage?"

She smiled but didn't respond. He stared at her with his head cocked to the side as if waiting for her to say something. Patrice smiled slyly.

"Come on Sean. You know there's no such thing as a pretty marriage."

They hugged. She kissed his cheek, he kissed her hand, then she slid into her car.

THE END

About the Author

Melissa Dawn is a psychologist by day and multi-genre writer by night. Her first book was a children's picture book entitled *What Do I Sound Like?* She is also the author of the short fiction e-book *Goddess of Wisdom and War*. She lives and works in Maryland with her family and enjoys bringing characters to life.